Roman Ivory

Roman Ivory

A Novel

by

Robert Bruegmann

Beautiful Dreamer Press

*for SBJ
and the memory of JWS*

Contents

Roman Ivory

Part One:

Robert's Story

Prologue:

In the Pit

Paris, rue de Seine, 21 May 1879

It is quiet and dark down here. Nothing is moving, but I feel a slight draught. The cool air grazes my freshly shaved arse cheeks and sends a chill through me.

I am in the basement of Fabrizio's gallery in the rue de Seine. I am lying face down, naked, on a bench padded with black leather, my wrists and ankles tied to the legs of the bench. There is a gag in my mouth. The leather has a surprisingly sweet taste.

The room is dark except for some flickering behind me—the votive candles that Fabrizio loves. The floor is paved with stone blocks, darkened by age and glistening with damp. I cannot raise my head far, but by the candlelight I can see the rough stone walls. Painted black, they absorb any light that reaches them.

Looking to the side and upward as far as the leather bands allow, I can see a part of the ceiling with its ancient wood beams, scarred by fire, almost entirely black. There is a stale odour from the stone and wood, and I think I hear the faint drip of water from somewhere.

I have been in this room in this position before, tied down with my body immobilized and my buttocks shaved and fully exposed, waiting to see what Fabrizio wants to do with me. It is humiliating and wildly exciting.

Then I notice something new. Right in front of me on a low ledge is a piece of carved ivory, tubular but topped by an obscenely bulging head with a narrow slit that makes it abundantly clear that it was modelled on the male anatomy. I can barely distinguish its outline and the carved image at the centre, but I'm reasonably sure it is identical to the piece I saw on my trip to the Capitoline Museum in Rome, a piece used in a gruesome murder. I now know, despite what Fabrizio has told me, that the murder occurred while he was in Rome, and that he departed for Paris immediately afterwards.

The sight of the ivory feels like a blow to my body. Fabrizio must have discovered what I learned in Rome. The erotic excitement stops instantly, pushed aside by a much more powerful emotion. In place of the tingling below my waist is a much stronger one above: a churning in the pit of my stomach. I am suddenly not well. I am afraid I may retch.

Although it is cool down here, my skin is hot and clammy. I feel perspiration from my back dripping down my sides. My heart is pounding, and I am having trouble breathing.

I have no idea what Fabrizio plans to do. The more I think about it, the more I am aware how dangerous my situation is. If Fabrizio knows what I learned in Rome, could he ever let me out of this pit alive?

No friend or family member knows I am in Paris, let alone in this basement. Certainly no one on the street outside or in the building above would hear any noise coming from this subterranean chamber.

I am terrified, but all I can do is wait. It has been only seventeen months since my father died and a year since I met Fabrizio. Everything about my life has changed in those seventeen months. Will I live to see an eighteenth?

Chapter 1:

My Father's Will

My father, Joseph Stapleton, the 1st Viscount Barrington and the head of the Stapleton Private Bank, passed away of rheumatic fever unexpectedly at our country estate, Barrington Hall, near Guildford in Surrey, on 12 December 1877. That was a year and a half ago. He was just fifty. I received the telegram from my mother that morning in my rooms at New College. On a bleak, heavily overcast December afternoon, I took the train for the journey south.

I had just turned nineteen and was soon to begin my final two terms reading Greats at Oxford. What I would do afterwards was not at all clear. My parents had long hoped I would work at the family bank and eventually take over the management from my father as he had from his, but I was decidedly unenthusiastic.

The afternoon of my arrival at Barrington Hall, my mother, my sister, her husband, and assorted cousins, uncles and aunts all gathered around the ponderous oak desk in Father's study. This had been his domain, a place where he spent hours by himself with the door shut. Henry Stewart, my father's solicitor, droned on about the will and codicils.

I knew about most of the will's provisions from conversations with my father before his death. As I listened, Stewart confirmed that I, Robert Stapleton, would become the 2nd Viscount Barrington and inherit Barrington House in London, Barrington Hall where we were sitting, and the bulk of the estate, save for some funds held in trust for my mother and sister. There were the usual bequests to various members of the extended family and the household staff in London and Surrey. That much I expected.

But there were surprises. There were, for example, small bequests to several men no one seemed to know. And there was one even more puzzling entry, a house on Carlton Hill in St John's Wood, London. I knew nothing about it, but no one in the family seemed surprised to hear of it.

My first thought was that my father had used the house as a pied-à-terre to meet women. That part of London had a certain notoriety for that kind of activity, and I had heard vague remarks from several of my father's fellow club members that, in his younger years, my father was considered something of a lady's man.

Based on comments made after the reading, I suspected my mother and my uncle Rupert, my father's younger brother, knew more. Later in the afternoon, I found Rupert alone in the downstairs hall. "Uncle, I was hoping you could tell me something about the house in St John's Wood."

He looked slightly embarrassed. "Robert, I'm on my way out for the evening. I think it would be better if we talked about this at my house in town. I suspect there is a great deal that you never knew about your father. Can we talk after I return from Amsterdam in a week?"

"Of course."

Chapter 2:

A Trip to St John's Wood

While waiting for my uncle to return, I decided to visit the mysterious house on Carlton Hill. I asked my father's personal secretary, Harold Griswold, to accompany me. Griswold was an old man who had worked for my grandfather before becoming secretary to my father. He always seemed to be frowning. However, he was competent and efficient and, perhaps most important, he got along well with my mother. During our ride to St John's Wood, I asked him when my father had bought the house and for what purpose.

"I think all your questions will be answered once we arrive," was all he said. I was slightly annoyed but did not press him further.

The house turned out to be an unobtrusive two-storey structure on a quite respectable-looking street lined with solid, if old-fashioned, houses. The house itself, like most of its neighbours, was built in the early decades of the century, and like many of them had severe rectangular lines softened slightly by scrolled brackets under the eaves, the whole rendered in pale cream stucco with white trim. Set back discreetly from the street behind a low brick wall and tall hedge, it was a pale English reflection of an Italian villa.

Griswold rang the bell, and we were admitted by the housekeeper, a Mrs. Farrell, a plump elderly woman dressed in a dark skirt with white apron, flowery blouse, and a tasselled shawl. A great mass of white hair was partly covered by a cream-coloured lace headscarf. With her pink face and fixed smile, she looked like an old China doll.

"Yes, yes, yes," Mrs. Farrell twittered as we entered, waving her arms in a welcoming gesture. "Please do come in. Such a pleasure to meet you finally, Your Lordship, Lord Barrington. Of course, I've heard tell—"

"Thank you, Mrs. Farrell," Griswold cut in roughly. He walked past her into the front hall and then the parlour, a spacious room whose plaster walls, ceiling, and furnishings were all rendered in a delicate palette of pastel tints.

Mrs. Farrell looked abashed but continued to mutter as she followed Griswold into the room. I followed Griswold's example and settled into an armchair facing Mrs. Farrell, who ensconced herself on the elegant settee opposite. "'Twas my privilege, my honour, my duty, to be managing this house for your late father. As you know we've an uncommon small staff for a house this size, but I've always done my best to keep things tidy, dare I say, as perfect as possible," she said with more waving of arms, "considering, of course, the problem of the roof this spring, making it difficult to—"

"Yes. Thank you, Mrs. Farrell," Griswold cut in once again. "Lord Barrington does not have a great deal of time. He was surprised to hear about this house and naturally wanted to see it."

I decided I needed to interject myself into the conversation. "I hadn't known about this place. I wonder why my father bought it and what he did here."

"Your Father, the late Lord Barrington, may he rest in peace, such a fine man, always so considerate and kind, and such a gentleman—" She paused as she noted a disapproving glare from Griswold. "Um, I am not sure when he bought it, but he used it for meetings, for gatherings—you know how necessary this would be for such an important businessman as your father and a distinguished scholar as well. His business associates would be staying here. And he'd be studying his collection of classical whatnots, and he'd be doing his writing, you know, on statues and things."

Mrs. Farrell said this with a completely straight face, but surely she would have known if my father had brought women back here. I looked at Griswold. His expression, as usual, was completely impassive. He excused himself, saying he wished to examine the account books for the house.

Although I was impatient to see the rest of the house, Mrs. Farrell launched into a minute and garbled description of the house and every detail of its history, features, and upkeep. My eye was caught by a collection of bronze figures standing on a massive table covered with a turkey carpet along the wall opposite me, mostly hidden behind Mrs. Farrell's energetically bobbing head. I wanted to examine them more closely, but Mrs. Farrell was obviously pleased to have this opportunity to describe her stewardship of the house, and I didn't wish to offend her by interrupting.

Finally, Griswold returned and rescued me. Without sitting down, he once again cut the housekeeper off in mid-sentence. "Thank you very much, Mrs. Farrell. We are obliged to you. We will find you if we need any further information." She reluctantly retreated to the kitchen with what sounded like resentful muttering.

I walked directly to the table with the bronzes. At first glance there was nothing unusual about them. I knew it was common for English gentlemen making the Grand Tour to pick up castings of antique models and newly created pieces. We had a few at Barrington Hall. Here, they were more numerous and, exhibited on a table directly opposite the entrance, more conspicuous. I had recently done some study of antique sculpture and had learned about the originals for many of them. Here in gleaming bronze were some of my old friends, mostly known only as engravings in books, small enough that I could pick them up and examine them at will.

There was something deeply satisfying about holding them in my hand. The Borghese Warrior, for example. I loved the heft of him, his cool, smooth surface and the gleaming dark patina he had acquired as the bronze had aged. There was something heroic about the confident manner in which, as small as he was, he strode across a verde antico base. I could easily understand why my father had worked to assemble this tabletop array. They were not only marvellous objects themselves, but together they were like a miniature museum of the some of the world's greatest sculpture.

I was also almost immediately aware that both the casts and the contemporary pieces were variations on a similar theme. The figures were all young men or boys, Apollos or Jasons, with no Dianas or Athenas in sight. Meant to represent gods, soldiers or athletes, they had titles like *Pro Patria* or *Pax Labor*, and the spears, plows, discuses, and other implements they carried suggested they represented high ideals in athletics, labour, love of country, and so forth.

The poses, however, suggested something quite other. Regardless of their occupation, they were all young, handsome, and naked—or almost naked except for a belt or sash or piece of drapery fluttering incongruously below their waists, ostensibly hiding but actually drawing attention to the genitals swelling beneath them. The real subject matter was the beauty of the young male body.

The more I studied them, the more I felt my face flushing as I started to have completely unexpected thoughts about my father. I imagined him in a loose robe and slippers in this room caressing one of these pieces as I was doing or even handling some actual young man in the same manner. The thought appalled me.

What made it worse was I could not help but notice that handling the bronzes was arousing me. It brought into sharp focus a world of emotions I had been trying to keep at bay for years. I quickly put the Warrior down and pushed these thoughts away. I hoped that Griswold had not noticed anything. I was grateful that he didn't say a word.

Griswold then led me to the back of the house. There, with windows overlooking the garden, was a room handsomely panelled in oak with a large desk in the centre. Griswold walked directly over to a large wardrobe and opened it. I started to remove some of the contents. The first boxes I opened contained nothing more than everyday papers, invoices and letters. But towards the back I found a small portfolio of charcoal sketches on Arches paper. The principal figure in each case was a handsome youth of about sixteen, naked or nearly so.

In one sketch the boy was dressed in military boots and a short Roman toga that barely covered his buttocks and genitals. In another he was wearing just a hat but with a bow in his hand and a quiver of arrows held by a strap over his shoulder that just grazed his right nipple—as if he were about to go out hunting in the nude. In yet another, the boy was standing with his head thrown back either in agony or in ecstasy. It was difficult to tell.

In the most carefully worked sketch, the boy was seated in profile on a tabletop draped with heavy cloth, clasping his legs with his arms. It had an inscription, now faded to faint sepia: "Pour Joseph, de ton ami dévoué, Jean-Louis, Souvenir de Rome, 1853." This must have been some kind of present from the artist.

My eyes were burning. Where did my father acquire the drawings? Did he know the artist? Did he know the boy? Maybe most painful of all, why was I aroused? I glanced at Griswold, but he seemed unsurprised. He, like my mother and uncle, obviously knew more about my father's life than I did. However, when I tried to elicit further information from him, he only said my father brought the sketches back from Rome along with a many other pieces of art.

The rising consternation I felt was soon eclipsed by what we found in the drawer of the big mahogany desk. It was locked, but we pried it open. Inside, in a handsome intarsia box, also locked but with the key still in the keyhole, was a set of objects, each enclosed in a maroon velvet bag secured with a drawstring and carefully swaddled in layers of muslin. As we opened the bags, we found shards of pottery, pieces of carved ivory, and numerous coins. All the objects appeared to be ancient, and all the imagery erotic.

The object in the largest bag appeared to have been carved from an elephant tusk. The cylindrical shaft tapered slightly, but at one end was a large bulbous swelling, an almost completely smooth helmet-like protuberance that must have been a separate piece affixed to the cylinder, the joint so neatly done it was all but undetectable. The piece was unmistakably phallic.

I was so embarrassed holding this piece of ivory with Griswold standing next to me that I turned away, pretending to focus my attention on a small painting on the opposite wall of sheep grazing. When I could compose myself sufficiently to examine the object more closely, I saw that at the centre of the cylinder was a beautifully rendered scene, executed in high relief and set in a medallion.

It showed two men standing in profile. The older, bearded, figure was shown in the act of handing a shallow bowl to the youth opposite him. I had seen enough Greek pottery to know that this scene represented the presentation of a kylix, a gift, a token of love, from an older man, the *erastes*, to his younger friend, the *eromenos*. Outside the medallion, the entire surface of the ivory was filled with low relief figures of men and boys wrestling, caressing, and copulating.

I jumped when Griswold said in the most matter-of-fact way, "Is it possible that it is the same boy as in the sketch signed by Jean-Louis?" No sooner had the words left his mouth than I knew he was correct, and that this was not a new observation for him.

"Yes," I replied, "and I suspect, given how similar they are in style, both images were done by the same artist—no doubt the Jean-Louis who wrote the inscription to my father." As I said this, I became intensely embarrassed. "Did you already know this?"

Always tactful, Griswold evaded the question. "I am sorry, Sir, but I'm woefully ignorant about the finer points of art. Your father was a great scholar. He sometimes tried to talk to me about art, but I have no head for it."

The revelations at the house on Carlton Hill so agitated me that I barely remember leaving and starting the journey back to Barrington Hall. On the way I was too embarrassed to ask Griswold directly about my father's activities, but I posed a number of what I imagined were innocuous questions hoping to elicit some information. However, Griswold was remarkably adept at answering every question without disclosing anything. No matter how I turned it over in my mind, I could only reach one conclusion: my father, seemingly the most conventional of men, had led a double life for many years,

After the shock of the trip subsided, I found myself thinking more about my father's life than I ever had when he was alive. Despite his average size and unexceptional appearance, he dominated any crowd he was in. I could never understand why. His features were regular but unexceptional. He always dressed in suits so impeccably tailored that no one would have guessed how expensive they were. By middle age he had gained a fair amount of weight the way many Englishmen do. By the time I was born, he was already starting to lose his hair and require thick spectacles. Nevertheless, he seemed to tower over everyone else by sheer force of personality. I wondered how such a father could have had a son like me. People told me I looked a good deal like him, but I seemed to be as timid and indecisive as he was forceful. I was constantly worried that he was disappointed in me.

Beyond this, thoughts about my father were hopelessly muddled. I knew he was a faithful member of the Established Church. He would have known that any intimate activity with members of his own sex was a sin. But even so, it now seemed clear to me he defied this clear prohibition. He must have concluded his need for intimacy was so urgent that he was willing to violate his faith and his vows.

As these thoughts passed through my mind, I wondered about my own attraction to men. In the past, I had told myself it was only temporary, but after my discoveries at my father's house, I felt deeply uneasy. Was this disposition hereditary? Was it possible I would one day find myself in the same position? My ruminations became so painful I pushed the matter from my mind.

In the days that followed, I was angry with my father for deceiving me and everyone else. If he had not had an alternate life in London, he would have had more time and inclination to know me better. But then I decided I was at least as much to blame for not trying to know him. I found myself almost pitying him. His need was so compelling he was willing to jeopardize everything that was most important to him—his family and his business. He must have been conflicted and unhappy.

I tried to think back on what clues I might have missed. From all reports, he was a good but far from brilliant student, and that at Oxford he became passionate about art. After he finished his studies, he hoped to be a painter, but my grandfather, a stern and forbidding patriarch from another era, expected him to enter the family banking business.

I could well imagine how difficult it would be to counter grandfather's wishes. Still, my father persisted, and after working at the bank for two years, he received permission to travel to Rome and Paris to study art. The idea was to allow him to see if he had sufficient talent to make a successful career for himself. After what I saw at the house on Carlton Hill, I wondered if his real reason for going was to escape the family and explore life more freely on his own.

For reasons never discussed by the family, he abandoned his dream. He came back to England and resumed work at the bank. A few years later, when grandfather died, he took over as head of the enterprise. He was extremely successful in expanding the business, and, due to his zealous attention to some financial transactions with the British Navy, became a trusted financial advisor to members of Her Majesty's government. In gratitude, a group of high officials in the Admiralty persuaded Her Majesty to raise him to the status of viscount while I was still a boy. I remember being proud of him.

He was the very picture of success. He bought a grand house in Berkeley Square in London's Mayfair that he renamed Barrington House and remodelled it in what I, in my youthful arrogance, considered the unfortunate taste of the previous generation. Several years later, he secured a country seat by purchasing a large and recently built house in Surrey, which he expanded and remodelled. I dismissed the dark stone and thin plaster details as an unsuccessful attempt to evoke the medieval style. Almost immediately after his death and the transfer of both houses to my ownership, I started to remember the many things I appreciated about them, and I deeply regretted some of the comments I had made.

Over the years my father amassed a significant art collection that was displayed in both houses, and, I now realized, at the house in St John's Wood. The nucleus was the assortment of antiquities he had brought back to England from his sojourn on the Continent. To that he added paintings, sculpture, tapestries, and objects of all kinds.

In addition to his success at the bank, my father was widely seen as successful in his role as a head of household. He married Emily Tallmadge, the attractive and accomplished daughter of Admiral Augustus Tallmadge. My parents appeared to all to be a prosperous and happy couple, eminently respectable, the kind of people who never raised their voices and to whom no scandal ever attached. They raised two children, my sister and myself, and guests came away with the impression we were a model family.

By the time I reached my tenth birthday, however, I was aware of changes in our household. Even though I was usually too absorbed in my own world to pay much attention to the lives of my parents, it became obvious even to me that they were leading increasingly separate lives, with my father in town much of the time while my mother remained in the country.

She seemed to lose all interest in London society and started spending most of her time with my sister and me and a few of the neighbouring ladies. She started dressing mostly in greys and blacks with little jewellery and pulled her hair tightly back. She rarely ventured into London except to manage affairs at our house there or to participate in the Ladies' Committee of the Bishop's Home Mission.

She was, in fact, quite efficient at running both households. Despite her quiet, unassuming manner, my mother had a remarkable head for business, and I believe she was the driving force, although always behind the scenes, in many of the crucial decisions that were made at the bank. She was remarkably skilled in managing people, and I imagine she might have done even better at running the business than he.

My mother was quite attentive to my sister Alicia and me. I was close to Alicia, who was three years older than I. Despite the fact that I was the male descendant and heir, she always took the lead in whatever we did, and I rarely complained. While I was away at school she married Roger Forrest, a suitable husband quite widely and accurately regarded as the dullest man in England. He was immediately drawn tightly into the family circle, lunching with my father at his club and expected at some point to take over leadership of the Stapleton Bank.

After I returned to Barrington Hall, I was surprised that neither my mother nor my sister had any interest in hearing what I found at the house on Carlton Hill. One day, as we were sitting in the library, I decided to ask them directly, "Did you know about the house in St John's Wood?"

My mother put down her book, stood up, and walked toward the fireplace so I could not see her face. "All men like to have a place of their own," she said, "and Carlton Hill was your father's. I never gave a thought to it. In any case, it is yours now." There was a rare and unmistakable strain in her voice. I knew she was not telling the truth.

I tried again. "Did you know anything about the Greek and Roman antiquities he kept there?" Mother didn't answer. When the silence became oppressive, Alicia responded. "Father was interested in classical art and wished to write about it for scholarly journals. He needed a place away from his business and from demands we might have on his time."

My mother turned sharply toward us, and I could see on her face they had divulged more than they intended. I was embarrassed for them and vowed to avoid any further mention of it.

Chapter 3:

At the British Museum

While I was waiting to speak to my Uncle Rupert, I made an appointment to see the keeper of the Department of Greek and Roman Antiquities at the British Museum, a Mr. Charles Thomas Newton. I wanted to ask him about the antiquities at Carlton Hill.

In preparation, I made an unannounced return trip to the house to retrieve the portfolio of sketches and the box of Greek and Roman artifacts. While I was there, I spoke briefly to Mrs Farrell. I asked her some further questions about my father. She rambled on in her incoherent way about his kindness as an employer and what she imagined was the loss to the world that he had not concluded his research. I was only half listening, but then she said something that caught my attention.

"Your father was so kind to be inviting young artists to come here, you know, for his advice. Some of them he would be allowing to stay. One or two of them for months. He would be doing everything in his power to help them and their careers. But sure I am that you already know that."

"No, I have heard nothing about his helping young artists," I said. "Who were these young men and how did my father come to know them?"

Mrs. Farrell visibly shrank back, wringing her hands. "Oh my! Perhaps I have said what I oughtn't. I don't know nothing about these boys—young men, I sh'd say, them what is come to the house." Acute distress was obvious in her even more than usually garbled language. Embarrassed by the discomfort I had caused and realizing I was not likely to learn more, I took my leave. I was certain now. Mrs. Farrell also knew what my father did in that house.

Several days later, on an unseasonably warm afternoon, I walked up the Portland stone steps to the great classical colonnade of the British Museum. Inside, passing through the public galleries towards the rear to find the keepers' offices, I was reminded of the way countrymen like my father had gathered art from across the world and shipped it back to the heart of the Empire. In the dim galleries devoted to Greek and Roman art, I was struck as never before by the sheer volume of artifacts that had arrived here as a result of England's wealth and the relative poverty of southern Europe.

I was also struck by the high percentage of artifacts depicting handsome young men, mostly in the nude, and often in the company of older men who were—quite obvious to anyone looking at them carefully—their lovers. It made me marvel about the priggish attitude of the Oxford dons who revered Greek and Roman art but rejected the sensuality that was one of the most conspicuous components of it.

I found Mr. Newton, a plump middle-aged man with deep-set eyes, tortoise-shell spectacles, and a formidable salt-and-pepper beard, in a tiny, cluttered office deep in the bowels of the vast building. I knew Newton was an eminent archaeologist, the celebrated discoverer of the remains of the Temple of Halicarnassus, and a prominent member, like my father, of the Society of Dilettanti.

"I am pleased to meet you, Lord Barrington," Newton rumbled as I entered his office. "My condolences on the loss of your father. We often had occasion to discuss antique art and the paper he was writing on Roman copies of Greek sculpture in English collections. I regret that he never finished it. A real loss to classical scholarship. Please have a seat."

After I settled into the chair opposite his desk, I told him I had brought with me a case with a few samples from the house in St John's Wood. I didn't know whether my father had mentioned the nature of his collection to him, and I was concerned he might be shocked.

I need not have worried. He winced when he saw some of the objects but said only, "Let me assure you that the Greeks and Romans produced this kind of work in considerable quantities. Generations of gentlemen making the Grand Tour have brought them back, and examples are to be found all across Europe and America, and, I should add, in the collections of serious institutions such as this one.

"To own them does not endorse the odious behaviour they portray. Institutions such as ours collect them because of their artistry. Whatever their subject matter, they are valuable to serious scholars for the light they shine on the development of style in the ancient world. Of course, because of the shameful subject matter, we rarely make them accessible to the general public, which would likely be interested in them for the wrong reasons. They are kept in the Private Case."

After looking carefully at some of the coins and shards of pottery, he said, "I believe that most of these artifacts are genuine Greek or Roman work, but some were probably made recently. I am afraid it is sometimes quite difficult to distinguish between the two, all the more so since the Romans themselves often created blatant forgeries of Greek originals.

"In addition, although our artists today might not be able to rival Phidias or Polykleitos in creating new works of art, recent advances in technology allow artisans today to make better forgeries than the Romans did, and they produce them in copious quantities. The result is that almost all collections have a mix of more and less authentic artifacts. We may never know for certain which is which."

Finally, I took out the ivory piece carved from an elephant tusk. Even before I could hand it to him, he pulled back suddenly. I could see that he was highly agitated. He began slowly and deliberately. "This is a *fascinum*, supposedly a sacred ithyphallic object, a *medicus invidiae*, so to speak. But, like the human member on which it was modelled, it obviously had, ahem, other uses, if you know what I mean." I quickly looked away to hide my embarrassment.

"Quite a few of these pieces, in wood and metal, less commonly in ivory, which was a rare material, have come down to us. But this one," and here Newton seemed even more uncomfortable, "I hesitate even to say . . . I am almost certain that this piece, or at least a piece almost identical, is known to most serious students of antique art, because, um, its involvement in a scandalous event in Rome several decades ago."

"A scandalous event?"

"Yes. A grisly murder. The victim was a German scholar and dealer in antiquities, many of them apparently inauthentic, named Johann Gottlieb. I am not sure how the ivory was, um, ahem, involved."

Newton seemed to choke on the words. "I believe that after the murder, the ivory in question was deposited in a museum in Rome. I assume it is still there, so perhaps this piece was once half of a pair."

Then, with a small snort of relief, "Or perhaps the resemblance is just accidental." A long pause. "Yes, that must be it." Newton's eyes drifted away. "Still, it is exactly like the images I have seen of the Roman ivory, and the reports could not have escaped Joseph's attention. I wonder how he . . . why he . . ." Newton paused again. His jovial manner had disappeared completely. He looked as embarrassed as I was.

I didn't know what to say. Yet another distressing revelation. It was impossible to imagine my father, so reserved and cautious, being involved with a dealer in stolen antiquities, let alone a murder. On the other hand, I would never have guessed he led a secret life in St John's Wood.

Finally, Newton shook his head as if clearing it and continued in his most professorial manner. "I would be hard-pressed to say whether this is a real work from antiquity or a recent forgery. The sheer volume of erotic art that has survived since antiquity is surprising, and the percentage of it devoted to unnatural acts more surprising still." His voice trailed off and his gaze drifted towards the tiny window.

I don't remember what else Newton might have said during the few minutes I remained in his office. I was suddenly overwhelmed with a desire to find out what I could about the ivory and the sketches, why my father had them, and what his life had been like on the Continent before he returned to England.

I had already formulated a plan to do a tour of the Continent at the completion of my studies. I wanted this trip to complete my education and perhaps give me a clearer sense of what kind of career I wanted. Now I had an additional motive. I still had Hilary and Trinity terms to finish at Oxford, but I decided to postpone my studies there and travel as soon as possible.

Chapter 4:

Return to Oxford

I already knew something about intimate relations between men. At dusk one day when I was still quite young, walking idly around the outbuildings at Barrington Hall, I turned a corner and caught a brief glimpse of Oliver, our Irish stable boy. He was only a few years older than I but was already much more developed. He was leaning over a railing in the stable with his pants around his ankles. A burly older man whose face I could not make out was standing behind him, thrusting himself against Oliver's backside.

At the time, I had only the most general idea of what was going on, but it was clear that I had interrupted something I should not have seen. I turned and fled and tried to forget the image, but it stayed with me. I was too embarrassed to ask Oliver about it.

Several years later, I had an initiation of my own at the hands of my cousin Alastair in a stone cottage that members of our family occupied along the coast near Penzance during the summertime. Three of my male cousins and I slept in a loft at the top of one of the cottages. Accessible only by a narrow ladder on the exterior, that little room was all but closed off from the adult world below.

One night Alastair climbed into my bed after the other two had fallen asleep. He was only two or three years older than I, but he seemed much older, as if he were already a man. He was almost a foot taller and already had a powerful body and dark hair covering his chest. I, on the other hand, was thin and almost hairless below the head. I thought Alastair very handsome and would have loved to have him as a friend and ally, but until that night he had studiously avoided me except when contact was unavoidable. In those cases, he usually made some mildly insulting remark, particularly if there was another cousin nearby.

Needless to say, I was astonished when he got into bed with me, pulled off his nightshirt and drawers and hissed into my ear "Frig me." By this time, I had already had ample experience frigging myself, and I was certainly not averse to having my handsome cousin in my bed, but I was so startled by his demand that I froze. He grabbed my hand, cupped it around his member and started pushing it up and down. I was amazed how large it grew under my touch. He started to buck his hips and I saw a stream of hot creamy liquid spatter across his chest. Alastair laughed, cleaned himself using my sheet and quickly retreated to his own bed.

At first, I was appalled. The next time he came to my bed at night I tried to stop him. "Alastair, I think that what you are doing—we are doing—is a sin."

Alastair just laughed. "Silly boy. It is entirely natural for a virile young man like myself to find relief where I can. Besides, you seem to be the kind of boy who likes it," he said, reaching down to grab my half hard member. I was mortified but said nothing. Then he grabbed my head and kissed me on the lips. "You are more like a girl than a boy anyway." Now I was angry and started to object, but he cut me off abruptly. "I need it, and you like it. If you say one word to anyone, I will tell everyone what you are."

His occasional visits lasted all summer. Some nights, he would thrust his member up against my stomach or rub it between my thighs until he spent himself on me and my sheets. When I protested, he said, "You should be grateful that I am not actually penetrating you. Men who allow themselves to be penetrated are the lowest of the low. They are sodomites." It helped only slightly to think that as long as what we were doing was against my will, the blame was mostly his.

Still, I spent hours in anguish over the fact I was complicit in one of the gravest sins in the Bible. My shame was enhanced by the fact that, if my cousins were awake, they would undoubtedly have understood what we were doing. In the morning, there was the embarrassment of knowing that the housekeeper would see the sheets and think that I had soiled them. Still, that was nothing compared to the shame I had knowing Alastair had told the truth about at least one thing. The encounters were intensely arousing to me.

When I was away at school at Winchester College, it was impossible to escape the undertone of young male lust that permeated the place, the constant soft noises and faint odour that resulted from pervasive fervid couplings. Although I was sorely tempted, I was too timid to engage in the activity around me. I convinced myself that any feelings I had for older men were natural for my age and that I would eventually find myself more attracted to women. I prayed obsessively that God would deliver me from my terrible longings.

By the time I got to Oxford, most of my friends had passed out of what had been for them an experimental phase and were interested only in women. This only intensified my mortification. There were, of course, boys who continued to sin with members of their own sex. I was acutely aware of the hypocrisy at the school. Although any intimate act between members of the same sex was officially frowned on, it was clearly a long-standing part of the culture of the place. Some of the tutors delighted in having us read passages from Aristophanes, Plato, Lucretius, Catullus, Martial, Petronius, and Ovid that unmistakably described unnatural acts.

I knew about Achilles and Patroclus, Orpheus on his return from Hades, David and Jonathan, Socrates and Alcibiades, Antinous and Hadrian, Julius Caesar, the "wife to all husbands and husband to all wives," Michelangelo, Frederick the Great of Prussia, Beethoven, the American poet Walt Whitman. And I had heard recently an extraordinarily funny fragment of doggerel about the "Arsebishop," Percy Jocelyn, the Lord Bishop of Clogher, a town whose name was pronounced, "Clugger":

The Devil to prove the Church was a farce
Went out to fish for a Bugger.
He baited his hook with a Soldier's arse
And pulled up the Bishop of Clogher.

Clandestine drawings, mostly crude but some remarkably accomplished, were produced in quantity and passed around or drawn on toilet stalls. Of course, it was bad form to talk openly about any of this.

At Oxford I finally became aware that my attraction to men was not a passing fancy. This was a bitter realisation. Throughout my childhood I had tried to be the perfect son and, in a refrain I heard constantly from my mother, "a credit to the family." In their eyes, I succeeded. My parents rarely scolded me, and my sister complained that it was all too obvious I was their favourite child. For me, to seem perfect in their eyes but harbour a terrible secret only heightened my anxiety.

I thought at least I could try to avoid impure thoughts. I became friendly with Athena Briggs, a pretty young woman from a wealthy Baltimore family living in London. I met her at Christchurch College through her brother William. William was tall and athletic and looked striking in his cricket whites, which set off perfectly the slightly olive tone of his face and the sturdiness of his legs and arms.

William had a friendly, open manner and dazzling smile, and everyone seemed either to admire or be jealous of him. Athena was like him in many ways, and it was probably that similarity that drew me to her. I think that she aspired to a literary career, and I never doubted she had at least the ambition necessary to make a go of it. We could sit for hours and talk about the latest novels serialized in the newspapers.

My parents kept encouraging me to court Athena, which I did. We became good friends. I even imagined that there was no reason why, if we married, I could not learn to love her. We talked about becoming engaged, though I don't think either of us was really serious. Still, the suggestion we were thinking of marriage seemed to please both of our families and relieved a little my sense of guilt.

Her willingness to discuss an engagement did reassure me on another score. I had long feared that my appearance was not likely to attract anyone. When I looked in the mirror, I saw a face that was not ugly, but plain. Like my father's but without the fire of ambition that seemed to light his features. My hair was lacklustre and my figure middling. In short, nothing to be ashamed of but quite out of the league of some of the most popular boys at school.

All these thoughts were in my mind when I made a quick trip to Oxford to put my affairs there in order. By chance, I happened across a particularly effeminate young man everyone called Mallory. Someone had told me that his actual name was Olivier Maloof but that he wished to obscure any connection to his wealthy Levantine family. It was rumoured that his father had sent him to Oxford with a generous allowance if he promised not to return home. He was also rumoured to be the lover of one of the dons in Magdalen College.

Maloof was slowly walking down Merton Street toward the Canterbury Gate, looking absently-mindedly at the upper floors of the adjoining buildings. He was tall and thin, wearing some sort of odd, vaguely oriental outfit of ballooning green pants, scarlet waistcoat, flowing grey coat and no overcoat, despite the biting wind. An enormous green silk scarf was elaborately tied around his neck, falling down his back almost to his green pigskin boots.

It felt like Fate had put him on that street for me to encounter. I thought that perhaps I could speak to him in a way that I could not to family or friends. I walked across the street. "Hello. You're Maloof, are you not?"

"Yes, I am. But why, I ask myself, would this young son of British nobility, who has never spoken to me before, suddenly be addressing the notorious brown fellow from halfway around the world?" Maloof's English was lightly perfumed with a French accent.

Startled, I looked around to see if anyone was observing us. Maloof did the same. "You are quite safe, my dear boy. There is no one here to witness your accosting the flamboyant Olivier Maloof."

I recovered enough to say, "I wondered if I might have a chat with you."

"How intriguing. A chat. Well, yes, I think that might be possible, indeed even desirable. Where would you imagine we would, um, consummate our little chat?"

"How about tomorrow at four at the Bullingdon Club?" It would be highly unlikely we would meet anyone I knew there.

"That would be perfect. I'm positively burning with curiosity to discover the nature of our chat. *À bientôt, mon chéri.*" And with that he twirled away down the street.

I arrived early the next afternoon and picked a table in the rear where we would be inconspicuous. Unfortunately, my plan backfired. Maloof had to traverse the length of the room to reach the table. By the time he made his way to me, his loud voice and brilliant plumage had attracted the attention of everyone in the place. Every eye in the room was on us when I stood up to shake his hand.

He extended his as though he expected me to kiss it. I grabbed it quickly, gave it a firm shake, and promptly released it. He looked amused. We sat. I asked him what I should order and was not surprised when he requested a sweet Italian liqueur. I ordered ale.

I cannot remember the first half hour of our visit except that it was mostly local gossip, dominated by Maloof. As the hour dragged on, I started to worry he would leave before I came to the point, so I summoned up the courage to tell him about the death of my father and the discovery of the artifacts in the house in St John's Wood. I was greatly relieved when the mere mention of St John's Wood set Maloof off on a monologue that made it quite clear he understood what I was trying to ask.

"Ah yes. St John's Wood," he said. "I believe I can enlighten you a little. But my dear boy, I don't wish to offend your delicate sensibilities."

"I don't think that anything you tell me will offend my sensibilities," I replied.

"About that I am dubious, but I will proceed. I also should specify that anything I say needs to stay strictly *entre nous*. There is nothing worse than a loose tongue. I deplore the way some men prattle on about matters that should remain entirely confidential."

"Yes, of course." Before I could say anything more, Maloof was talking again.

"I myself may have been a guest at one of the better residences in that vicinity, although I must say it ain't really the fashionable place for young gentlemen like myself."

I just nodded.

"Most, but certainly not all, of what transpires there involves affluent older gentlemen and younger specimens of the so-called fair sex, although I must say that to my mind nothing is more fair than a handsome boy. Leaving this linguistic curiosity aside, I'm not surprised that your father, like a few gentlemen of my acquaintance, would want a pied-à-terre in that neighbourhood to carry on affairs with members of the *not*-so-fair sex.

"Of course I'm referring to 'trade,' the practice whereby gentlemen elect to meet a companion who can provide the services they require for five or ten shillings. Young clerks, tailors' assistants, shoeblacks, and all those divine soldiers, the First, the Foot Guards and the Blues. Above all the Blues, what with those divine uniforms supposedly designed by Michelangelo, you know . . ." Maloof paused. As he was speaking, I realised my father might well have paid for the companionship of boys, but the idea scandalized me.

Maloof continued, "Of course, a gentleman could complete the entire transaction in a molly house, but for those who can afford it, a private house away from family and public scrutiny is much safer and more discreet, and—"

I finally broke in, "I understand what you are saying, but I confess that I don't understand how my father would meet a boy of this kind in the first place."

"Nothing could be simpler. For those with offices in the City, the boys who deliver goods or telegrams. For those without offices, there are the arcades of the Royal Exchange or Covent Garden, street corners in Drury Lane, the Regent Street Crescent, Bird Cage Alley. And then there are the more impromptu gatherings, the parties, the *bals masqués*, private events at the Ranelagh Gardens and places of outdoor resort. Not that I have ever observed any of this activity myself," he said with a smirk. "However, they are all available to members of the club."

"The club?"

"I speak metaphorically. To put it crudely, any individual who might be called a practitioner of *paiderastia*, the *more pecundam*, the *crimen sodomitae,* or, as the great Doctor Angelicus Thomas Aquinas put it: the *peccatum contra naturam.* One who engages in *paedicatio* or *irrumatio*, a *Knabenschander*, buggerer, sodomite, catamite, chestnut gatherer, *bichon*, not to mention many terms more colourful but even less polite. I'm afraid now I *have* shocked you."

"No, not all," I replied, although the hue of my face undoubtedly indicated otherwise. I was abashed by this verbal torrent and appalled that anyone might have overheard it.

"Very good," Maloof continued. "I should add that there are a surprisingly large number of gentlemen with such proclivities even in a provincial little backwater like Oxford."

"Here in Oxford?"

"This venerable institution has been a bastion of what the Germans call 'warm relations.' You have heard, I'm sure, about one of our university's brightest lights, the author of *Studies in the History of the Renaissance.*"

"Walter Pater? I have certainly read him. In fact, I'm a great admirer of—"

"Then you know about his fervent admiration for classical Greek art and its attention to the beauty of the young male body."

I was only half listening. I was thinking that Maloof's thin body, his dusky complexion, long eyelashes, jet black eyes, and

31

full reddish lips made him exotic and not unattractive. I was usually only drawn to older men, but I found myself wondering what it would be like to kiss Maloof. But he was still talking.

"As you may know, our revered Mr. Pater was a student a generation ago at Queen's College. Later, a fellow at Brasenose, he had his rooms painted primrose. They became the preferred meeting place of a certain exclusive set. You may be acquainted with one of his regular acolytes, the Irish boy Oscar Wilde, a brilliant youth who is reading Greats at Magdalen. Young Wilde has adopted some of Walter's more curious affectations and added his own. The peacock feathers, the outrageously chequered suits of clothes. He makes me look quite modest by comparison."

"Yes, I have met Wilde." I said. I doubted that Wilde, even at his most precious, could be more ostentatious than Maloof. "And I have heard about him and Pater, and how their devotion to beauty is inspired by classical art and contemporary youths."

"I suppose no one wished to offend you by mentioning the *scandale* involving our Mister Pater and a certain young man whose name, out of my natural disinclination to gossip, I decline to mention."

"I have not heard about any scandal."

"It appears that a certain William Money Hardinge—oh dear, I seem to have let that slip—was a boy who, because of his enthusiasm for certain Greek customs, earned himself the sobriquet 'the Balliol Bugger.' But you seem a sweet innocent boy who would never dream such abominations exist."

"Well, I very much doubt that I'm as sweet and innocent as you think." I was now both embarrassed and annoyed. Speaking more loudly than I should have, I said, "And I don't think of myself as a boy."

"I can assure you that I meant no disrespect. For many men of a certain persuasion, the word 'boy' is a capacious term and can apply to men of all ages if they take the passive role."

I think by this point even Maloof was aware that I was desperate to leave. I was relieved when he took the initiative, standing, bidding me farewell, and once again drawing all eyes to him as he exited the room. I waited a few minutes before I walked out as well.

Unfortunately, the wait accomplished nothing. Almost every man in the room had their eyes fixed on me as I left. I was grateful to Maloof for opening my eyes to many things I had never suspected, but if anything, our chat had only deepened my anxieties about myself and my future.

Chapter 5:

Uncle Rupert's Revelations

The house in St John's Wood and meeting with Maloof put my relationship with my father in a new light. Before, I had felt sorry about his death, but it was mostly a vague regret. Now I became much more engaged with my memories of him, curious what his life had been like, and deeply sorry that he had passed away before I could know him better. I would not have had the courage to ask him directly about what he did in Rome or Paris or St John's Wood, but maybe one day he would have revealed some hints.

I hoped my Uncle Rupert could tell me more. Three years younger than my father and twenty years my senior, he had been an oarsman at Oxford and was still a frequent polo player. He was fit, dressed well, and cut a dashing figure. He radiated wellbeing and smiled often. When he did, it lit up his face and seemed to draw people to him.

He did something at the family bank, although no one seemed to know what. He appeared to be more interested in art and circulating in London society than in matters mercantile. Growing up, I spent quite a considerable amount of time with my uncle discussing art. Rupert had one of the most impressive collections of modern art in Britain and knew many of the foremost artists.

On our frequent trips to the galleries and museums I found my own tastes mirroring his. He loved big historical canvases by artists like Lord Leighton, Alma-Tadema, and Gérôme. He had a huge painting by Alma-Tadema of Roman gladiators that almost completely covered one wall of his dining room. My uncle and I deemed this kind of painting infinitely superior to the crude canvases of certain French artists who called themselves "Impressionists."

After the revelations about my father, I started to wonder if Uncle Rupert, given his taste for art, certain mannerisms, and the fact that he never married, had similar inclinations. I was amazed this thought had not occurred to me earlier.

On a cool, overcast afternoon in March, I walked up the limestone steps to his house on Holland Villas Road. It was a substantial stuccoed building that he had purchased just after it was completed. Before he moved in, he had several of the rooms redone in the Moorish style with mounds of cushions in oriental fabrics, antique painted wooden panels pierced with arabesque designs, great brass hookah pipes, and clouds of sheer billowing draperies. The rooms were the talk of the town. My parents had only sarcastic comments about them, and even I, visiting as a young boy, wondered about these exotic affectations.

Rupert's man ushered me into the glass-walled conservatory. The room was heated by hissing radiators and heavily perfumed from my uncle's exotic brugmansias, which opened only after dark but whose pungent scent lingered all day.

Uncle Rupert took a seat on a low divan and motioned for me to sit opposite him. Between us was a small Moorish table with a beaten brass top. A servant girl brought in tea and scones with clotted cream and jam.

Rupert smiled. "My dear boy, I understand from old Griswold that you visited the house on Carlton Hill. Of course, he didn't say it in so many words, but it was clear from what he did that you tried to hide your discomfort with what you saw. I'm sorry you had to find out about your father this way."

"Yes, I confess I was startled. I hope you can help me understand."

"Let me try to explain. As you know, Joseph worked at the family bank for a few years after Oxford. He was thorough and diligent. Everyone expected he would take over from your grandfather."

"Yes, I knew that much."

"I followed Joseph to Oxford and then to the bank three years later, assuming I would play only a minor role. However, when

Joseph decided to leave for the Continent, suddenly I found my-self the family member next in line to take over. I am sorry to say my performance didn't auger well for my eventual leadership of the firm.

"I must apologise for what I'm about to say. I have no idea how much you have guessed, or how much I ought to tell you, but now that your father is gone, I feel you have a right to know, and I'm sure that neither your mother nor your sister would be comfortable telling you, so the duty falls to me. It is not an alto-gether edifying tale. Are you sure you want to hear?"

"Yes, please. I'm not as naïve as you might think."

"I'm not sure about that, but we shall see. I must caution you to keep what I'm about to tell you entirely to yourself. There is no point in blackening the reputation your late father earned over many years as head of a family and head of a bank, or in casting any shadow on either institution. If what I'm about to tell you would become public, it could have serious consequences, even for you and me."

"Of course, I understand."

"Very good. To return to the story: just as my utter lack of skill in managing a bank was becoming clear to everyone, we started hearing rumours about a liaison your father had made with a young man—more a boy than a man, really—in Paris. Your grandfather was livid when these rumours reached his ears. He applied considerable pressure on Joseph to relinquish that rela-tionship and take his rightful place here. When that failed to produce the desired effect, I was dispatched to Paris to confront him, urge him to abandon the liaison and return home.

"I pushed him hard but not because I had any qualms about his relationship. I have known a few men with his proclivities. As far as I can see, they lead sad and lonely lives and are subject to ridicule, blackmail, and worse. However, as long as Joseph caused no scandal and brought no stain to the family name, I considered it a matter between him and his Maker." Rupert picked up his teacup and took a sip.

"I confess that my motives were more selfish. I wanted him back because my role at the bank was becoming increasingly uncomfortable, and I knew Joseph was ideally suited to the task. Your grandfather and I even briefly discussed the possibility of bringing the boy here to London and accommodating him in some manner. We went so far as to contemplate settling on him a small apartment and an allowance of two hundred a year, which my research indicated was a not atypical arrangement, although, of course, more often used for young women than young men."

This was shocking. Members of my family knew about my father's activities and were prepared to turn a blind eye, even to have them continue in London.

"In the end, I never really knew whether Joseph returned because of some feeling of loyalty toward the family, a crisis with the boy, or something else. We never talked about it. In fact, we were so happy to see him back in England that even your grandfather agreed to ask no questions. In the years that followed, hardly anything related to the subject crossed the lips of anyone in the family."

I was watching Rupert closely as he talked. He seemed to be distancing himself from my father's proclivities, yet everything about him seemed to suggest he was cut from the same cloth.

He continued. "At first, Joseph buried himself in work. He would stay at the bank until all hours, and he proved an effective manager. Within a year, your grandfather turned over full control to him. After Joseph was married and you and your sister were born, everyone breathed a sigh of relief and thought that maybe he had put the business in Paris out of mind. However, a few years later, after the death of your grandfather and Joseph's ascent to the peerage, he bought the house in St John's Wood and started spending considerable time there.

"He told the family that he had bought the place because it was a convenient location to have meetings, entertain business acquaintances away from the office, and to study Greek and Roman sculpture in the library he had assembled. He said he was preparing a paper to be published by the Society of Dilettanti on some subject. I have forgotten what. However, that essay seemed always to require more research. As far as I know, it never materialized."

"Yes, I heard as much from Newton at the British Museum."

"You have spoken to Newton? I see you have made a serious start to your research. Over the years," he continued, "I heard several remarkable stories about what happened at Joseph's house in St. John's Wood. They didn't seem at all in character with your father as we knew him, but after your grandfather died, he apparently felt he could resume some of the, um, activity that he had enjoyed on the Continent. I eventually learned from Griswold that your father had been lodging young men at the house, and I guessed the rest."

"Did my mother suspect?"

"This is only conjecture because I have never spoken to her about it, but your mother is extraordinarily perceptive. I dare say she must have known about your father long before I did. If so, she apparently decided that her marriage and the upbringing of her children were too important to jeopardise by creating a fuss. I assume that she deliberately turned a blind eye."

"So, you knew about all this, as did Griswold, and Mrs. Farrell, and my mother and sister. Was I the only one who had no idea?"

"My dear boy, you are intelligent and quick-witted, but you have an open and trusting personality that makes you slow to suspect that what people tell you isn't always the truth. I don't say this as a criticism. It is part of your good nature and charm. But it also means you probably miss a good deal when it comes to understanding other people."

"I'm grateful for your candour." I paused, trying to formulate my next question. "I hope you will not mind my asking you something quite personal. And, of course, if you don't feel it is appropriate. . . I . . . I don't know how to say this, but—" I became flustered, but to my great relief, my uncle intervened.

"No, Robert. I think I know what you want to ask me. The answer is that even if I'm not the marrying kind, I am otherwise quite conventional—although I can see," he said with a sweep of his arm, "why you or anyone else might think otherwise. I suppose it is one of Nature's cruel tricks that when She made your father and me, She made each of us what we were. Because of my all-too-public experiences with members of the opposite sex, I have rarely had to battle suspicion."

"Thank you for everything you have told me," I said.

"You are most welcome. I'm just sorry that I couldn't speak to you more openly in the past, but your father made it clear to me that he wanted family members to know as little as possible about his life in Paris or at the house on Carlton Hill."

He paused there and seemed lost in thought for a moment. "I do think that in the last few years he might have had some change of heart, though. He might have thought that, after you left Oxford, he might tell you a little more himself."

"I imagine that would have been an awkward conversation," I replied, "but I do wish that he had been able to confide in me."

"Robert, I am aware I'm now wading into dangerous waters, and forgive me if I'm being too presumptuous, but I sometimes had the impression that he might have thought you might be a . . . might be a member of the same congregation."

"Member of the. . . ? Please, Uncle . . ." I started to stand.

My uncle reached across the table and put his hand on my shoulder. "I'm sorry if I have spoken out of turn, Robert. I beg your pardon."

I pondered for what must have seemed a long time before I said, "You are not the first person to make comments about my, um, interests. I don't know why so many people seem to think I have such tendencies. It isn't something I am comfortable discussing."

"Of course. Of course. Once again, my apologies. If you will permit me to make one further observation on the subject—I think I, and apparently others, have reached that conclusion because you are—and please take it as a compliment—quite attractive in a straightforward kind of way, quiet and serious, and no one has ever linked you to a young woman."

"I am almost engaged."

"Of course, you are. The delightful Miss Briggs. We will not mention it again."

After an awkward pause, the conversation turned to other subjects. Rupert was charming as ever as we discussed the latest news from the galleries and the Royal Society. By the time I left, it was already dark, and the gaslights had come on. The rain had let up a little, but there was still a slight drizzle, and the stone pavement was glistening. I walked a short distance, then stopped at a corner, listening to the rain bouncing off my umbrella and trying to put my thoughts in order. I tried to connect what I had just heard from Uncle Rupert with the image I had of my father, my family and myself. Most of all, myself. Could I have admitted to my uncle that my interest in understanding my father's life was inevitably connected with questions I had about myself?

Chapter 6:

Planning My Tour of the Continent

Before my father's death, when I thought about a trip to the Continent after university, it had been primarily to finish my education and explore some possibilities for my future. My family's position meant that if I wanted, I could have had a life of leisure in London or in the country. However, I knew I wanted some kind of profession.

I knew from an early age that I was intensely interested in art, but I was never certain what kind of career I might pursue. At one point I thought I wanted to be a painter. My parents counselled that, unless I felt a real passion for painting, perhaps architecture might be more practical. My father arranged to take me to visit the offices of Edward Barry, the son of the famous Charles Barry, designer of the Houses of Parliament. He was remarkably solicitous of a young man uncertain of his future and painted a glowing future for me as an architect. But I had a sinking feeling as I looked at row after row of draughtsmen hunched over their tables.

Another possibility had slowly come into focus. I had known for some time that I felt a lack of something in my life, but I had never been able to determine what that something might be. At first, I imagined it might be spiritual. While at Oxford, my friend Samuel persuaded me to accompany him a number of times to the church of St Aloysius. My parents would have been horrified to hear I had entered this bastion of Roman popery, but I had read and was deeply impressed by Cardinal Newman's *Apologia Pro Vita Sua*, and I had several revealing conversations with a man called Gerard Manley Hopkins who had just come to the church as curate. I wondered if the teachings of the Church might help me eradicate my unnatural attractions. At times I even felt I might have a calling in the priesthood.

In retrospect, I see that my interest in the Church had very little to do with its teachings. I had been influenced in part by the enthusiasm of Catholicism's most ardent advocates and particularly that of my friend Samuel. It eventually became clear, however, as I sat with him near the front of the nave studying the stained glass of the chancel and the reredos with its ranks of saints in their niches, that I was more interested in the architecture and interior decoration favored by the Church of Rome than in its theology or liturgy.

Ironically, my interest in art and architecture seemed to make me swing from one side of the spectrum to the other, from Cardinal Newman to Walter Pater, the historian and critic of art who was considered by many of the Oxford community to be a pagan, an enemy of the Church, and a dangerous advocate of sensuality in art and life. I loved Pater's commitment to living life to the fullest and to cherishing beauty wherever it could be found. I could quote paragraphs of Pater, and I'm afraid I did, and all too often. Samuel was appalled, and I saw less and less of him.

I was particularly thrilled at Pater's famous dictum: "To burn always with this hard, gemlike flame, to maintain this ecstasy." I thought to myself: ecstasy. That is certainly one thing I have been missing. My life had been totally without ecstasy. Intellectual, emotional or physical.

The search for ecstasy was connected in my mind in a powerful but highly confusing way with a desire that had been growing more urgent for some time: to experience love. Unfortunately, I had little idea how to find it or what it would feel like when I did. I only suspected that my search would probably be easier far from home. It crossed my mind that this reason for going abroad probably mirrored that of my father.

I wondered briefly whether I could leave England so soon after the death of my father. Fortunately, when I suggested to my mother that I was thinking of leaving earlier than expected for the Continent, she heartily approved of my plan, perhaps thinking that it was my way of dealing with grief. She assured me that management of the bank and the household were in secure hands. She took it on herself to ask my brother-in-law Roger whether he would be interested in the position of General Manager of the bank. He was obviously thrilled to accept the job when it was formally offered. As for the household, to be honest, I think my mother was relieved that I had no interest in inserting myself into her smoothly running operation.

My mother pressed me to take along my father's elderly valet Walters, whom I had inherited along with the real estate and tangible property. Walters was short and slightly stooped with grey eyes and grey teeth and walked with a bit of a limp. He invariably wore a valet's uniform, entirely black, even the buttons, with just a little white of his shirt and collar showing under his waistcoat. His face was extraordinary in its impassive anonymity, the way it never appeared to betray the slightest emotion. He moved silently like a ghost. He would suddenly appear out of nowhere to help me dress or undress or ask if I needed anything.

Walters, like Griswold, had worked for my family since my grandfather's day. Because he undoubtedly knew more about the personal life of my father than anyone else, with the possible exception of my mother, I had hoped he might have the answer to many of my questions, but he had the same uncanny ability as Griswold to appear to answer without revealing anything I wanted to know.

My father seemed to have been quite comfortable talking with both Griswold and Walters. I wondered whether my inability to communicate with them was primarily because I was less outgoing and confident than he or because I was still so young.

I was a little afraid that Walters' age would make him more of a hindrance than a help. Still, I thought, he had accompanied us on family trips and all my father's trips in the past, and he might be helpful with arrangements. Although it was almost impossible to gauge his reaction to anything, from what I could tell, he was gratified I wanted him along.

Chapter 7:

Paris

We left Charing Cross station on a typical murky June morning and endured a choppy crossing of the Channel. After arriving in Paris at the Gare du Nord, we took a cab to the hotel Le Meurice on the rue de Rivoli.

My parents, sister, and I had often stayed at this hotel, which was a great favourite of Englishmen wishing to avoid as much as possible the intrusion of anything foreign during their stay abroad. Walters had advised me which suite of rooms my father had reserved on previous trips, and I took the same.

I was surprised when the hotel manager, a M. Scheurich, came out to the desk himself to welcome us. I remembered him from previous trips as a somewhat imperious figure in a formidable black tailcoat and stiff collar. I was surprised to find him smiling and affable.

"It is my honour to welcome you back to Paris and to Le Meurice. I had the pleasure of knowing your late father for many years. I was sorry to hear of his passing. And, of course, I remember you, your charming mother and sister as well."

I wondered how many times my father had stayed at the hotel without us and what M. Scheurich knew of his activities.

"May I accompany you to your rooms, Lord Barrington?" he said, turning back briefly to snap his fingers at a porter who was standing by our luggage. Walters started giving him instructions.

"Yes. That would be most kind." I was not yet used to being called Lord Barrington, a name I always associated with my father. The deference of the hotel manager suddenly made it clear to me how my standing in the eyes of the world had changed.

Scheurich accompanied us to a set of rooms on the second level. He threw back the velvet curtains in the drawing room and pulled open the windows that extended from the floor almost to the ceiling. Beyond the intricate wrought iron scrolls of a small balcony's railing, I could look directly down on the carriages passing by on the rue de Rivoli and at the Tuileries Garden beyond. It felt like all Paris was at my feet. The feeling was intoxicating and a little frightening.

While Walters unpacked our trunks, I watched children playing in the Terrasse des Feuillants and the *allées* of chestnut trees behind it in the park below. Nearby, the nannies were chattering among themselves on the benches. Altogether, it looked exactly like some of the paintings by Bazille and Caillebotte I had seen in galleries on previous trips. They were perhaps the only painters in the new French manner whom I really appreciated. They seemed to bring a new spontaneity to their views of contemporary Paris without sacrificing traditional painting skills.

I turned away from the window and watched Walters in an adjacent room hanging some of my clothes in a ponderous mahogany and brass armoire in the style of Louis XIV. I didn't expect to learn much, but I thought I would ask anyway. "Why did my father like this hotel?"

"Lord Barrington—the late Lord Barrington I mean, if you will excuse me, Sir—thought that it was the best location in Paris. He said it was close to the Louvre and to the apartments of people he knew. It was the first place he stayed when he arrived here to study art before he moved to the small studio he rented in Montmartre."

I was amazed at what for Walters was a torrent of words. He continued, "He particularly loved being near the Tuileries. It was different then. The Tuileries Palace at the end of the garden was still occupied by the Emperor. Your father loved to walk in the gardens of an evening. He could spend hours strolling there."

"Did my father have many friends in Paris?"

"Not when we first arrived, but after only a few days he

seemed to have an entire circle of young friends. He was young then and sociable."

Could it possibly have been a suppressed smile that passed briefly across those thin, tight lips? I wanted to press him about the "circle of young friends," but by then Walters had moved away. I didn't follow up because I suspected I would learn more from him if he volunteered the information.

My last trip to the city with my parents had taken place shortly after the fall of Paris to the Commune following the war with Prussia in 1871. At that time the city streets still bore the marks of damage caused during the violence. Since then, almost everything had been repaired. Smart carriages filled the streets. The new tree-shaded boulevards were bustling with fashionable ladies and gentlemen on foot and in carriages. The city sparkled. The area around the hotel made even the best quarters of London seem shabby by comparison.

That evening, I decided to go to a performance at the recently completed opera house. It was a fine early summer evening as I set out on foot from the hotel, with the sun just about to set. The pavement on the rue de Rivoli was thronged with gentlemen in gleaming black top hats returning home from their offices, aproned nannies with children in tow, and eager tourists studying their Baedekers.

My route took me through the Place Vendôme. My father had taken me several times to the expensive shops around the Place to buy gifts for my mother and clothes for me. Although for himself he preferred English tailoring, he felt I should keep abreast of what fashionable young men in Paris were wearing. We would also invariably stop in at the Banque de Londres et Paris, the corresponding bank to my family's own establishment, where my father liked to introduce me to his French counterparts.

By the time I reached the Place de l'Opéra it was almost completely dark, but the brilliant Jablakoff lights turned this entire corner of Paris into a brightly lit stage set. Before me stood the grand colonnade of the Opéra, the copper dome covering the great staircase within and, above it all, the crowning figure of Apollo holding aloft a gilt lyre, gloriously nude, gleaming against the last light of the pale Parisian sky.

I paused to examine the sculptural groups representing the various arts that flanked the entrance portals. Three of them were exactly the kind of sedate allegorical exercises one might have expected. Decidedly not so the fourth, representing La Danse, by the sculptor Antoine Carpeaux. I had read a good deal about it. The day the hoarding in front of it came down, notices about it appeared in all the newspapers. It was a masterpiece, some said. It was obscene, said others, confidently asserting that it would henceforth be impossible for respectable ladies and girls to attend the opera. Days later someone splashed ink on the stone, making it necessary to remove the piece for restoration. There was talk of replacing it with something less provocative.

I stopped directly in front of the plinth holding the sculpture just above head height. Seeing it in person was startling but not because of the women dancing at the base, which certain journalists castigated as wanton and lacking in decorum. My eyes instead were instantly drawn to the central figure, the Genius of the Dance. His naked body, erupting out of the ring of women at the base, was bursting with youth and vitality, his quivering flesh almost palpable. Where the figure of Apollo high atop the building was godlike in his splendid manhood, aloof in manner, the young dancer seemed to explode out of the stone.

The way he threw his arms up over his head, arched his chest backward and thrust his hips forward, allowed an unimpeded view of his wonderfully lithe and seductive body, captured by Carpeaux just at the moment when it was turning from that of a boy into that of a man. His genitalia, which would have occupied almost the exact centre of the composition, were hidden by a tiny piece of improbably bunched fabric. This piece of cloth frustrated the eye and made the figure seem even more lascivious to me than many completely exposed sculptural figures I had seen.

And the ecstatic expression on the young dancer's face! Exactly how I imagined such a boy would look at the moment of spending. It took my breath away. I thought back to everything I had read about the work. Remarkably, I had found not a single word about that face and that body. I was certain that at least some of the journalists viewing the piece must have had reactions similar to mine, but presumably describing what they felt would have been considered too great an attack on public morality. The sculptor could express what the writer could not.

Remembering where I was, I quickly looked around. I was relieved to find that no one seemed to be giving him or me more than a glance. I suppose that many people see only what they expect to see.

On entering the building, I was so absorbed by my reflections on Carpeaux's sculpture that it required a few minutes to fully react to the grandeur of the interiors as I walked through the foyer to the grand staircase. The brilliant lighting, the voluptuous sculpted female figures holding torchieres, and the staircase itself, flowing upward beneath tiers of balconies lined with men dressed in black and ladies arrayed in gowns of swirling silk, created a spectacle that put to shame anything we had to offer in London. It occurred to me that this was perhaps the closest our century could come in architecture to the great medieval cathedrals.

I now had an idea for a career. If I could just describe in words what I found so moving in the architecture and decoration of a building like this one, that kind of writing could be my métier—advocating for a modern art that could be as inspired as anything created by the great masters of the past. I decided that I would make copious notes after I returned to the hotel to use for a piece on the Opéra that I would submit to one of the English journals. But would I dare to say anything about the Genius of the Dance?

Chapter 8:

Pederasty in Paris

My first social event in Paris was a dinner party in my honour hosted by an officer at the British Embassy whose wife was a friend of Uncle Rupert's. It was a small but elegant gathering at a pavilion masquerading as a Swiss chalet on an island in the Bois de Boulogne.

Among the guests were a number of officers, present and past, of the British Embassy and some artists of Rupert's acquaintance. One of these, I soon discovered, had been at the Académie Mersault with my father in the mid-1850s. He confirmed what I already knew—that my father had studied privately with the painter Tony Robert-Fleury and then enrolled at the Mersault in preparation for entry into the celebrated École des Beaux-Arts. He remembered my father as a lively young man but without the driving ambition or egotism necessary to become a successful artist.

The individual who seemed to have known my father best was a man named Vincent Outerbridge, who had recently retired from his job as an attaché at the embassy. We chatted at length about British residents of Paris but didn't get to the subject of my father until after the *glace plombières*.

"I have no idea about your father's skill as a painter," he said, "but he was part of a circle of artists and architects, most of them older than he, who were constantly making the rounds of the salons, the restaurants, the theatres. And they gave rather notorious private parties. But I'm not sure I should tell you more, particularly so soon after your father's death."

"Please. I'm interested in learning as much as I can no matter where this information leads me."

"I understand, but let's take a walk away from the others. What I say is for your ears only."

"Yes, of course."

Outerbridge picked up his walking stick and waved his gloved hand for me to follow. We left the island over a small wrought iron bridge and walked along a gravel path edged with boxwood until the pavilion was out of sight. He motioned for me to sit on a rustic bench.

"I believe we can now speak freely. As I said, I believe your father moved in an elegant circle of men involved in the arts. In the years he was in Paris, I heard persistent rumours about masked balls this group would organize modelled on the famous yearly events organized by students at the École des Beaux-Arts. As I understand it, although most of the attendees were older gentlemen from abroad, including, I believe, your father, there was invariably a group of local youths in attendance. My impression was that most of them were hired. Are you shocked by this suggestion about the nature of your father's life here in Paris? Should I go on?"

"I am not shocked. I learned about my father's, um, preferences almost immediately following his death. Please go on."

"I have heard from friends that these boys were unusually attractive and often wore outrageous costumes fitting the theme of the evening. Or at least they arrived in costume. By the end of the evening many of the lads would be mostly or entirely unclothed, sitting in the lap of this eminent German author or that wealthy Dutch merchant."

I felt like I was peering through a hole in the glossy surface of polite society into a shadowy world I had never imagined. I was almost certain Outerbridge was part of that world. By this time, I had learned to identify some of the telltale signs, for example his suit of clothes that fit just a little too snugly, and the slightly too-insistent shades of pink and green in his waistcoat. Of course, there was also the fact that he was sitting uncomfortably close to me.

Outerbridge continued, "Many of these men were from Germany and England. The English in particular have always come here in some numbers to find a freedom they don't enjoy back home. It is difficult to imagine today, but as recently as one hundred years ago, sodomites were routinely burned alive all across Europe. In France, the lawmakers in the first years of the Republic took the remarkable step of striking down all penalties for pederasty, the term the French use instead of sodomy. They did this on the perfectly reasonable grounds that the state should not interfere with the private affairs of its citizens, at least after they have reached puberty. For reasons of his own, the first Napoleon did nothing to change that policy."

I had heard Maloof use the term "sodomy" among many others, but it still startled me when I heard it.

"A number of nations followed the lead of France. In Germany, many states abolished penalties for pederasty, and Germany has given us some of the boldest men in the fight against the absurd prejudice against men who love men. Unfortunately, the unification of the country was done under the aegis of the Prussians, and they have extended their own repressive laws across the entire realm. A real tragedy."

I was fascinated and appalled. Maloof, with his cynical manner, might have said similar things, but it didn't shock me. He could not hide who he was. Outerbridge, on the other hand, appeared quite normal. He seemed perfectly content to describe in an offhand manner behavior that I was struggling to consider anything but sinful. I wanted to end the conversation, but I also wanted to hear more. "And in Britain?"

"Britain, I'm sorry to say, is even more benighted than Germany. Buggery—please excuse the term—was still a capital crime until 1861, although I don't think anyone had been put to death for that offence for several decades before then. Today it is no longer a capital offense, but men can be arrested for public indecency and put into the pillory and sent to prison."

I interjected, "I'm probably being quite naïve, but aside from the legalities, isn't there a moral or religious problem with this kind of activity, and even more so, paying for it?"

"These men, as a rule, don't see it that way. They ask, 'How can it be wrong if it is a fair exchange, and both parties obtain what they need or want without hurting anyone else?'" Outerbridge was becoming quite agitated. "I am a member in good standing of St George's Anglican Church here in Paris, and I know that the rector would say the same. In private, of course. Why should we regard the injunctions against sodomy in the Old Testament as anything other than customs of primitive nomadic tribes in a benighted part of the world? "

I was shocked to hear Outerbridge all but openly condone what I thought every right-minded Christian considered a sin, but I could think of no suitable response, so Outerbridge continued, "In England, for those in the upper classes there are only rarely unfortunate consequences, even when there is attempted blackmail. Most of the intended victims simply refuse to pay. If the boy insists and goes to the police, it usually comes down to the word of a highly respected barrister or physician or gentleman against that of a young man of no position who usually has had previous problems with the constabulary.

"In fact, the laws make it difficult to prosecute even the most notorious individuals. First the authorities would have to prove that an act of buggery or penetration—" Outerbridge must have seen the look on my face. "Please stop me if I am embarrassing you." I was even more embarrassed by "penetration" than by "buggery" or "sodomy." It was just too specific and graphic, but I was also curious to hear more, so I signaled him to continue—"an act of buggery or penetration actually took place which, as you can imagine, in most cases is all but impossible. On the other hand, there are periodic scandals in which some individuals are badly hurt. Are you aware of the Park and Boulton affair in London? It was widely reported in the press."

"I remember something about a young man who dressed as a woman and called himself, um, herself Stella of the Strand. I believe that she and a partner had a considerable career on the stage."

"Yes, Stella and Fanny. As improbable as it seemed, they were apparently intimate with a distinguished nobleman, Lord Arthur Clark. Stella and Fanny escaped unscathed in the scandal and court proceedings that followed because no act *per anum* could be proven. In fact, they became heroes of a sort to a certain sector of society. Poor Arthur, however, did not fare so well and took his own life. Or, as some believe, decamped to the south of France and hasn't been heard of since. In either case, it was a real tragedy. He was a young man with a most promising political career."

"Did you know Lord Clark?"

"I am proud to have counted among his friends," Outerbridge responded with some vehemence. "In any event, in the days after the start of his trial the trains to Paris were packed with gentlemen, some single but a surprising number married, who suddenly remembered urgent business on the Continent. As usual, the authorities made no effort to stop them. Waves of men have fled to Paris over the years every time a major scandal of this kind appeared in the British newspapers."

Outerbridge paused his monologue as an amorous young couple strolled near enough to be able to hear us. After they passed, I asked, "I assume it is safer for these men here in Paris?"

"In many ways, yes. Pederastic activity isn't itself illegal, but Parisians are not very tolerant. Activity of this sort in public is dealt with harshly. There have been repeated raids by the police, and every year hundreds of men are arrested and prosecuted. Even some highly placed gentlemen.

"Things were bad enough before the doctors got involved. A silly man named Tardieu wrote a book about 20 years ago claiming that he could always identify a pederast by a physical examination. According to the doctor, the pederast who played the active role often developed a pointed penis, and the passive partner an 'infundibuliform deformation of the anus' or funnel-shaped arsehole." Outerbridge laughed heartily. I was now truly appalled by how lightly he seemed to be treating the entire matter.

"You seem to have made a thorough study of this subject," I said, with more emphasis on the word "subject" than I had intended.

"Not the matter of the funnel-shaped arseholes, mind you," he said, still choking on his laughter, "but yes, I was obliged to learn a good deal about this particular world because of my position at the embassy. Fortunately, during my time here, even with the increased public scrutiny, there was never much of a problem. Many pederasts married and were able, with or without their wives' knowledge, to carry on with boys or other men. Then as now, being wealthy and powerful is the best defence against threats to one's reputation."

I broke in. "Where do all these men meet?"

"Men who are looking for partners can easily meet them. There are the *maisons de passe* or what we would call molly houses in London, the arcades of the rue de Rivoli, the baths on the rue de Penthièvre, the Palais Royale, the Tuileries—"

I remembered what Walters had told me about my father strolling for hours in the evening in the Tuileries. "Really! The Palais Royale, the Tuileries? How can this be? I have heard of similar places in London but nothing quite so public."

"For decades the Tuileries was perhaps the most notorious place of assignation in Paris. More recently much of the activity has moved to the wooded area adjacent to the Champs Elysées. Unfortunately, many of the men who frequent these places are entrapped and prosecuted."

"You don't suppose that my father—"

"Your father was quite a well-known figure here in Paris. Young, titled, wealthy, and well-connected, he aroused admiration and envy. I'm afraid most of my information comes from the envious, so I cannot vouch for its veracity."

"Are you suggesting. . ."

"I have heard that your father was a constant presence in the world I have described. He apparently enjoyed the freedom the city offered for several years but then left quite abruptly. Some of my friends informed me he had to leave because he was being blackmailed. Others said he was forced by his family to move back to England to take over the family business. Or because word of a relationship with a boy had reached their ears, and they threatened to cut him off. I'm sorry if this information distresses you. I certainly hope I haven't offended."

I assured Outerbridge that I was grateful for what I had learned, but I was troubled and eager to end our interview. We returned to the pavilion in time for me to thank my hosts and take my leave. On my way to my hotel, I reflected that Outerbridge seemed to confirm much of what Uncle Rupert had told me. Thoughts about my father, though, were pushed aside by the turmoil in my own mind as I struggled with Outerbridge's apparently complacent attitude toward behavior that I had always been told was sinful.

Chapter 9:

St Sebastian at the Louvre

The next day, with what I had heard from Outerbridge still on my mind, I paid a visit to the Musée du Louvre hoping to find someone to help identify the Jean-Louis whose sketches I had seen in the house on Carlton Hill. I was directed to the office of Octave de Roquelaure, a large room in the south wing of the Louvre, littered with books, papers, and art objects sitting on shelves and propped against the walls.

De Roquelaure was at least in his mid-sixties and visibly in poor health. Thin, probably tightly corseted, he wore a close-fitting suit in a cream colour that made him look even thinner. His dark hair, the colour apparently the result of some chemical enhancement, stood in dramatic contrast with the pallor of his face except for his cheeks, which had an incongruous rosy tint, almost certainly the result of the application of rouge.

I greeted him in French, but he addressed me in a stiff and formal English with a heavy French accent. "Lord Barrington, I imagine that you must be the son of a Lord Barrington with whom I had the honour of a slight acquaintanceship several decades ago?"

As I replied in the affirmative, he motioned for me to sit opposite his desk in an elaborate ebony and gilt chair in the style of Louis XIV. After what seemed like endless unenthusiastic pleasantries, he asked how he could be of service. I opened the portfolio I had brought and showed him several sketches including the one with the inscription to my father. The sight of the sketches transformed him. He became animated, pulled his chair forward, and started to speak with noticeable excitement. "Remarkable! Yes, I do know who J-L was. Come with me."

I was thrilled to hear this news, but before I could say anything, de Roquelaure abruptly rose and headed for the door without waiting for me to replace the sketches in the portfolio. I caught up with him in the corridor and followed him as he walked through the grand galleries of the south wing. These sumptuous rooms, created during the reign of Napoleon III, housed paintings of the French School by David, Gericault, and others, but he didn't stop, instead continuing into the galleries surrounding the old square courtyard of the Louvre and up a set of stairs into a small, cramped space on the top floor. Its walls were painted a deep blood red and were crammed almost from the floor to the ceiling with paintings in elaborate gold frames.

He stopped in front of a painting that I instantly recognised from the sketches. The brass plaque on the frame read "The young Saint Sebastian praying near his home in Gallia Narbonensis, Jean-Louis Fortin, École Française, Salon of 1853." In the picture a handsome boy, clearly the same one as in the sketches, sat atop a rocky hill, nude, legs clasped in front of him, peering off into the distance. Although the painting was smaller than some of the immense historical scenes around it, in its reserve and simplicity it was in some ways even more compelling.

"The sketches you showed me were clearly made in preparation for this picture. It created a sensation when it was shown at the annual Salon some twenty-five years ago."

My initial reaction was puzzlement. It did not look like any portrayal of St. Sebastian that I had seen. I knew of several well-known paintings of the subject, but they almost always depicted a young man tied to a stake or tree, his body riddled with arrows and writhing in agony. As I scanned the picture, I eventually noticed a small bow and some arrows hidden in the grass in the lower right corner, but M. Fortin's Sebastian appeared to be just a boy, an extremely attractive boy, sitting serenely on his hill, completely alone with his sheep.

More visitors clustered around this picture than any other in the gallery. Several men—they were almost all men—were seated in front of easels making copies in charcoal or oil. Because of the press of individuals, de Roquelaure led me back to his office after only a brief pause.

"From all reports, Fortin as a young man was enormously precocious. Even as a student he gained a reputation as a prodigy. He succeeded in winning the Prix de Rome on his first attempt and departed for the French Academy in Rome with everyone expecting great things. The St. Sebastian we just saw was the first piece he sent back from Rome.

"The work was highly controversial. Several prominent individuals, especially church officials, were scandalized and wrote scathing pieces in the journals."

"What was the objection?"

De Roquelaure seemed embarrassed by the question and stammered. "They claimed that the young saint, um, looked more like a nineteenth-century boy of loose morals than a young man destined to become a martyr of the early Christian Church." He stared fixedly at me for a moment as if trying to read my thoughts, then said, "I think that most of this was foolish prudery. That kind of attitude would condemn much of the work of the ancient Greeks, of Michelangelo, Guido Reni, and so on and so forth.

"Fortunately for us here at the Louvre, Fortin's St. Sebastian had passionate advocates as well, and one of these, a gentleman in a government ministry, acquired it for the State. It hung for a number of years in the Luxembourg Palace before it found its way here to the gallery you saw along with many recent paintings awaiting a more appropriate setting elsewhere in the museum. Young Sebastian remains extremely popular with a certain crowd, if you know what I mean."

By this time, I had learned exactly what "if you know what I mean" meant. I could feel de Roquelaure staring at me once again to gauge my reaction. Trying to avoid revealing anything, I said, "Certainly the artist had a masterful technique."

De Roquelaure looked slightly disappointed, but he continued, "From a few things I have heard, I have gathered that Fortin's time in Rome was a good deal more turbulent than his friends in Paris were aware. From what they tell me, he lived a thoroughly dissolute life, and his early career was marked by a series of scandals.

"Then, as unlikely as it seems, this man, apparently notorious in Rome, moved to Paris and became celebrated for his piety. He did a series of frescoes for suburban churches that were well received by the priests and their parishioners. I, and almost all my colleagues, think they are dull, deadly dull. But Fortin became extremely successful, becoming one of the *immortels* of the French Academy. His death occasioned one of the largest funerals for an artist ever seen in Paris. Altogether an astonishing story."

Several minutes later, after I had thanked the keeper and started to take my leave, he stopped me. "One minute, please. I think that there was a short notice with some illustrations in the *Gazette des beaux-arts* some years back. Let me see if I can find it here." He pulled several leather-bound volumes down from the shelves and leafed through them. Finally, he pushed an open volume across the desk to me. "Here are engravings of two more paintings done by Fortin while he was in Rome."

De Roquelaure walked around his desk and pulled up a chair next to mine. The subject of the first image was identified as the young St. Philip. For some reason Fortin portrayed him as a blacksmith, although I didn't remember any mention of this in the Bible. In the painting, he had thick trousers of a rough material and a heavy leather apron. He wore no shirt even though he had a hammer in his right hand and in the left a pair of tongs holding a red-hot metal bar that seemed to be perilously close to the tangle of dark hair on his chest and a prominent brown left nipple jutting out erect through the hair. Where Fortin's St. Sebastian was a sublime boy, his Philip, although apparently only a few years older, was already a fully formed young man. Even in a small black-and-white engraving, the image of Philip sent a shiver through my body. I imagined that it probably gave a good idea of what Fortin's Sebastian would have looked like in full manhood.

The other engraving reproduced a painting quite different in character. It showed a small, bespectacled man of perhaps sixty years sitting at a table in front of a wall lined with shelves laden with what looked like Greek or Roman antiquities—portrait busts, Greek vases, and small sculptural objects. The caption read, "The Antiquarian."

"I believe this was a man named Gottlieb," de Roquelaure said. "Johann Joachim Gottlieb, a German scholar from Hamburg who went to Rome in the 1840s and became a leading expert on Greek and Roman art and a dealer in antiquities. It was later determined that much of what he sold was either obtained illegally or forged. He managed to sell some of these to our own institution. He came to a bad end. Murdered. A considerable scandal."

"Yes, I have heard about Gottlieb." This was startling news: Fortin, apparently a good friend of my father's, had known Gottlieb well enough to do this portrait. Even more startling was the fact that, sitting on a shelf immediately behind Gottlieb in the painting, was a piece of ivory that appeared to be identical to the one I had seen on Carlton Hill. Everything seemed to confirm some connection between my father and the murder of Gottlieb. I said nothing about any of this to de Roquelaure.

He was obviously keen on continuing our conversation and even suggested a visit to his apartment later that week. I thanked him, made some excuse, and started to leave a second time.

"Before you go," he said, "if you are interested in finding further information about Fortin and his St. Sebastian, I can suggest one or two men you might wish to consult.

"Narcisse Fortin, the son of Jean-Louis, is also an artist. He is primarily a portraitist but not a successful one. I can also suggest one other name. Fabrizio Croce is an Italian art dealer in Paris who seems to have known every significant French and Italian artist of the last several decades. He cuts a wide swath through society, partly because he is so well informed about ancient and modern art, but also because his wife is the daughter of a prominent family in Normandy. Croce isn't exactly a friend, but you can mention my name."

With that, de Roquelaure pulled out a leather-bound notebook from a top drawer in his desk and consulted several pages. On a piece of paper with his name and a crest embossed on the top he wrote, in a florid hand, the names and addresses of the two men.

Before departing the Louvre, I decided to pay Sebastian a second visit. Fortunately, it was now late in the day, and the gallery was less crowded. As I reached the painting, the effect was the same as it had been the first time I saw it—immediate and electric. Sebastian, almost life size, seemed to sit just beyond the plane of the picture surface. The illusion was so complete that it felt like I could almost reach through the frame and touch him. Every detail was rendered with a fidelity to life that was breathtaking. The glowing colours and the smooth handling of the paint made Sebastian's body seem to glow from within, as if the ever-so-slight olive cast of his skin was suffused with a warmth from deep within. As I brought my face as close to the canvas as I dared, I had a sudden impulse to caress the painted surface. I refrained from acting on that impulse.

The other emotion I felt was a sharp stab of envy. Sebastian was perhaps five years younger than I. Although he was just a boy and not, in my mind, nearly as handsome as he undoubtedly would later become, I recognised that this was exactly the kind of youthful beauty extolled by the Greeks. I felt an intense longing to possess even a fraction of that beauty.

As I stared at the canvas, I found myself looking again at Sebastian's pose, the way the positioning of the front leg must have just barely concealed the genitalia which, except for the placement of the leg, would have occupied the exact centre of the canvas. I looked to see if there was any evidence of their shadow on the leg behind. There was none, but the thought led to my considering further the model posing for the picture.

I wondered how Fortin had found him and how faithfully he had portrayed him. Was the boy embarrassed to be sitting naked in front of the fully dressed artist? That thought, in turn, led me to imagine myself posing in the same position, without clothes, on a table, directly in front of a handsome mature artist. The thought once again made me shiver, both from arousal and embarrassment.

After I left the gallery, I continued to ruminate about the painting and my reaction to it. Was it an inspired new interpretation of a familiar story? Or was it pandering to the basest instinct of the men who gathered around it? And to my own? But surely it was acceptable to admire the beauty of the boy. After all, he was part of God's creation. How could there be sin in that? And how could I convey that thought without being accused of indecency?

Whether I ultimately approved of the painting or not, I could not deny that my experience of it, like my experience in front of the Genius of the Dance at the Opéra, had inspired in me something of the ecstasy described by Walter Pater. I was now convinced that my calling was to give others some introduction to the passion that could be aroused by works of art.

I was fired by an ambition to become a scholar and critic in service to a new, more modern art, one that exploded the hoary conventions, spoke directly to our time, and, like the art of the ancient Greeks, celebrated the beauty of man as a reflection of the divine. There was, I reasoned with myself, nothing sinful in my admiration of the beauty of the human body. I just needed to avoid defiling that beauty with carnal urges. Of course, even as I was having this thought, I was aware that I had been experiencing just those urges.

Putting that troubling consideration aside, I thought of two potential projects. One would be a study of the way St. Sebastian had been depicted in art since the Renaissance by painters stretching from Botticelli and Mantegna through Titian, Rubens, and Reni and finally to Fortin. I imagined a work somewhat on the model of the two volumes penned by Mrs. Jameson and Lady Eastlake on depictions of Christ. A related project, if I could find sufficient information, would be a monograph on the work of Jean-Louis Fortin. I would use it as a starting point for an argument about whether it represented a vigorous, viable Christian art for the nineteenth century or something much less noble.

By this time, the sky was already dark. As I was walking along the rue de Rivoli toward the hotel, the comments about the Tuileries made by Walters and Outerbridge came to mind. I figured there was no harm in paying a short visit. I entered the gardens near the Arc de Triomphe du Carrousel and skirted the circular water basin. It was so quiet that I imagined anyone in the park would hear the crunch of gravel under my feet. I walked westward along the central *allée*. Only glimmers from the gas lamps on the rue de Rivoli penetrated the rows of chestnut trees.

The place looked entirely different from the way it had appeared during the day. Only a few hours before it would have been animated by hundreds of men and women strolling along the paths and children playing among the trees. Now it had a slightly sinister appearance heightened by the view of the ruins of the old palace in front of me. The park appeared deserted. However, after a few additional steps I started to see moving shadows and flickers of light among the trees on either side of the central allée. I moved to one side and watched.

Soon a young man, probably about my age, apparently from the working classes by the look of his clothes, walked by and looked me up and down in a quite brazen manner. I suspected his interest was sparked by the cut of my clothing. In any case he was too young to be of interest to me.

After about ten minutes, during which time another half dozen men walked by, I was ready to leave when I noticed a gentleman of about forty or fifty appraising me from about ten feet away. Although he was in deep shade, I could discern a robust figure and an elegant coat and top hat. He reached into a waistcoat pocket, took out a cigar and lit it. While the match was illuminated, I could make out a handsome face with a close-cropped beard and sensuous lips. He moved a few feet closer.

My heart was pounding. I had come only to look, but here was a distinguished gentleman who seemed ready to establish contact.

Was there any harm in speaking with him? Although by this time I knew I could no longer ignore my attraction to men, to older men particularly, this attraction had always before been somewhat hypothetical. Now, I could no longer ignore the truth. I had a pounding desire to see this man with his clothes off, to run my hands through the hair on his chest, to kiss him, to feel his. . . I knew I couldn't act on any of this, but maybe I could just speak to him? However, I knew that a mere word had the potential to start a conversation, and that conversation could lead to much more. I could not remember ever feeling so excited. Or nervous. By this point the gentleman was only a few feet away and seemed about to speak.

I could not do it. I stammered, "Excuse me. I'm sorry," or some such thing, stupidly in English, and started to walk away as fast as I could.

"No need to flee, young man. I will not bite," he said in perfect but slightly accented English. I didn't stop. "Well, another time, then. You look to be a fine young man, and I would love to make your acquaintance."

I returned to my hotel as quickly as I could, shaking violently from the encounter and deeply ashamed of myself for walking into the park knowing what I might find there.

On the way through the lobby, the desk clerk alerted me I had a letter. I was surprised to see it was from my mother. I opened it and glanced at it briefly. What caught my eye was the news that Athena Briggs would be visiting Paris with an aunt in three weeks and hoped that we could meet.

It felt like Fate was playing a cruel trick on me, forcing me to think of Athena when my mind was filled with the memory of the gentleman in the park. Reaching my room, I laid down on the bed, still trembling. Despite my belief, by now wavering but still far from extinguished, that the desire I felt for that man was wrong and a sin, I could not decide whether I wished I had spoken or not.

Even if I had done nothing more than speak, it felt like it would have been crossing an invisible threshold, one from which there might be no return. I did what I knew I must do to relieve the tension; however, even after I had cleaned up and downed a tumbler of cognac, I knew I would not be able to sleep. I knew that the vision under the chestnut trees would haunt my thoughts for days to come.

The next day I sent a note back to my mother telling her that I would be delighted to see Athena again. After that, my thoughts returned to the St. Sebastian in the Louvre. I asked Walters if he remembered anything about an artist named Fortin in Rome. "His Lordship knew many artists. I think that there was a French painter with a name like Fortin who did a famous painting of a young man. A painting his Lordship admired, and that he told me was in the big museum here. I believe we visited his studio."

This was conclusive evidence. My father knew Fortin. Was it more than just a friendship? And what about the boy who posed as Sebastian? Did my father know him? Was the sketch by Fortin perhaps a souvenir of an intimate encounter with one or the other?

Chapter 10:

Fabrizio

Several days later, on an overcast afternoon, I followed up on de Roquelaure's suggestion and sent a note to Fabrizio Croce, proposing to pay a visit to his gallery in the Faubourg Saint-Germain. He proposed a date on a late afternoon three days later.

I had the carriage drop me off in front of the church of Saint-Germain-des-Près, so I could walk a bit through the quarter before meeting Croce. Over the previous several years, the Right Bank had become the preferred locale for residences of the new aristocracy, and this little pocket of the Left Bank near the École des Beaux-Arts had acquired a genteel and pleasantly antiquated air perfectly appropriate for a gallery of Greek and Roman artifacts.

I walked to the Place de Furstemberg, up the rue de Seine, stopping just before the imposing buildings housing the Institut de France. Fabrizio Croce's gallery was located next to the Galerie Eude dit Michel Jeune, a well-regarded establishment I knew from previous trips. I had not noticed Croce's before.

The gallery was on the ground floor of a typical French apartment building. Large plate glass windows filled the space between the iron columns. In the central window were arranged a pair of large marble urns flanking a group of Greek *kraters* on a low plinth. "Galerie Croce, Arts Antiques" was spelled out in gold letters outlined in black.

As I entered the shop, a bell hanging on the back of the door announced my entrance. A figure at the back, a handsome man, about forty years of age, powerfully built, turned to see who had walked in. Probably weighing some 14 stone, and standing at least six feet in height, he made me feel insubstantial by comparison. He walked directly over to greet me.

"Croce, Fabrizio Croce," he said, extending his hand. "You must be Lord Barrington. I received your note, and I'm pleased to meet you. Welcome to the Galerie Croce." His piercing dark eyes seemed to look right through me in a way that might have been frightening except for the smile on his lips. His French was impeccable, aristocratic even, with only the slightest accent.

Up close, he was even more handsome than I had noticed on entering. He had a perfectly chiselled face with a rakish beard and a head of closely cropped lustrous black hair sprinkled with grey. His head looked remarkably like that on a portrait bust of the Emperor Hadrian that I had recently seen in the Louvre.

With trousers of a soft cream colour set off by a dark stripe at the outer seams, a crimson and lime embroidered waistcoat, a tightly fitted coat of a beautiful dark wool fabric, and an old-fashioned ruffled shirt open at the throat with soft turned-down collar in the manner of Lord Byron, he might have been either a French aristocrat or a Bohemian artist. It was clear from the fit of his clothes that they concealed a highly developed body. I was trying to decide whether he was the most handsome man I had ever met when he interrupted my thoughts.

"I understand from your note that you have some drawings by the artist Fortin that were in the possession of your late father," he said, continuing to look at me in that unnervingly direct way.

"Yes, M. Croce," I replied, indicating the portfolio I had brought with me. Before I could say anything further, he broke into a broad smile that allowed a glimpse of a set of impeccable teeth. "I apologise for my lack of hospitality. May I offer you some coffee or tea or maybe you would prefer whisky?"

I declined.

He motioned for me to follow him as he walked to a door at the back of the gallery that led to a small office. No one else appeared to be in the gallery. As we sat on chairs in front of his desk, he said, "May I express my condolences for your father? Your note said he was in Rome between 1851 and 1854. I was born in Rome, and my family lived there until moving to Paris in 1853, but I was only 15 when I left, and there is no reason my parents would have met your father."

"Are your parents still alive?" I asked.

"No, I'm sorry to say they died some years ago."

I murmured some condolences of my own and pulled out three of the sketches I had brought. Croce gave them only a cursory glance. "I can tell you little about Fortin in Rome. I believe he returned to Paris in the early 1860s and started doing all those dreadful murals he inflicted on new churches in the suburbs. I met him here in Paris towards the end of his life and would see him occasionally at public functions, but I barely knew him. At least several of these sketches, as I am sure you have already learned, were done in preparation for the famous St. Sebastian in the Louvre."

I asked him what he thought of that work. To my surprise, he merely shrugged his shoulders and murmured something I could not quite hear.

As he talked, I could not stop staring at him. He was so handsome, so sure of himself, so masculine in his bearing, his dark eyes so deep and intense. Even the air surrounding him seemed to crackle. At the same time I was trying to listen to him, I was desperately thinking about what I could do or say that would prolong our meeting or lead to another.

I also became aware that I was forming some vague images at the back of my mind about what his body would look like out of his clothes. As soon as I was aware of the nature of these thoughts, I tried to put them out of mind. I knew I ought to be ashamed, but I was not. In his presence it all seemed so natural.

"Do you know anything about a German scholar and dealer in antiquities named Gottlieb," I asked.

"Yes, I remember hearing about Gottlieb. I had some interest in classic antiquities even when young, so even though we had already moved to Paris, I naturally heard about this bad business. At the time I was vaguely aware that there was a scandal connected with his death, but it was only later that I heard some of the details. I gather that the police think it was a robbery or some kind of action by a criminal element."

I was disappointed that I was learning nothing new from Croce. On the other hand, any disappointment I felt was overshadowed by my intense awareness of his physical presence. We had been sitting closer together than one would normally consider polite, and he seemed to be watching and listening to me with extraordinary intensity. It was making me nervous, but I did not want to leave. When he offered to take me on a tour of his gallery, I readily accepted.

"My apartment is in the adjacent building. I live there with my wife and two daughters," he explained. "They are away on the English Channel in Houlgate where we have a summer house, not far from the house of my wife's family in Caen. My main business here in the gallery is selling Greek and Roman sculpture and artifacts from the classical era. For example," he said, leading me over to a marble sculpture, "this remarkable Hellenistic head of a faun that turned up two years ago near Monreale. He is my pet. I rub his head every morning for good luck."

Croce was now speaking fluently, completely at ease. "I procure most of my antiquities in Sicily. I like to show them like this, in a gallery set up like a salon with contemporary furniture, because it gives potential customers some idea of how the sculpture and other classical artifacts might look in their own drawing rooms." He made a rapid tour of the gallery pointing out objects of particular note, almost all of exceptional quality and beautifully displayed.

After the tour of the gallery, we returned to his office. I sat down in the chair I had previously occupied, and he pulled his own even closer, this time so close that our knees almost touched. I looked down at the gap between them. If either of us moved half an inch we would be touching, but he didn't move, and I dared not. In my imagination I thought I could feel the heat from his legs. I was always terribly shy around handsome and accomplished older men, and I'm sure at that point I was quite red in the face.

Croce then asked me about myself. I was so nervous I was not sure what I was saying but found myself telling him about my childhood, my somewhat distant relationship with my father, my ambition to write about art. I suppose I felt so flattered he was showing an interest that I allowed him to coax a good deal of information out of me that I would not have divulged to my intimate friends, let alone someone I had just met.

When I paused, I realised that I had been talking for several minutes, probably somewhat incoherently, and had probably made a terrible first impression. At the conclusion of our visit, I thanked Croce and turned to leave. He put his hand on my shoulder. "I see you are interested in the kind of antiquities I sell in this shop. I would love to tell you more if you would be willing to honour me with a return visit."

Stupidly, my first thought was that I had learned all I would from him about my father, Fortin, and Gottlieb, so I thanked him and made some vague promise to return and left. However, no sooner had I left his shop, than I knew that I would return, and soon. During my trip back to my hotel, I could not put his image out of my mind. That well-constructed body, the hair, those dark intense eyes, the dazzling smile. I also knew that there had been some kind of powerful current between us. I was by now not so innocent that I wasn't aware of the unspoken communication between and under our words.

I wanted to return. It became an obsession. I could hardly think of anything else. Every day over the next few days I determined that I should go, but every time I considered it, I decided I did not want to seem overly eager and that no good could come from a return visit. However, exactly one week later I sent him a note to which he promptly replied. And, after even greater agitation between receiving the note and the appointed day, I did return. And I did again several days after that.

On that third trip, as we were examining a bronze bust of a Roman emperor—I have forgotten which now, only that it was a nineteenth century copy after a Roman original—I had placed my hand on the back of the emperor's head. Croce put his own hand gently but firmly over mine. It felt like an electric jolt passing through my hand up my arm to my head where the blood rushed immediately to my face. I could feel my body shake but somehow managed to keep my hand where it was. When I didn't withdraw, he pulled his hand away and walked behind me. Then I felt his hands on my shoulders, his lips on the back of my neck, and his body pressed up against my back. I must have made a sudden motion because he quickly pulled his hands away.

"I'm sorry. Maybe I have misread your eyes and body? If so, I'm very sorry to have embarrassed you. I hope you will forgive me."

"No, I'm the one . . . I think—no, I know—I ought to be the one who should apologise," I blurted out. "I'm not sure what my eyes were saying," I stammered while continuing to stare at the bronze bust, "but you are married. I thought that . . ."

"Yes, I am married, but my wife isn't here, and I don't think she would mind my making a new friend."

Then, after a long pause between us, I continued, "You talked about what my eyes were saying. Whatever you were hearing from them was probably exactly what they were saying. I just have had little experience with this kind of thing." I found myself blushing furiously as I finally allowed myself to turn my eyes to his face.

"What is 'this kind of thing?'" he asked with a mischievous glint in his eye. I quickly looked away, overcome with embarrassment.

"Having someone touch me like that. At least someone I want to touch me." I could not bring myself to look at him again.

He stepped around the bust and took my face in both hands. At that, I looked into his eyes. I could not believe what was happening. All thought left my mind. He leaned over to kiss me on the cheek. He pulled back and asked, "Was that acceptable?"

"I don't know. Yes, I suppose it was acceptable." I suddenly caught myself, "But I would not want you to think that I am leading you on to something sinful." As soon as I said it, I recognised how stupid that must have sounded. He was the one who had taken the lead.

He ignored my comment. "You have such a beautiful mouth. I assume you have used it to kiss a man before, have you not?"

I was more taken aback by the compliment than the question. I had received few compliments about my appearance, and certainly none about my mouth. I thought he was playing some kind of cruel trick. I was about to turn and walk away but decided that I had already accepted a kiss from him. What harm could there be in answering the question? "Not exactly, M. Croce. I may have dallied with some boys my age and a cousin. Some of them kissed me or wanted to, but I didn't like it and usually pushed them away." How could I be saying these things to an almost total stranger?

He put his hand back on top of my hand and leaned forward so his face was only inches away from mine. I could feel his warm, slightly herbal breath on my face. "So can I infer from what you just said that you have never had any intimate relationship with a man?"

Now I knew that my face must have blazed scarlet. Did what I had done with Alastair count as an intimate relationship? When I couldn't decide what to say, Fabrizio continued,

"Would you like to fill in that part of your personal education with me? May I kiss you on the lips?" he asked in a low voice. "And please, call me Fabrizio."

"I'm sorry, um, Fabrizio. This is all so sudden. I don't think that I can . . ." I was choking not only with embarrassment but also fear. I might be on the verge of doing something I would regret for the rest of my life.

Once again, he pulled back. "I'm the one who should apologise. I should be more careful. I should have considered the fact that you have had little experience. We certainly don't have to kiss or do anything else today. Or this week or this month, or ever, for that matter. We have all the time in the world for you to decide what you would like to do, if anything."

"Thank you very much. I'm flattered by your attention." I

turned and started towards the door. However, after a few steps I stopped and turned around. "No, no. I mean yes. The answer to your question about kissing is 'Yes.' I have waited too long already. To be honest I have thought about little else for days. I am afraid that what you are proposing might lead to a terrible sin, but I seem unable to resist."

"It is no sin, Robert. There have been many men like us throughout the centuries. Some of the most illustrious men of their times. Today, a growing number of enlightened individuals across Europe, especially in Germany, have already started a campaign to pull us out of medieval superstition and prejudice. I would be happy to discuss any of this with you."

I made no reply but instead started to cry, whether from joy or fear to this day I can't tell you. Fabrizio pulled me gently toward him, gave me another light kiss on my cheek and held me in his arms. For the next ten or twenty minutes he held me tight, reassuring me that my reaction was quite normal and that there was nothing for me to be ashamed of.

Finally, I was able to speak. "Of course, I know about the Greeks, famous writers and artists, kings. But what about the teachings of the Church? I apologise for being so direct, but I really would like to understand better. Is it not a problem for you that the Bible forbids such activity?"

Fabrizio replied, "I believe that men should live by the Commandments and the teachings of Jesus. I don't think that we should feel obliged to follow all the rules imposed by tribal custom in the Orient two thousand years ago. Holy Scriptures contain injunctions that no one has followed for centuries. And," he added, "surely God could never have devised a world in which something so natural was sinful. I believe that the Greeks with their acceptance of the beauty of the human body had the right idea about how to view man made in the image of the Divine."

I desperately wanted to believe Fabrizio. I hugged him tightly. Fabrizio asked, "Are you at all reassured?"

"I don't know. I will need some time to think."

"Of course," Fabrizio said, stepping back from me. "You should take all the time you need. If you wish to proceed any further . . ."

"I don't know what I think, but it appears that my body has decided for me. I suppose that having come this far, I have already crossed the line in my mind and might as well go the rest of the way with my body."

"Are you sure?"

I paused for a long moment. I knew that this was the moment: the moment I had long anticipated and feared. "Yes, I'm sure."

Fabrizio smiled, took my hand and unlocked a door at the back of the gallery near the one leading to his office. We climbed a narrow staircase to another, smaller gallery space on the upper level. "I will take you on a tour of this gallery later," he said.

He guided me into a suite of rooms at the back containing a small bedroom whose windows opened onto the building's central courtyard. As soon as we were through the door, he pulled me toward him, and I could see he wanted to kiss me on the lips. I had experienced brief pecks on the lips from Alastair and Samuel and some other boys my age, but they hardly resembled the passages in sentimental novels where men and women kiss passionately. I assumed that in theory two men might kiss in the same way, but I had little idea what kissing a man like Fabrizio would feel like.

As he took my head in his hands and touched his lips to mine, I was startled by the way his beard brushed against my face. It was not a bad sensation, but for some reason it was completely unexpected. That was followed by surprise that his lips were remarkably soft and had a slight taste of something sweet. For such a powerfully built man, he was surprisingly gentle. At first, he just touched his lips to mine tentatively as if to see how I would react.

When I made no effort to pull back, he continued but with more conviction. Soon I found myself pinned against the wall with Fabrizio pressing hard against me and kissing me passionately. I felt his lips push mine apart and his tongue enter my mouth. It felt like he was trying to devour me whole. I'm afraid I was so nervous and amazed how quickly everything was happening that that I just stood against the wall and made no attempt to reciprocate. I was acutely conscious of a pounding in my heart. Also, in my member as it strained against my trousers. I could feel his as well.

After a few minutes, he pulled me away from the wall, turned me around and gently led me back toward the foot of the bed. He removed my coat and waistcoat, carefully folded them and placed them on a chair. Then he unbuttoned my trousers and pulled them down to my ankles. After that he pushed me backward, carefully, onto the bed.

Then he knelt down in front of me and slowly removed one of my boots and stockings, then the other. I could not move. I felt detached from reality, almost as if I were watching a scene in a theatre. I was lying on the bed in front of him in just my drawers and shirt while he remained fully clothed. Even though the room was warm, I was shivering uncontrollably. I was acutely aware of the fact that my full stand was pushing out the front of my drawers. Although it was just few feet from his face, Fabrizio seemed not to pay any attention. He stood up again.

I pushed up on my elbows to watch while, very slowly, he took off first his coat, then his waistcoat, then his boots and finally his trousers. He folded them methodically and put them on top of the pile of my clothes. My eyes remained fixed on his face, but I could clearly make out his powerful, compact body, the kind usually seen only on men who perform manual labour.

I finally allowed my eyes to move lower down his body. Around his neck was a simple, narrow gold chain with some kind of small gold object that lay in the cleft of his chest. It caught the light and glittered against the dark hair that covered his upper body. His torso perfectly matched his handsome face, at once massive but supple. Below that, I could not help but notice his drawers were as fully tented out as my own.

As I looked down at myself, I was embarrassed to see that not only was I continuing to display a full stand through my drawers, but there was also a growing wet spot seeping through the front of the cotton fabric. I'm not sure what expression I had on my face, but whatever it was, it caused Fabrizio to issue a deep rumbling laugh. He stepped towards me, knelt down and, to my astonishment, shoved his hands under my arse cheeks, lifted my hips, bent slightly, and licked the wet spot on my drawers with his tongue.

Then he rose, bent over me and, grasping my two hands, pinned my arms back behind my head and pressed his entire body down on top of me for more kissing. I was still nervous, but as I gradually overcame my surprise and anxiety, I started to feel something like the euphoria described in passages by the lady novelists. The physical sensation of his weight on top of me and his mouth on mine now felt natural, almost familiar, but I still marvelled that something I had so long dreamed of and dreaded was finally happening and, most astonishingly, with such an impossibly handsome man.

Finally, he pulled back and stood once more in front of me. I closed my eyes and waited to see what he would do next. To my amazement, he knelt on the floor between my legs, slowly pulled my member out from my drawers, kissed it gently, and licked the viscous liquid that was oozing from the tip. "May I proceed?" he asked in a low voice.

By this point I was trembling all over again, my eyes tightly shut, but I nodded in assent. He murmured some words about trying to relax and that he would stop immediately at any point if I were uncomfortable. I opened my eyes and looked directly at him, but I could not manage any words. Instead, almost by instinct, I found myself raising my hips upward toward his face. It felt like my body was acting on its own.

He smiled. Then he took my entire member in his mouth and started to move his head up and down using his tongue to massage the head. Very quickly, much too quickly, I felt an increasing warmth spread through my body, and within a minute or two I knew I was about to spend. I started bucking my hips and forcing my member into his mouth. He gagged several times but never stopped. Finally, I let out a roar that passers-by on the street must have heard as I felt the rush of hot liquid explode into his mouth. It was the most intense sensation that I had ever experienced.

The entire episode could not have lasted more than a few minutes, but it felt like an eternity had passed since we had entered the chamber. After I had spent, he licked my still tumescent member clean and gently pushed it back into my drawers. I was still shaking. "Was that good for you?" he asked, lying down beside me and putting his arm under my head.

My initial reaction was acute embarrassment about the way I had acted, so unlike the genteel sentiments in the novels. I sat up and hid my face in the crook of his neck. "I'm so sorry," I blurted out. "It was just too—" To my intense embarrassment I found myself starting to cry again. But Fabrizio gently pulled my head from his neck and put his finger to my mouth, a signal for me to stop speaking. He then covered my mouth with his hand and just left it there. "Shhhh. There is nothing at all to be sorry about."

At that moment the emotion that was uppermost in my mind was relief. After years wondering whether I really preferred men to women, I had found out the answer in less than an hour's time. Despite all my fears this act might lead to eternal damnation, I could not bring myself to believe that anything so natural and loving could be sinful. It was entirely different from what I had experienced with Alastair.

But I was confused about what should happen next. He finally removed his hand from my mouth. "It was wonderful for me. Thank you, thank you," I gushed. "But how about you? May I . . . Would you like me to . . . ?" I was too embarrassed to continue.

"Only if you want to." I was slightly apprehensive, but I knew I did want to. And I wanted to the next day and most of the days for the next weeks. My willingness to provide that service was fortunate, because after that first day, Fabrizio didn't seem inclined to return the favour. I did not mind. It felt as though it was my role to give pleasure and his to receive. He was older, stronger, more experienced, more forceful in his personality. There was something irresistible about the feel and taste of Fabrizio's body, the way he could take control of me, and I loved the way it felt completely natural for me to yield and give him pleasure.

I cannot claim that in the days that followed I did not have some moments of terror that I had succumbed to pure lust and that my actions would lead me to endless degradation. I thought of my father and wondered what his first experience had been like, how he felt about it afterwards, how he dealt with the kinds of deception necessary to continue. However, after several weeks, although never really convincing myself that what I was doing was not sinful, I had dropped all feeling of guilt.

My encounters with Fabrizio did, of course, make me confront some questions that had long puzzled me. "Why do you think I'm drawn to men and not to women? And to older men and not to those my own age?" I asked him. "Was it something about my upbringing? Some kind of disease? Do you think it could be in my blood, inherited from my father?"

"As far as I know, no one has a good answer to questions like these, Robert," he told me. "Of only one thing I am certain. You are blameless."

I decided that Fabrizio was correct. I had never asked to be the way I was, so I should not blame myself. Most of the time, I was able to believe this.

But . . . But . . . What I had done involved a married man. Surely violating the sanctity of the marital bond must be wrong. I could not bring myself to say anything to Fabrizio on that subject, though. Once again, it was as though Fabrizio could read my thoughts. "I love my wife, and I'm happy about the time I spend with her in our apartment and in our bed, but it is never like what I just felt with you.

"Amélie and I never talk about it, but I believe she must have divined my inclinations. In fact, I suspect that our marriage could not have lasted—or been as amicable as it has been—without an arrangement giving me some freedom. I suspect that perhaps it is the same for her."

I was shocked that any wife could look the other way when her husband was carrying on a passionate relationship with another person, man or woman. But then I thought of my mother, how she probably knew what my father was doing but chose, perhaps for the sake of our family, to turn a blind eye. I left for another day any thoughts about the sanctity of marriage, or even any desire to understand exactly my status in the mind of Fabrizio. My overwhelming feeling was gratitude. That someone so handsome, so virile, so successful, and apparently so happy with himself could accept an individual of his own sex as a lover made it so much easier for me to accept my own inclinations.

We settled into a routine. I would come by the gallery in the evening and leave several hours later. Occasionally I would come earlier, and we would have a small dinner in the tiny dining room at the back of the gallery. Or sometimes I would stay until the morning and share breakfast with Fabrizio.

The meals were prepared by the cook in Fabrizio's apartment in the adjacent building. There was an inconspicuous door hidden in the panelling on the gallery side leading to a passage connecting to the kitchen next door. The door was always kept locked from the gallery side, but when a meal was ready the housekeeper would ring a bell that sounded in the gallery, and Fabrizio would unlock the door and roll in a table fully set up for the meal. After we finished, he would return the table with the dirty dishes to the other side.

We kept entirely to ourselves during my visits. I usually arrived after the gallery closed and departed before it re-opened in the morning. On the rare occasions when Fabrizio came to my hotel, I made sure Walters was away on an errand.

I learned a great deal from Fabrizio about art and particularly about some vexing questions involving copies, fakes and forgeries. "The real antiquities are very expensive," he continued. "Only a handful of men are willing to pay for them. Most of my customers are happy with reproductions. I order these from a group of skilled craftsmen I know in southern Italy. These men have been carrying on this trade for generations, probably all the way back to classical antiquity.

"The pieces most in demand are modeled, at reduced scale, after famous original Greek and Roman pieces—the Doryphoros, the Apoxyomenos, the Belvedere Torso, and so on. Or copies of later works—the David of Donatello or any number of works of Michelangelo, for example.

"Please don't mention to anyone I said this, but I honestly think that some of these reproductions are actually better than the originals. I know that some of my competitors try to pass them off as original antique works. I will not do this, but I have been to houses across Europe where it is easy to see that the antique pieces and the fake are mixed together indiscriminately with the owners blissfully unaware."

As the days passed and I continued to visit Fabrizio, we started to adjust to each other in hundreds of ways, both small and large. One major change involved our pattern of lovemaking. In what must have been our fifth or sixth week together, while everything was still new to me, Fabrizio did something unexpected. Immediately after entering the chamber Fabrizio ordered me, in surprisingly peremptory fashion, to strip down to my drawers, clasp my hands behind my back and stand at attention. He then slowly circled around me, probing, now caressingly, now rudely, every part of my body. He must have felt the way my entire body was shivering, but he said nothing. While he was standing behind me, I felt something rough, a coarse rope, no doubt, being used to secure my wrists

Standing once again in front of me, he reached behind my neck and ran both hands gently across the nape, then along my shoulders. From there he slid them down my chest, pinching one nipple and then the another. Lightly at first, then hard enough to cause me to squirm. Then his hands moved lower across my stomach, stopping to pull sharply on the sparse hairs that led down into my drawers. He did this in a way that was not really painful but was quite uncomfortable, and having to stand still and let him do this to me was humiliating. This only seemed to heighten my excitement. And his.

Then his hand slipped under the fabric of my drawers. My member was now twitching wildly with anticipation, but he didn't touch it. Instead, he started to run both hands down the outer side of my legs and then back up the inner sides of the calves and thighs, once again up into to my drawers, this time moving his hands up, so they were brushing my testicles. He squeezed them lightly, then pulled them harder causing me to bend my knees to try to relieve the pressure. I waited for him to do something, anything, to relieve the pressure that was building in my member, which continued to twitch uncontrollably.

I continued to stand there transfixed, shaking with anticipation, flushed deep red by the humiliation of being almost naked and letting Fabrizio fondle and prod at will. Seeing that I made no attempt to break free or move, he then started to pinch my nipples and squeeze my balls considerably harder than before. Once again, it was not so much that it hurt, although it did, as the way it felt like a violation of my body. The humiliation made me even more excited. I let out a slight moan. He quickly reached up and covered my mouth with his hand.

Then he inserted the finger of his right hand into my mouth and then a second and third finger. This was even more unexpected and at first unwelcome. I briefly thought about asking him to stop, but then I could feel the heat rising in me and realised that this latest intrusion was as exciting as it was humiliating. While his fingers were still inserted, he said, "Do you like having fingers in your mouth?"

"If it . . . ooof . . ." I started to say but then stopped in mid-sentence when it was coming out completely garbled. I was keenly aware that saliva was dripping from his fingers to my chest as he pushed his fingers in and out.

"You need to enunciate more clearly. I can't understand you," he ordered in a loud voice.

"I . . ." I started to say but could do no more than make guttural noises.

"Do you like having my fingers in your mouth?" Fabrizio barked at me again.

I tried to say, "Uncomfortable," but it was unrecognisable, so I just grunted, "Yes."

I'm not sure if even that was intelligible, but Fabrizio seemed satisfied. "That's what I thought," he said, laughing. He then pushed his fingers even further into my mouth gagging me. I tried to pull away, but with his free hand he held of the back of my head forcefully in place. "You need to answer me when I ask you a question. And you need to speak up so I can hear you. Now, I want to hear you answer my question clearly. Do you like having my fingers in your mouth?" He spat out.

"Yes!" I tried to shout.

"That's what I like to hear. Now stay," he commanded as he took his fingers out of my mouth. I obeyed.

He walked behind me and slid a finger down my back, running it across each vertebra and then over the rope that tied my wrists together and then under my drawers and down the cleft between my arse cheeks and then, suddenly, pushed it into my hole. I could feel my sphincter muscles resisting but then suddenly relaxing and opening. I was so startled I pulled forward and let out a yelp.

Fabrizio stepped forward with me so that he could keep his finger inserted. "Is what I'm doing hurting you?" he asked in a gentle tone of voice.

"I'm sorry. I didn't mean to pull away. It was just that I was so surprised." I stammered. "It does not hurt at all, Sir. But it is embarrassing."

"Are you unhappy with that, with what I'm doing? Should I stop?"

"No. I'm just sorry I'm so inexperienced, Sir." I'm not sure why I was saying "Sir" instead of Fabrizio's name, but his smile indicated he was pleased.

Fabrizio then pulled me gently down onto the bed where we kissed for several minutes as he murmured reassurances about how glad he was that I was there with him and that he would never hurt me, all the while keeping his finger inserted and moving it around. Then, after I had calmed down, his tone suddenly changed.

"On your stomach, Boy," he ordered.

I did as commanded, and once on my stomach, saw him pull a small vial out of a drawer in a chest beside the bed. "We have sampled the French way of making love," he said. "May I introduce you to the Greek method?"

The image of the man thrusting himself against Oliver leapt to my mind. At the time it had repelled me as much as excited me. I remembered what I had heard from Alastair and others about men allowing themselves to be penetrated. I turned my head towards Fabrizio, trying to think what I could say.

It was once again as though Fabrizio read my thoughts. "You have probably heard that it is demeaning for an adult male to play the passive role in lovemaking. But what rational basis could there be for this superstition? Like a dance, it requires two people. Why would one role be inferior to the other if it results in pleasure for both? But, Robert, I will only continue if you are sure that you want me to."

I started to tremble even more than before. Fabrizio kissed me on the back of my neck, murmured more soothing words. I was so overcome with anticipation I could not speak but nodded my assent.

I felt a cool liquid trickle down the crack of my arse and his finger again, rubbing and probing. I then felt his member pushing tentatively against the hole. I held my breath. He entered slowly and gently. It hurt at first, but he kept asking if he should continue and, badly wanting to please him, I kept saying, "Yes, Sir," even though I was uncertain whether I could bear it. But after a certain amount of time, he was fully in, and I started to feel some pleasure. Another Rubicon had been crossed.

That first experience with penetration was difficult, but over the ensuing days I learned to relax and found that it was something I looked forward to. I was surprised to find that I loved the feeling of having him inside me, submitting to his strength and power, having him take the lead and dominate, letting him order me to do anything that he wanted. I became obsessed with having him inside me at every possible occasion, but sometimes he refused to do anything until I asked. This was embarrassing. He would sometimes compound the feeling by making me beg.

As we came to know each other better, our roles in lovemaking became more and more defined. He gave orders; I obeyed. I was his to do with as he pleased, and what pleased him was more and more aggressive. To my surprise, it also pleased me. I could never decide whether it was the physical sensation or the submission and humiliation that aroused me the most. Or why I craved this kind of treatment.

"Yes, please, Sir," I would say as I got onto my hands and knees on the floor, and he got out the cane. I found it completely perplexing how something I hated so much as a schoolboy could now be so exciting. I found that the more Fabrizio made me submit, the more affection I felt towards him.

Maybe it had to do with trust. I let him take complete control. He never abused that trust. He somehow knew exactly how much discomfort and humiliation would enflame my passion without ever pushing over the edge where it became too much. The closer it came, the more I wanted to cover him with kisses, to lick every inch of his body, to push my nose into his private parts and his arm pits and take in the dark masculine smell.

Fabrizio was endlessly inventive. It almost always ended with him penetrating me, but even in that act there was great variety. I was astonished to find how many positions Fabrizio could manoeuvre us into. And in how many places. In the bed, on the floor, against the wall, with me bending over a table, a large urn, a bronze horse. On several occasions we coupled outdoors in the dark shadows along the river accompanied by the sound of water lapping on the stone and the low murmur of other men engaged in similar activity around us.

And, on one occasion, late in the evening, Fabrizio took me as I was bent over the railing in an open window of an apartment of one of his friends along one of the city's new boulevards. Although it was mostly dark outside, there would have been enough illumination from the streetlights for someone on the sidewalk below to make out what we were doing. That realisation only increased the excitement for both of us.

Sometimes at home he would take out pieces of clothing or equipment that he kept for the purpose of lovemaking. For example, a French sailor's uniform or a priest's robe.

Our activities in bed were often observed by Fabrizio's cat, Queen Victoria. Fabrizio told me that, due to that British sovereign's long reign, three successive felines bore the name of the empress. The latest feline, Vicky, was actually a male cat. She—or rather he—was usually sweet, but he clearly didn't approve of all the attention I was receiving. When we were making love, he would make a low hissing noise and occasionally leap onto the bed. Fabrizio would shove him rudely onto the floor, and Victoria would usually spend the rest of the time in a corner glowering at us.

Fabrizio asked once or twice if I wanted to reverse our roles. I told him truthfully that, although I might like to try switching our roles in the future, for the time being I was happy continuing to go on the way we were. Laughingly, he told me that I should take the opportunity to practice because I would almost certainly outlive him, and when that happened, I would want to take younger lovers and have them submit to me. When he said that, I put a finger on his lips to stop him. I was so happy with the way things were that I didn't want to imagine the future a month hence, let alone decades.

After lovemaking, Fabrizio almost invariably took me in his

arms, and we kissed and talked. I think I eventually loved these periods of affection and companionship even more than the coupling. By this time, I had pushed out of mind any lingering thoughts of guilt. Maybe in the future I would regret what I was doing, but for the moment I was willing to follow Fabrizio's lead and assume that, as long as we were hurting no one, we were not violating anything that Jesus had preached.

With increasing frequency, I would stay the night with him in that small chamber at the back of the gallery. He would hold me from behind while we both fell asleep. "Spooning," he called it. I came to love that feeling of being safe and protected as I fell asleep.

Fabrizio almost always arose before I did. I usually awoke to the pressure of his reawakened member and his arms pulling me back against him. After we finished, he or I would open the door to the passage and roll in the tiny table we had used for dinner. On it would be an assortment of breads and pastries, jellies made from fruit grown in the gardens at his house on the Channel, cheeses from all corners of France, rich sausages, the bitter coffee Fabrizio favoured, and hot chocolate or tea for me.

Sometimes he would signal me to duck under the table as we were eating breakfast. I would crawl towards him and open his robe. He would pull my head forward and continue to eat until he ejaculated in my mouth. Once I told him, after I had swallowed his seed, that it had the taste of jujube. He laughed uproariously.

Chapter 11:

A Contretemps with Narcisse Fortin

A few days after my third trip to Fabrizio's shop, I sent a note to Narcisse Fortin explaining my interest in his father's work, particularly the St. Sebastian, and asking to see him.

I received an extremely curt response indicating that the artist had no interest in discussing his father's work with me and particularly the early work which he considered to be the result of his father's youthful folly. I was taken aback. When I happened to mention this episode to an English couple, Paul and Cecile Herington, friends of my parents' and longtime residents of Paris, they explained that the younger Fortin was notoriously difficult and seemed to have few friends among the artists in the city.

By complete chance, they had been invited to an opening for a show of portrait paintings in a small gallery in the rue Lafitte that included a canvas by Fortin. They had not intended to go but suggested that if I accompanied them I might be able to convince Fortin to speak with me.

The gallery was really just a single large room entered through a door that opened directly onto the street. The walls were covered in a deep maroon fabric and densely hung with portrait paintings almost to the ceiling. Paul Herington explained to me that this kind of gallery featured artists who were not successful. For a fee the gallery allowed artists to hang their work. It also took a commission on any pieces that were sold. Fortin's portrait of a young woman seated in a lavish drawing room was hung in an inconspicuous location in a far corner of the room.

Cecile Herington located Fortin in the crowd and pointed him out. A small, slightly dishevelled young man only a few years older than I, he had a sharp, angular face with a flaming coloration that suggested a highly choleric temperament. Paul Herington introduced me. I could see that Fortin recognised my name and was not happy to meet me, but I told him that my note probably gave him the wrong impression. He looked at me suspiciously. I told him that I was more interested in trying to understand more about my father's time in Rome, and that his father and mine knew each other there.

"I'm sorry, but I have nothing to tell you. You sent a note asking to speak to me. I declined. And now you assail me in public. I deeply resent this intrusion. But since you are here, I will tell you that I know little about my father's time in Rome. I think he himself tried to put it behind him."

With no prompting from me, he continued, "So many artists now are atheists, socialists, pederasts. I cannot even go to the annual exhibition at the Salon because it is so upsetting. Artists are sending paintings that mock religion and the Church or have licentious subject matter I would not want my wife or children to see. French society in general has deteriorated, and artists seem to be leading the way."

Because he was becoming more heated by the minute and attracting the attention of the people standing nearby, I made polite apologies and turned to leave. "I absolutely forbid you to write anything about the work that my father did in Rome," he shouted at my back as I exited the gallery.

I was startled. And angry. I had stepped into the street but turned and faced him as he stood in the door glaring at me. "You have no right to tell me what I can or cannot write," I said, more loudly than I had intended. I could tell the Heringtons, who were standing next to me in a small crowd gathered to witness the altercation, were astonished to hear me speak so forcefully. "My father had sketches for the Sebastian that is now in the Louvre. He and many others thought it was a fine painting. I agree with that. I will write about it and other work if I choose."

Fortin could barely contain himself. He was trembling with anger. "My father renounced that work! So do I. It only appeals to degenerates and pederasts. I suppose your father was one of those and you as well."

By now everyone in the room behind him and the street around me had stopped talking and was watching with rapt attention. I was so angry I was ready to strike him, but I caught myself and decided that it was best for me to maintain my dignity and leave. I said in a low voice, as biting as I could make it, "I resent your accusations about my father and myself and would respond, but you are a bitter and rude man, and your comments don't merit a response."

With that I turned my back to him and walked away followed by the Heringtons. As I left, I was astonished to hear a scattering of applause, and one "Bravo!" Several minutes later, while I was still shaking with anger, Cecile Herington turned to me, "Robert, I'm so proud of you. I didn't know you had it in you, but I think you were superb. Fortin deserved exactly what you gave him. Your father would have been gratified by the way you defended your honour and that of your family."

I was not so sure. Some of what Fortin implied was true. I was deeply shaken by his accusations. And I was startled by the way I had acted. Never in my life had I done anything so conspicuous in public. Like the rest of my family, I was always correct and restrained if anyone was nearby.

On the other hand, I could not help but feel some pride. I had clearly changed in the short time since I left England. I wondered how much of that was due to my newly discovered confidence after meeting Fabrizio. And I wondered what he would have thought of the encounter.

Two days later I was startled to receive a note from Athena Briggs announcing that she had already arrived in Paris with her aunt. With the excitement of meeting Fabrizio and my confrontation with Narcisse Fortin, I had completely forgotten about her. Since I had last seen her, I had become a different person. My encounter with Fabrizio had dispelled once and for all any idea that I could love a woman in the same way I could love a man.

I was afraid of what might happen if we met, suspecting she might want to press me, undoubtedly in the most genteel but still insistent way, to announce our engagement. I considered whether I could invent an excuse for not seeing her but couldn't think of anything plausible enough, so I sent a note proposing to meet her at her hotel on the Boulevard des Capucines. Meeting her in the hotel lobby, I was surprised to find her alone. She explained that her aunt was doing a tour of Parisian churches. Few women of my acquaintance would have appeared unaccompanied at a meeting with a single gentleman.

We walked to a café opposite the Opéra. She was always pretty, but in her new Parisian clothes—she had obviously been shopping—she was quite striking. I could see several gentlemen on the pavement appraising her in a not altogether discreet manner. Once we were seated, my immediate impression was once again the resemblance to her brother William, whose image was still indelibly lodged in my mind. Her conversation was animated, and to my relief contained nothing about a possible engagement.

Paradoxically, I found myself wondering whether a marriage with her might be possible, even if it lacked the passion I had with Fabrizio. I knew that eventually I would need to wed if I wished to avoid undue scrutiny. I decided I might as well broach the subject. "Do your parents and mine still expect us to marry?" I asked.

To my surprise her response was a hearty laugh. "No, I think that they have given up hope. I personally think we might have made a go of it, but I suspect that it would probably have inhibited both of us in our ambitions. I had an interesting conversation with my brother a few weeks ago. Do you remember William?"

"Of course." How could I have forgotten? I was unable to keep from blushing. I had a vision of William as I last saw him standing in the drawing room of the Briggs's house. I remembered my difficulty in following the conversation as my eyes kept drifting to his fine face and robust figure fairly bursting out of his suit of clothes. However, as usual, he seemed to pay little attention to me.

"I'm not sure if you know that William has married. We were relieved when he announced his engagement. He had been seen in the company of several women of dubious repute in London. But in the end, he married a completely respectable woman. She is the daughter of an immensely wealthy baronet."

"I'm pleased to hear it. Please convey to him my most hearty congratulations. I saw him frequently at your house, but I cannot say we were ever close or that he took much notice of me."

"William is a surprisingly acute observer of people," Athena replied. "He remembered you quite well. That is why I thought of asking him whether he thought you would make a good husband. He asked me if you were a passionate suitor. I was surprised by the question. When I told him you were attentive and kind, but that you were in no way what I would call passionate—I do hope you won't mind my having said that—he replied in the oddest way. He said that he had a suspicion that you could be quite passionate with the right person. Was he right?"

This statement so unnerved me that I could barely speak. I was surprised that William would have ventured any opinion about me at all, but at least as reported by Athena, his choice of the word "passion" was surprising, and the fact that he used "person" and not "woman" was even more so. I said the first thing that came to mind. "Athena! Really! You certainly have become the modern woman. You do speak your mind."

"Does what I said offend you? Was William quite wrong?" she asked.

I could think of nothing further to say. Fortunately, seeing my confusion, Athena came to my rescue. "I told him I suspected he was right, and that you would amaze all of us when you broke free of the grip of your family and all the expectations everyone has for you."

I was completely taken aback. Was Athena telling me she and William realised some time ago what I had only recently discovered about myself? I changed the subject. "Tell me about yourself. If we are permitted to talk of passion, what are you passionate about?"

"I know it is probably a silly ambition, but I have started writing a novel. My uncle Leonard—I believe I introduced you to him in London?—runs a publishing house and has promised to take a look at it. I have taken up lodging in the city with a girl I met who has similar aspirations—I would like you to meet her—and have decided to devote full time to my writing."

I was again taken aback. What was Athena trying to tell me now? All that I could get out was, "I'm confident that you will produce something noteworthy. Will you let me see it when you are ready?" We continued talking for a few more minutes, and I became increasingly charmed by her warm and generous personality.

The more we talked, the more comfortable we became with each other. I wondered if one day I might be able to tell her about Fabrizio. If she were to accept my relationship with him, would it be possible to ask her to marry me? I knew that there would be immense pressure to marry someone and produce an heir, and I wondered if I might do that with Athena without sacrificing too much of my independence and privacy. I tried to imagine myself in bed with Athena, wondering if I might be able to fulfil my marital duty.

I had long been pre-occupied by this question. I had even thought, several times during my time at the University, of going with some friends to a molly house to see whether I was able to perform. I was too embarrassed to follow through. But the question came back to me forcefully while I was talking with Athena.

While we were chatting, I started to imagine her brother William stripped down to his flannel cricket trousers, holding me and kissing me the way Fabrizio had done so many times. I was thrilled by the stirring in my trousers. I decided that, using some similar mental manipulation, I might very well be able to marry and produce an heir when the time came.

However, I worried that doing so might be unfair to the woman I married or any children we would have. Still, I knew that many men before me, including my father and Fabrizio, had been able to make a similar arrangement work, and I wondered if perhaps it would suit me and Athena as well.

94

Chapter 12:

Parisian Discoveries and Distractions

While Fabrizio spent his days in his gallery, I used my time to explore Paris. One of my first priorities was to make the rounds of the museums, galleries and artists' studios. I stopped in to pay my respects at the studio of Lord Ronald Gower, a Scottish friend of my uncle's. Gower showed me some of his own work but also images of some sculpture he greatly admired by an artist named Rodin whose *Age of Bronze* had garnered an enormous amount of attention when it was shown publicly the year before. It was so lifelike that some critics claimed it had been cast from life, and was therefore merely a mechanical exercise, but M. Rodin had photographs of himself working on the piece with the model, a Belgian soldier, proving that he had modelled it by hand.

I was troubled by the implication of this debate. Why was it so important how a piece was created? Shouldn't any work of art be judged on its own merit? When I saw images of it, though, all these questions were forgotten. No mere mechanical process could have created anything so sublime. I was thrilled. Here was a true successor to Michelangelo. I determined to write a piece on Rodin and attempted to meet him, but he was not in town.

I also paid several visits to the great International Exposition on the Champs de Mars. Although my overall impression was not positive, I did have two notable experiences. The first was my visit to the enormous head of Liberty by Bartholdi. It was part of a colossal piece of metal sculpture destined for the harbour of New York City. I stood in line to walk up the steps to the top, which afforded an interesting view of the exhibition.

This encounter triggered thoughts of the United States. My father knew that it would be prudent to ally himself with one of the great American banks, but he had no interest in crossing the Atlantic. I, on the other hand, longed to go, perhaps even move there to participate in the new world and new life that was incubating far from Europe.

The other experience that impressed me was a device by the American wizard Thomas Alva Edison which he called the phonograph. I joined dozens of other fairgoers in putting a listening device over my ears to experience the uncanny way the machine could reproduce voices and music. It seemed to prove that in our time almost everything can be reproduced. Pointing machines and mechanical drills and chisels can shape stone, allowing remarkable copies of sculpture at any scale. Photography allows a painter to capture a view in mere seconds. Advances in chemical analysis allow the skillful forger to produce paintings almost indistinguishable from the originals. Thanks to the genius of Mr. Edison, now even human voices can be replicated.

I decided to write a short essay along these lines to submit to a British periodical. With Fabrizio's help, I wrote draught after draught. I finally submitted my piece to the *Edinburgh Review* and was thrilled when they accepted and published it. It was my first published work, the beginning of what I hoped would be a career.

I composed a note to my mother alerting her to the publication. In her reply she wrote, "My Dearest Son. I am pleased that you are exploring a possible Career in Writing about the Fine Arts. I know your late Father wanted you to follow him at the Bank, but he did once admit to me that he had resigned himself to the idea that you needed to be free to choose any Career where you could make a Contribution to Society and live your Life in your own way. Thanks to your Father, our Family is now financially secure, and Times have changed. I believe it is now more acceptable for a Young Man to follow his own Path. I know that, however you decide to order your Life, you will be a Credit to our Family." I read that letter over and over wondering what my mother was thinking when she wrote it. Did she know about me?

Of course, I felt that, as a visitor to Paris, it was my duty at least to sample some of the more frivolous entertainments English gentlemen are expected to experience. I watched horseracing at Longchamps, went riding in the Bois de Boulogne, dined at the Grand Véfour, and, of course, visited the Folies Bergère where I saw an amusing Negro review called "Mason et Dixon."

And, speaking of frivolity, Serge, a distant cousin, took me to an entertainment given by Count Robert de Montesquiou in the immense apartment of the count's parents overlooking the Quai d'Orsay. It was a brilliant affair. The room was filled with distinguished older gentlemen, some in exquisitely tailored suits, a few in full military regalia and others with sashes, swords, turbans, and other exotic accoutrements. There was also a small set of young men. Among these were several in provocative costume—cycling suits, boxing shorts or the outfits worn by tightrope walkers—some so tightly fitting that every feature of the body underneath was clearly visible. These outfits were obviously intended to catch the eye of the older gentlemen, which they obviously did.

Finally, there were several women, or so I thought until I looked more closely. They wore the most lavish costumes of all and had the loudest voices. To my great surprise, one of these "women" was being escorted by Olivier Maloof from Oxford. He was wearing a violently red frock coat and making conversation that could easily be heard across the room. I was almost successful avoiding him but ended up having to endure yet another embarrassing monologue.

I tried to make conversation with some of the other guests, but it was so noisy and the conversation so painfully brilliant that after a short time I was eager to leave. As my cousin and I reached the landing on our way out, I noticed a distinguished bearded gentleman in a grey cape and old-fashioned top hat who was just about to enter. I was startled. Even though I had caught only the barest glimpse of the gentleman in the shadows in the Tuileries, I was almost certain this was the same man.

He cast a glance in my direction, smiled slightly, tipped his hat, and paused on the landing as if waiting to speak to me. I made a slight nod and continued to walk quickly down the stairs, hoping my haste wasn't seen as impolite. I realized by the time I reached the street that the damage had already been done. In a gathering of this kind, it would not take long for him to determine who I was and send a note to my hotel. I decided that I should probably be more selective in accepting any further invitations. Even a completely innocent conversation might reveal clues about my relationship with Fabrizio.

Chapter 13:

The Chapel

and the Pit

My visits to Fabrizio's gallery became increasingly frequent. During the day when no one else was in the gallery, Fabrizio would sometimes tell me about the objects on display. Although I had grown up with the extensive collection of art in my parents' houses and had learned a good deal in school, most of what I knew had come from books. Fabrizio taught me to observe each object carefully, finding the telltale signs that suggested the era in which a piece was made and the vicissitudes of its history.

He was particularly keen on teaching me how to distinguish between genuine works of antiquity and recent copies and forgeries, for example by examining the patina to determine whether it had been the result of centuries of weathering or induced all at once by the application of chemical agents. He would hold up a marble head and challenge me to explain to him why I thought it was a Greek original, a Roman copy or a more recent forgery. These sessions fired my imagination.

Several weeks after our first night together Fabrizio took me to a room towards the rear of the second floor that we had not yet entered. He called it the Chapel. It was usually opened only for specific customers upon request. The room's walls were lined with superb antique wood panelling that Fabrizio told me came from a decrepit medieval rectory in the Périgord. On all four walls and on pedestals and easels were artifacts of the kind that the British Museum would have relegated to the Private Case. There were boys and men, mostly naked, either alone in provocative poses or in scenes of coupling, rapes or orgies. There were hermaphrodites, athletes, soldiers, Christian martyrs, and Priapus figures with obscenely large members.

"I do a brisk trade with men interested in this kind of art," Fabrizio told me as he walked through the room. "With the possible exception of the Fulminetti shop in Rome and two galleries owned by a pair of professors in Berlin, I suspect that you see before you the largest inventory of this kind of art in Europe."

I said, "Don't you think you are tempting fate to call this room a chapel when you use it to house such profane art?"

Not surprisingly, Fabrizio laughed at my question. "It is too late for either of us to worry about fate when we are already terrible sinners in the eyes of the Church." Fabrizio found it amusing that I still attended services at the Cathedral of the Holy Trinity, the Anglican church frequented by Americans in Paris, and that I still wished to champion the cause of art that could revivify religious faith.

He facetiously suggested that to further my research on spirituality in art I might wish to visit his best customer, an elderly German nobleman whom he called Count C. "Count C, or Pansy as we call him behind his back, is a devout Catholic. He is particularly fond of pictures by artists using beautiful young models posing, mostly undressed, in provocative positions. You can imagine how much he appreciates work like Fortin's St. Sebastian. I have heard that in his enormous palace in Dresden he displays them in a room lined in black velvet, illuminated with votive candles and furnished with an antique altar up front.

Of course, being a learned man, he is also interested in history and Greek and Roman mythology. I understand he has a large collection of what he calls his 'doomed boys'—beautiful young men from history or myth who died young before they lost their beauty. Antinous, who sacrificed himself for his lover Hadrian, Hyacinth, who was transformed into a flower, or Cyparissus, who became a tree.

He moved to a set of shelves along one wall and laughed as he took down a set of books bound in green Moroccan leather with titles stamped in gold and marbleized endpapers. "These are pieces of fiction that I commission in small, numbered editions for special collectors. Personally, I find them ridiculous, but they sell remarkably well, so I assume that there are people who find them effective for their intended use.

"They have a style all their own. Let me give you a sample." He picked up one of the volumes and opened at random a page near the middle. "Ah, yes. Here we have 'a young shepherd stroking his arbor vitae' who is interrupted by a Satyr who subjects him to a 'rampant rear entry,' finally shooting 'streams of creamy exudations into the boy's very soul.' 'Creamy exudations,' indeed! And into his very soul. I wonder how that would work anatomically. In any case, I think I have given you some taste, as it were, of the verbal 'exudations' contained in these volumes." By this time Fabrizio was laughing so hard that the book in his hands was shaking violently.

When he finally regained his composure, he added, "The most amusing thing about these 'exudations' is that my source is a demure English lady, a Miss S, who has been residing here in Paris for many years with her companion, a well-known American sculptress. In addition to producing earnest novels about poor girls who overcome all obstacles to become successful novelists or selfless nurses—books that she has privately printed but, as far as I can tell, no one reads—she seems to have found her true métier in chronicling what she delicately describes as 'affairs of the heart' between men."

At first, I was shocked by the way the subject matter of the books and the art in this room was obviously intended to arouse the baser passions. After some reflection, I decided that it was not the subject matter nor even its intended effect that troubled me. After all, I felt no such reservations with the passion aroused in me by the Belvedere Torso or the magnificent bodies in the art of Michelangelo or, for that matter, the *Genius of the Dance* at the Paris Opéra. I wanted to believe it was the quality of the art in Fabrizio's Chapel. Much of it was so thin, so obviously intended to evoke only one response, whereas the great art of the past, the art of the Greeks or Michelangelo or Reni, could be seen in many different ways. Or so I very much wanted to believe.

The visit to the Chapel led to one to the Pit. One evening, instead of retiring to the chamber upstairs, Fabrizio had me follow him to the office at the back of the main gallery where he took down a painting of young Spartan athletes wrestling, put his hand into a small opening, and pulled. One entire panel of the wall pivoted open. On the other side was a narrow staircase leading down to a basement.

It took a while for my eyes to adjust after we reached the bottom of the stairs. The floor, walls, and ceiling were all black. Along the walls were multiple hooks hung with ropes and straps and metal objects that I could not identify. At one end of the room was a large platform with four thick columns at the corners and more hooks. At the other side of the room was a metal chair that I immediately identified as a medieval torture device. I was not sure whether I was amused, excited, or repulsed.

After a few minutes I decided I was excited. Over the next few days, Fabrizio would introduce me to one piece of equipment at a time. On the first day he ordered me to strip, tied my wrists in front of me, connected them to pieces of rope and ran the ropes to a pulley on the ceiling. He then used the rope to hoist me upward so that I could barely stand on my toes. I remember thinking how much my pose must have resembled that of a St. Sebastian in a painting by Guido Reni where the saint is standing against a tree with his wrists bound and stretched above his head in like manner.

Fabrizio then proceeded to frig me repeatedly, stopping short each time just as I could feel myself ready to spend. As my excitement became all but intolerable, I begged him to let me finish. He seemed to love to hear me beg. But instead of granting me my wish he pushed my fully engorged member into a metal device held firmly in place by a belt that he locked with a small key. I was frantic to have him unlock me and let me spend, but he let several days go by before he obliged. It was intensely embarrassing to be out in public wondering whether anyone passing on the street could make out the outlines of the device through my trousers.

Some of what Fabrizio did was clearly meant to hurt a little. When he hoisted me up onto my tiptoes, for example, my toes and legs ached from trying to relieve the strain on my arms. My arse and nipples soon became just as sore. For Fabrizio, it seemed to be less about causing any real pain and more about the psychological effect of feeling in control and having me bend to his will. I had never imagined that I would tolerate this kind of humiliation, but after the initial shock I soon found it thrilling.

I also became aware, after a while, that although he was the one who nominally dictated what we did, in reality he was observing closely my reactions, and those reactions controlled his every action. He obviously found it arousing, but he was careful to make sure it had the same effect on me. Ironically, the discomfort and even pain made me want to be even more affectionate with him. I became aware that it wasn't the discomfort that I craved but the fact that, for the first time in my life, someone was paying such intense attention to me.

I loved these sessions. I loved watching the rippling of muscles as he moved and feeling the rasp of his moustache against my skin. I loved the taste and feel of his member as I took him in my mouth and felt him deep inside my body. And increasingly I was sure it was about a good deal more than physical sensation. After our play in the Pit, Fabrizio would usually lead me upstairs to the bed in the small room behind the gallery where we would kiss and caress and talk until I would fall asleep in his arms.

Lying in bed with Fabrizio already asleep, his leg carelessly thrown over mine, I would look at his face, listen to him breathe, and wonder how I could be so lucky. Despite my inability to banish the occasional pangs of guilt, I knew it was only after meeting Fabrizio that my life, like my body, began to feel full and complete. It was hard for me to believe that I had found someone seemingly so perfect and, incredibly, someone who seemed to reciprocate some of my feelings toward him.

I suppose, in retrospect, there were ample signs that might have led me to suspect how far from perfect he was. I should have been more troubled by how little I really knew about him. How I had never met any of his friends or family. How little I knew about his life before I met him. But I pushed any possible misgivings aside in my quest to please him in every way I could and avoid anything that would mar our happiness.

Chapter 14:

Sojourn in La Rochelle

In August, when everyone leaves Paris for a summer holiday, Fabrizio suggested we take a two-week trip as well. He didn't think it wise to go to any of the resort villages along the Normandy coast, where we might see people he or I knew. Instead, he proposed going to La Rochelle, where he was confident no one would recognise us.

He engaged a beautiful, recently constructed villa along the rue du Mail, the tree-lined boulevard along the seafront. It was a fanciful two-storey brick structure imitating medieval half-timber construction with spiky wooden ornamentation and a turret on the upper floor that afforded splendid views of the water. Fabrizio introduced us to the rental agents, without the slightest hesitation, as a M. Federico Craxi and his English nephew Roger Stockton. We occupied the main house. Leopold, Fabrizio's valet, lodged in a small outbuilding at the rear. I met him when Fabrizio and I boarded the train for La Rochelle and he had to enter our cabin with some question for Fabrizio about the baggage, but I rarely saw him during our stay since we preferred to do almost everything for ourselves, and he devised ample entertainments for himself.

The weeks in La Rochelle were the first time we felt free to go out in public together. We would sit at our favourite café, sipping glasses of pastis in the late afternoon and watch the passers-by. We would comment on the handsome men, on their manner and clothing, and wonder what they were thinking when they saw the two of us sitting together. Would they think we were father and son, uncle and nephew, or realise what we really were?

We went bathing in the ocean at least once a day. I noticed

how other bathers stole glances at Fabrizio's splendid body. He explained that when he was a small child, he was constantly bullied. His older brother Carlo persuaded him to use exercise and boxing to develop strength and stamina, a regimen he had continued to splendid effect.

I burned badly. Fabrizio, on the other hand, never burned, but his skin, slightly olive in tone in winter, turned to a shade of deep brown often seen on antique bronzes. The way the lighter skin covered by his bathing costume, extending from just above his knees to the thin strips on each shoulder, highlighted the central part of his body reminded me of images I had seen of the Belvedere Torso.

I loved to lie with him in bed in the evening running my hands through the hair on his chest and feeling the muscles rippling under the skin of his back. The salt air blowing in through the large balcony doors made the lace curtains billow, lightly caressing our naked bodies as we cuddled and kissed and, inevitably, made love.

I became so comfortable with Fabrizio that, one evening when we were lying in bed, I asked him about something that had puzzled me since I first met him. "Fabrizio, you are so handsome and accomplished. What is it that you see in me? I am plain, and I have not yet done anything to speak of with my life."

"You badly underestimate yourself, Robert. I will probably regret telling you this because it could destroy your modesty, one of your most agreeable traits, but you are mistaken about your appeal to others. You are more than just pleasant to look at. You have that northern European look with blue eyes and light-coloured hair which so many southern Europeans find irresistible.

"That in itself makes you attractive. But when you combine that with your British reserve, your sweet and generous character, your smile, it makes you beautiful. Even if you had none of these qualities, some men would find you beautiful because of your youth, your title, and your financial situation. Anyone other than you would have known long ago how desirable you are."

Fabrizio had never said anything like this before. I was amazed, and I didn't entirely believe it. I had another question for him. "Can you explain to me why so many people I meet who are of our sort just assume that I'm, well, the way I am when they never seem to assume that about you?"

"I have never completely understood how men of our sort recognise each other," he replied. "In some cases, there are clear signs. A fuchsia-coloured waistcoat, a heliotrope in the buttonhole. Sometimes you can divine a great deal from a glance held a second too long, a particular kind of smile, or the way someone carries himself. But, unlike our ridiculous Dr. Tardieu, I don't think that most of our kind can be detected in any obvious way. Certainly not you or me. Still, there is often something that provides a clue."

"I had no idea about you when first we met," I said, blushing. "Did you know about me?"

"I had a strong suspicion. You say many men have made similar assumptions, and strangers have actually approached you. Maybe they only guess but are bold because you are young and unthreatening. Somehow they sense you would not say something rude. Very few men act that way with me. I don't intend to be intimidating, but many say I am, so perhaps it is so. I sometimes wish it were otherwise."

"Did you know from the time we met that I would be, well, happy to let you take the lead, even be quite aggressive, in our lovemaking?"

"Yes, I had a good idea as well. Why, I cannot say. You are clean-shaven and well-spoken, but that is true of many young men. Is there some unspoken communication, some chemical we unknowingly emit, sensed only by those perfectly attuned to it?"

Fabrizio was smiling the big radiant smile that always made me melt. I covered his mouth and face with kisses. Then I thought about the clean-shaven comment. "Fabrizio, I sometimes feel like just a boy or a waiter without a beard. Don't you think it's time I grew one?"

"Please don't do that. I like you just the way you are."

By the end of the two weeks, it was hard to imagine going back to Paris, or to any place where we would be recognised. Our weeks at La Rochelle had dispelled any doubts that we could be comfortable together for more than a night at a time. For me, the fact that we had become closer was confirmed when Fabrizio suggested that we visit a photographer's studio to have our picture taken.

The photographer took us to the darkened back room of his studio and instructed us to sit on a park bench he had set up in the middle of the room with, behind us, a painted backdrop of the ocean executed in a florid eighteenth-century manner and, in front of us, a spindly tree branch with dead leaves painted green positioned to give the scene some depth. I noted with amusement that this arrangement was intended to imitate the actual scene only a few hundred yards away.

I sat on the bench with Fabrizio behind me. He pressed up hard against me with his hand on my shoulder. The photographer turned on some lights and adjusted his camera. We endured a series of flashes directly in our eyes as the photographer made slight adjustments to his camera, our positions, or the tree branch.

After we received the prints, I put one of them, encased in an elaborate cardboard mount, in a small binder that I always kept close at hand. In the photograph, I have a slightly forced smile while Fabrizio, his posture erect, his impressive frame clearly perceptible under his well-tailored suit, and his handsome face lit up by that dazzling smile, looked entirely at ease. I was astonished that Fabrizio would allow a photographer to create such a public record of our affection, but I suppose he imagined no one besides ourselves would ever see it, and even if they did, it could probably pass for the portrait of an uncle with his nephew that we were pretending to be.

At the beginning of our stay, I thought my feelings for Fabrizio might be a short-lived infatuation. By the end of our time in La Rochelle, I had changed my mind. I was not sure what I felt, but I knew it was deeper and more lasting than a mere infatuation. I was devastated by the prospect of having to hide when we returned to Paris.

I thought about all the obstacles to our spending more time together. He was much older than I. He had his family, his gallery, and his friends in Paris. I had my family in England, and I would almost certainly need to take a wife to avoid scrutiny. Our arrangement, however we might craft it, would be an arrangement unacknowledged by either family or unblessed by any church.

Still, I was sure there must be a way. One day I suggested that he might open a shop in New York. I knew he had wealthy customers who lived there. That way, even if both of us were married and wished to remain close to our families, we could spend at least part of the year together there. He didn't reject the idea out of hand, but after our initial discussion, he didn't mention it again.

On the last evening in La Rochelle, he handed me a small box wrapped in decorative green and white paper and tied with a crimson ribbon. Within the box I found, nestled in a bed of red velvet, a ring with a filigreed gold band holding a splendid antique cameo surrounded by a corona of brilliants. The cameo bore a fine image in the upper, lighter layer of stone that I immediately recognized as the head of the emperor Hadrian. It floated on a darker ground of pale blue. He kissed me and put the ring on the little finger of my right hand.

It was perfect. The image of Hadrian looked remarkably like Fabrizio. I found myself weeping profusely. "I am overwhelmed, so happy," I told him. "But I feel terrible that I don't have enough time to find a suitable gift for you in return."

"I thought of that," he told me. With that he held out his left hand. On his little finger I saw a ring with a matching setting and a similar cameo, but the face on the cameo was that of Antinous. "This cameo", he said, "was probably of late Roman manufacture. I had a jeweller match the setting of the one I just gave you. Pending your return to Paris, we can consider this ring your gift to me." I kissed it and held Fabrizio in a long embrace. We promised each other we would not remove the rings when I left Paris to continue my trip on the Continent. I had never felt as close to anyone. Alas, this feeling was not to last.

We returned to Paris. Fabrizio re-opened his gallery, and for a few days we saw each other as before, but it was clear our days of bliss were about to end. Amélie and the girls would be returning in a few weeks, and with the cooler weather minimizing the threat of malaria, it was also time for me to continue on to Rome. Despite my reluctance to leave Fabrizio, I was eager to learn more about Jean-Louis Fortin and my father, immerse myself in the study of art and antiquity, and perhaps write a few pieces for publication.

Both of us increasingly withdrew inside ourselves. Then, a week before my departure, we became embroiled in a painful argument. We had quarrelled before but had always reconciled within a few hours with tears and a particularly exciting session in the Pit. This time it was different. What touched it off I can't recall. It was probably something trivial, but it grew serious when he accused me of seeing other men.

I was dumbfounded. And furious. As I had come to know Fabrizio, I had gradually discovered that he had had affairs with many boys and young men before I arrived. I knew he kept in touch with at least a few of them. I didn't know whether he continued to invite them to his gallery when I wasn't there. I never had the courage to ask him directly. But just awareness of their existence made me intensely jealous. "You're the one with many boys," I nearly shouted at him. "Even if I were seeing other men— which I am not—I'd only be catching up to you." Rather than answering, he turned and walked away.

This had never happened before. I stopped talking to him. This was shocking behaviour for me. Particularly with Fabrizio I had always been polite and pliable, no doubt to a fault. Fabrizio made a few attempts to broker a truce, but I deflected them. He, in turn, became sullen and refused to talk to me. He even suggested that I leave Paris earlier than I had planned. I refused and decided to stay away from the rue de Seine.

Then, the day before I was scheduled to depart, I relented. I found him in the gallery and got down on my knees to beg his forgiveness. He barely looked at me. "Just go," he said. "If you come back to Paris for a day or two, do not come to see me. Just return to England. Better for us to say goodbye now." Then he turned away. I felt like the floor beneath my feet was collapsing, and I was hurtling downward.

Chapter 15:

Rome

I remember the rumble of the wheels of the cab over the paving stones as I made my way from my hotel to the Gare de Lyon. I was furious with Fabrizio for the way he had abandoned me, and I was furious with myself for believing he really cared for me. I wept profusely.

When the cab stopped, I made an effort to compose myself before stepping onto the pavement in front of the station. After checking to make sure that Walters had already arrived with our luggage, I then moved quickly through the thronged ticket area and platform shed and into my train compartment. I felt lonely and empty in a way I had never felt before.

The day started out cool with a slate grey sky—typical September weather in Paris. I don't remember much about the start of the trip. I was in emotional turmoil. I was aware that I ought to feel a real sense of accomplishment. In my quest to learn about my father's life on the Continent I had made some headway. I was now embarked on what promised to be a meaningful career as a writer and critic. And, finally, I had at long last discovered the passion that could be triggered by another human being. This last should have been the crowning achievement of my trip so far, but the enormous promise it held had turned to ashes.

As the train travelled southward, however, the day became warmer. Between Lyons and Aix-en-Provence, the sun started to break through the clouds. By the time we reached Nice, it was warm, and there was abundant sunshine. At the Hôtel de Luxembourg, my room had a fine view over the Promenade des Anglais and the Mediterranean as well as a splendid tropical garden behind the hotel where I could walk in the afternoon. Visiting

friends of my family and others for whom I had letters of introduction, I found the gardens along the French Riviera captivating.
However, the high point of my time in Nice was my exploration
of some of the nearby Roman ruins, especially the Pont du Gard
near Nîmes. I thought I knew it from publications I had read in
England, but it was much larger and more impressive than I had
imagined, my first real taste of the grandeur of the Roman Empire.
The sight made me so eager to reach the heart of the ancient empire that I cut short my stay and hurried south toward Rome, the
capital of the recently unified Kingdom of Italy.

On the journey I found myself still thinking every day about
Fabrizio and missing him terribly. Contemplating something
completely unrelated, I would hear a voice that sounded like his
or smell a gardenia like the one he wore in his coat buttonhole and
feel a stab of pain that shook my entire body. I had never felt that
way before and had no one with whom I could talk about it.

I thought about writing Fabrizio and begging again for his forgiveness but decided against it. Why should I be the one
apologizing? He was accustomed to getting his own way, especially with me. Did I really need to accept that? Our dispute was
senseless and as much his fault as mine. After a week, I did send
him a letter and then wrote occasionally, but I never said much of
consequence, and his occasional return letters were cursory and
revealed little. I was waiting for some sign that he wished to make
amends.

In reality, I was embarrassed to put my thoughts on paper because I feared Fabrizio hadn't felt towards me the way I felt
towards him. Even during our time in La Rochelle, we never actually discussed our feelings for each other or made any
commitments beyond the exchange of rings.

Arriving in Rome in early October, my mood improved considerably. Walters said that my father had stayed at the Hotel de
l'Angleterre but had considered it somewhat old-fashioned, so I
decided to try the recently constructed Bristol, a handsome edifice
on the Piazza Barberini. As I walked through the door, I noticed

that everything—the guests ensconced in heavily upholstered chairs, their pale complexion and drab attire, the snippets of conversation in English—made it seem as though the entire hotel had been transported intact from its namesake in England. As I threw open the draperies of my rooms, I was delighted to see that I had a splendid view of the piazza and a fountain identified by my Baedeker as the Tritone, the work of the great seventeenth-century sculptor Bernini.

While Walters unpacked our trunks, I took a bath, changed my clothes, and walked across the street to the Palazzo Barberini. I was disappointed. Although it was a grand building and housed some important paintings, many were in poor condition, badly hung, and dimly lit. What redeemed the trip was the great trompe l'oeil ceiling painting in the principal salon by Pietro da Cortona. I had heard that this was his masterpiece, but before seeing it, I was sceptical. It was intended as a hymn of praise to the ambitious and often decidedly less-than-admirable Barberini family. But as I stood in the middle of the great room and looked upward, the illusion of scores of robust figures ascending right through the cornice and up into heaven was spectacular. I no longer cared about the circumstances of its creation. It was a masterpiece.

I suddenly thought of my father. The palazzo had long been a favourite stop for tourists in Rome. He must have come and stood in exactly the same spot where I was standing to experience the full effect of the forced perspective. I wondered what his thoughts might have been. And whether he was alone or with someone or who he might have been planning to visit after his tour of the Palazzo.

In the days that followed, as I had done in Paris, I made the round of the usual tourist sites. I went to see the Roman ruins— the Pantheon, the Colosseum, and the Baths of Caracalla. After seeing the Pont du Gard, I thought I would be even more impressed by the heart of the Roman Empire, but I was a little disappointed. I suppose the awesome scenes of Rome in the prints of Piranesi and the spectacle of the Pont du Gard had spoiled me.

The one exception was the Colosseum. Although my visit there, on a hot and sunny day in November, made a considerable impression, I must confess that it was not primarily for reasons architectural or historical.

The area immediately around Colosseum had been excavated, but much of the rest of the Roman Forum was rural in appearance and nearly deserted. My Baedeker had a warning about thieves and pickpockets, but I saw few people of any kind. While I was there that afternoon the inhabitants consisted mostly of mangy dogs wandering the parched grounds sniffing at the litter strewn across the dusty ground.

For a small fee, the custodian allowed me to ascend to the Colosseum's upper levels. The building certainly looked impressive from there. What I had never realised, though, sitting in Oxford looking through illustrations, was the extent of the maze of dark passages inside the structure, now visible because the floor of the Colosseum covering them had long since collapsed.

Back at ground level, I spent some time roaming through these passages. I examined, amidst the accumulated rubbish left by generations of sightseers and furtive lovers, what I surmised were pens for wild animals and spaces for gladiators who participated in the extravagant entertainments so vividly described in the pages of Gibbon's grand opus on the decline of the empire.

In one of the dark passages, a few workmen were engaged in what I assumed were excavations. A few minutes later, as I exited the interior and emerged into the brilliant sunshine, I was startled to see one of the workmen leaning against an archway, perhaps twenty feet from me, one foot on the ground, the other resting against the wall behind him. Had he seen me coming and adopted the pose for my benefit?

He was a brawny man, perhaps thirty years of age with a thick neck, ruddy face, and shock of unruly black hair. His solidly built frame was stuffed into rough twill trousers caked with dirt. He had taken off his shirt and had tucked it into the back of his trousers exposing his prodigious biceps and a barrel-like chest.. Even from a distance the sight of rough leather braces just grazing the outer edge of his nipples set my heart racing.

As I stood there rooted to the spot, I wondered what it would be like to bury my nose in that unruly hair, how it would smell. I imagined he could lift me over his shoulder and carry me. He reminded me of engraved images of Samson or Hercules, and I found myself wondering about his thighs and other unseen parts, whether they were commensurate in size with his chest and massive arms and how they might compare with those of the Belvedere Torso. My gaze wandered down to his rippling stomach and then to the bulge at the front of his trousers.

When I became aware of what I was doing, I was embarrassed and raised my gaze briefly back to his face. He was looking directly at me. He had probably seen me staring at him for at least a minute. I froze, not sure what his intentions were.

He startled me by walking directly up to where I was standing, stopping so close that his head was just inches from my own. I could feel the heat radiating from his bare chest. Glistening with perspiration, it emitted a feral masculine odour. I could not look directly into his eyes, so I looked down. His nipples were startlingly pink and projected sharply out of dark circles the size of a British crown. The entire massive, half naked body exuded animal vitality. I felt small and effete and more than a little ridiculous standing in front of him in my tan linen suit and straw hat clutching my Baedeker in a sweaty hand.

He said something, presumably in some Italian dialect I could not understand. Then he made a crude gesture with his arm indicating all too clearly his intention. I could not move but was not sure whether it was because of fear or excitement. Then he grabbed my arm and roughly pulled me back into the shadow of one of the arches.

At that point he made his intentions quite explicit by thrusting me, face first, up against a wall below the springing of a vault and forcing himself against my backside. Even through his trousers I could feel something hard throbbing against my buttocks. He grabbed my head and turned it enough so I could see the gesture he made with his fingers suggesting a commercial transaction. I could smell red wine and garlic on his breath as well as the strong odour radiating from his body. I remember thinking that, with anyone else or in any other circumstance, I would have been repulsed, but in this case, it was intoxicating.

For a moment I could not make up my mind. His treatment strongly reminded me of my time with Fabrizio in the Pit, but this was a total stranger, and we were outdoors in a public place where anyone might walk by. There was something wildly exciting about allowing myself to be taken in public in this way and by someone so clearly from the working classes. And I felt a strong urge to do something to make me forget Fabrizio. He had claimed I had been unfaithful to him. As long as he believed that anyway, why not go ahead and discover what that would be like?

However, I remembered the warnings in the guidebook. Also, when I thought about Fabrizio, despite my lingering anger at him, I felt a sudden stab of affection that drove all the desire out of me. I was still overwhelmed by the memory of his body and reluctant to dilute those memories by exposure to another.

I shook my head and tried to leave. To my consternation, the man held me where I was. I was afraid he was going to force me and take my purse after he finished. Or worse. But to my immense relief, he released me, laughed, and asked in a rumbling bass voice, "Inglese?" I nodded and walked briskly away.

After fifty feet, I stopped, wondering if I really wanted to leave. I was still trembling with fear and excitement and decided that maybe it was not so dangerous after all. And I told myself, spending a few minutes with this man would have no negative effect on Fabrizio. Maybe I could take him somewhere where we could be in private, even have him bathe first. I turned around, but he had disappeared. I could not decide if I was disappointed or relieved. As I made my way back to the hotel, I amazed myself that I had even considered such an adventure.

Modern Rome, after I grew accustomed to the poverty, noise,

and dirt, proved to be every bit as magical as I had anticipated. I strolled the *passeggiata*, listened to the military band at dusk on the Pincio, and attended the opera at the Teatro Olympico. I secured *permessi* to view the pictures in the Villa Ludovisi and the Rospigliosi Casino as well as the gardens at the Villa Doria Pamphilj. A particularly striking expedition was a nighttime visit to the Casino of the Villa Borghese arranged by Madame C, whom I had met in Paris. Burnished by the warm flickering candlelight, some of the marble figures seemed almost alive. A fighting satyr, with his attributes dramatically lit from below, was so rousing that I had to pull myself away to avoid making my interest conspicuous to my companions.

I loved the way Rome had settled into its old age so gracefully, allowing its buildings and monuments to ripen without attempts to wipe away the traces of time. Stucco and stone glowed in the late afternoon light—so different from the grime of frantic London streets constantly under construction. Even the enormous press of people in the central part of the city, the acrid odours, the continuous assault on the senses until well into the night were somehow reassuring and less intrusive than the tumult of central London. I soon learned that nothing moved quickly in Rome. Time slowed. The weeks turned into months.

Among my first visits was an excursion to see a pair of sculptures from Hadrian's Villa depicting Antinous—a full figure piece in the Capitoline Museum and a relief in the Villa Albani. Fabrizio told me he thought little of Antinous when he himself was young, but as he had grown older, he grew obsessed with this tragic beauty.

Looking at the gloriously nude body and downcast eyes of the Capitoline Antinous, it was not difficult for me to see why Hadrian had been so besotted with him. Or Fabrizio. In them Antinous had ceased to be a boy but was not yet a man. I wondered if it might have the same effect on me after I reached Fabrizio's age.

I was also eager to see the famous works in the Vatican: the

Laocoön and the Apollo Belvedere in the Belvedere Courtyard; the Augustus of Prima Porta and the Doryphoros in the Chiaramonte Museum; and especially the Belvedere Torso in the Museo Pio Clementino. The Torso was a piece of sculpture that Fabrizio frequently mentioned as his favourite. He told me that it was assumed to represent Hercules, and it was signed, a rare practice in the ancient world. However, most authorities suspected the signature, "Apollonius, son of Nestor, Athenian," chiselled in Greek letters on the base, was inauthentic, and the work was a Roman copy or forgery, although a very skilful one.

I was astonished by my first sight of it. It was one of the few pieces of ancient sculpture in the Vatican collection that was left as it was found and not restored. I had not fully appreciated until that moment how the loss of arms, legs and head, instead of diminishing its impact, forced the viewer to concentrate on the massive trunk of the body, making it all the more impressive.

Hercules (if Hercules it was) sat on a base which lifted him well above the floor so that he loomed above me, his sheer bulk overwhelming. I spent a considerable amount of time walking around the figure to view him from all angles and admire the remarkable skill with which the sculptor had managed to convey action and anticipation even in a figure supposedly in repose. Hercules's back was particularly animated with a tremendous play of muscles rippling under the marble skin.

However, my eyes continually returned to the front of the figure and the junction where Hercules' massively developed thighs met the tautly compressed stomach and truncated but still mighty upper body. The way the sculpture was positioned on the base funnelled my vision directly into the narrowing gap between his powerful splayed legs.

This vision was so arousing that I had to look away when anyone else was nearby. I had the greatest urge to reach out and caress his thighs, the weighty sacks between his legs, and run my fingers over what remained of the marble member. Being well brought up, I didn't dare touch him as I had seen other visitors do, but in days to come the memory of those spread thighs, mixed with memories of the man in the Colosseum and of Fabrizio, haunted my thoughts, particularly when I first awakened.

In Rome, as in Paris, letters from members of my family arrived regularly. The first to arrive was from my sister, Alicia. I had to smile when I read it. After the usual pleasantries, she, who had paid scant attention to the family business while growing up, launched into a lengthy discussion of the profitability of the Stapleton Bank during the previous months and how well Roger, her husband, was working with our mother on business affairs.

The letter concluded with a perfunctory final sentence: "I am to tell you that everyone here, Roger and myself in particular, hope that you continue to have a rewarding time on the Continent, but of course we are eager for your return to us and, perhaps, to your rightful place at the bank."

Eager for my return to the bank! Ha! I could just imagine Alicia and Roger sitting side by side at her writing desk composing this far-from-subtle but harmless fabrication. They needn't have feared. I was not eager to return to England, and at such point as I might return, I had no interest in the affairs of the bank or in displacing Roger. I was, however, extremely pleased that he and my mother had everything well in hand; it would forestall any pressure for me to return.

Once I was well settled in Rome, I looked up acquaintances of my family's, especially those of my uncle and my tutor at Oxford. Many were writers or artists who lived or worked in the heart of the Foreigners' Quarter near the Spanish Steps. Walking down that staircase, I could not help but be awed by the knowledge that within a few hundred yards had lived and worked writers— Shelley, Keats, and Thackeray; sculptors—Thorvaldsen and Canova; painters—Sir Thomas Lawrence and Richard Evans.

I also noticed that, among the throngs of tourists standing or sitting on the steps, were quite a few boys, some of them alarmingly young, displaying themselves shamelessly along the outer walls of the stairway with their thin white shirts completely open, setting off their beautiful olive skin, brilliant white teeth, and lustrous black hair.

I suspected that eminent men of earlier generations probably saw a similar display. This was undoubtedly for some the chief attraction of the city. These boys were the inspiration for scores of paintings, pieces of sculpture, and love poems assumed by most readers to have been addressed to young women. That thought reminded me of the sketches in the house on Carlton Hill. I could well imagine Fortin finding his Sebastian displaying himself on these very steps.

I then tried to imagine my father standing on this spot observing the same spectacle. I didn't have much chance to pursue this line of thought, though. I must have been staring too obviously because, near the bottom of the steps, an elegantly dressed older man approached me and said, in lightly accented but otherwise flawless English, "Good afternoon, young gentleman. I would be most pleased to introduce you to some fine young women who could enhance your visit to Rome with some pleasant companionship." However, he had obviously already divined my real interests, because, without waiting for me to respond, he continued, "Or perhaps you would prefer a handsome boy?" This last accompanied by a broad conspiratorial smile.

The brazen proposition in broad daylight and in front of so many people shocked me, all the more so because it had issued from the mouth of a man who gave every indication of being a dignified gentleman. Although too startled to answer, I didn't turn away. I briefly toyed with the idea of engaging the services of one of the boys. After my encounter with the man in the Colosseum, I had been acutely aware of how much I missed the touch of another man. I would not normally be drawn to anyone as young the boys on offer, but somehow, in that setting with their bodies so casually displayed, they seemed desirable.

I had changed since I left England. I had gained some weight and, despite Fabrizio's disapproval while I was in Paris, had grown a beard. When I looked in the mirror, I was surprised by how mature I looked. Maybe even handsome. Standing on the Spanish Steps, I was even more surprised to find myself imagining what it would be like to be the one on top and in control. I felt a sudden, unexpected surge of confidence.

The thought occurred to me that I owed it to myself to accept the man's offer as a way to obtain the full traveller's experience of Rome. I wondered how much I would be expected to pay and whether there would be any danger of blackmail or physical harm. And then, by a curious shift of mind, I imagined that I might justify engaging the boy to provide myself with a little additional experience in the amorous arts which would benefit Fabrizio if we ever reconciled.

I also suddenly found myself wondering if my father had received the same offer and, if so, whether he had accepted. My thoughts were interrupted by the realisation that I was still looking at the boys on the steps. My prolonged scrutiny would have confirmed my interest to anyone watching me. Burning with embarrassment, I turned and walked away.

Seeing these young men in the flesh was unnerving. I could not imagine even their most brazen counterparts in London in such a public state of undress causing so little indignation in passers-by. Or so much agitation in myself. I decided that I was not ready for such an adventure. I also, for reasons I could not explain, continued to feel a sense of loyalty to Fabrizio. Even if my commitment was never voiced to him nor reciprocated, I resolved that I would only explore this aspect of Roman life through its art. To that end, I visited the studio of Gemito Vincenzo, whose paintings of Neapolitan fisher boys had attracted much attention, and stopped by the studio of Penry Williams, the Welsh painter well known for his scenes of Roman life, and met his longtime companion, the sculptor John Gibson, disciple of Canova.

Chapter 16:

Warm Friendships in Italy

"Can I be candid with you about some of our countrymen who have spent time here over the years and shown interest in, um, the local youths?" the elderly gentleman asked after an interminable set of pleasantries.

I was at the flat of Walter Townsend Bury in the Via Sistina. He had been a young man at the British Academy in Rome studying classical architecture when my father was there in the early 1850s and was one of the individuals whose name my uncle had given me.

Standing at the door to his apartment in a jaunty pose leaning on a walking stick with an elaborately wrought brass head, Bury extended a hand covered in a dove grey glove. His breeches, ruffled shirt, and elaborate cravat had not been seen in the clubs of London since the days of Beau Brummell, and looking more closely I could tell his elaborately coiffed hair was actually a powdered wig. I must have looked startled.

"My dear boy, I assure you that when I'm back in London I dress like any proper English gentleman," he told me, "but I have found that when my clients visit Rome, they want to feel like they are stepping back into a former era, and I like to encourage them in that illusion."

As we entered the apartment he continued, "I know about your search for information about your father and his activities in Rome. I have heard about your inquiries in Paris." He must have sensed my perplexity. "I dare say by now you have learned there is a fraternity among men of our kind in every major city in Europe. We know each other through business dealings, shared friends, and an appreciation for certain kinds of art, certain forms of beauty."

Men of our kind? I was no longer surprised to hear these words. I merely nodded and waited for him to resume.

After a long pause and a rolling upward of the eyes as if trying to recall something elusive, "The British colony in Rome was quite small in those days. All of us who went out in society tended to know one another. We would meet at church, at certain clubs, and at the salon of Contessa P. I am sorry to say, however, that I remember little about your father."

After all the promising preliminaries, I was sorely disappointed, but I replied, "The Contessa P?"

Yes, I am not sure whether she is still alive, but if so, she would likely be your best source of information about your father. She knew everyone."

"Do you know how I could find her?"

"I'm sorry. I have not heard anything about her for many years. I can, however, tell you something about a certain subset of men from northern Europe of which your father was a part. My friends tell me I can be quite candid with you. To put it crudely, many of them flock here because they find the boys more available, willing, and inexpensive than back home. And, in their quest for boys, the northerners are joined in considerable numbers by the Catholic clergy, despite the presence of an entire agency of the Church, called the Cardinal Vicarate, charged with investigating so-called offenses against morality. It is an open secret that some of the most powerful bishops and archbishops have relationships of this kind, and in some cases even flaunt them in public because they are protected by their superiors."

As he said this, a young man entered the room. His face was a rich olive colour like that of many Roman boys, but in his white jacket and cap he looked like he had just stepped off a cricket pitch. Bury didn't stop speaking but simply nodded to him. He made no objection as the young man sat next to him on the settee and gave him a quick squeeze of his thigh which he apparently assumed I wouldn't notice. Bury informed me that this was Eduardo, his assistant.

Attempting to avoid staring at Eduardo, I asked Bury what he might remember about Jean-Louis Fortin, but he gave only a vague answer. The same was true when I queried him about the murder of Johann Gottlieb.

Bury started to respond, "I remember the murder but few details. Many of my English friends departed immediately after it became public. Have you been to the British Embassy? They might—"

"The men there now have no reason to know anything," Eduardo interjected. I had not expected him to speak, and certainly not to cut Bury off mid-sentence, but Bury did not seem to find it surprising. He muttered something about how he relied on his assistant for all things Roman, and Eduardo continued. "You should go to the police station in the Foreigners' Quarter and ask which inspector was involved in the investigation. They are used to handling cases of this kind. Even if this murder occurred long ago, they would have records. If the men at the station are not forthcoming, I suggest you go to the office of the Commissioner of Police. He will listen to a gentleman from London."

I wondered how Eduardo knew so much about the police but knew it would be better not to ask. I thanked Bury and prepared to leave.

"Who will you visit next?" he asked.

"I will be seeing James Waterfield, a painter who had apparently been a friend of my father's."

"Waterfield!" Bury puffed. "He was certainly part of that high and mighty set a generation ago. He was far from young then but as vain as Narcissus. I'm surprised he's still alive. A thoroughly unpleasant man, a mediocre artist, a libertine and sybarite." Eduardo was pulling, discretely but insistently, at Bury's sleeve, muttering something about saying no more.

I walked back to my hotel. As I approached, I noticed Walters in front of the Tritone fountain speaking with an older woman. She was certainly not a lady, but, on the other hand, she was neatly dressed and nicely padded in the right places. To my amazement I saw him give her a quick peck on the cheek, then turn and enter the hotel.

As far as I knew, Walters knew no one in Rome. How could he have met that woman? I had never heard of him in connection with any woman in England. But here? How was it possible when Walters was always immediately available whenever I needed him? My frequent absences did give him at least a few hours most days to pursue his own interests, but I realised that I had no idea what he did during those hours. It reminded me how little most gentlemen know about their servants' lives but how much they knew about ours.

Chapter 17:

Detective Valenti

As Bury's "assistant" had predicted, I had a difficult time at the police station. It was located in an ancient quarter near the Piazza Navona, housed in an old building with a crumbling stucco façade, and filled with a motley assortment of denizens of the neighbourhood, almost all poorly dressed and talking loudly. It was chaotic.

The officers there spoke very fast, and I hardly recognised the language they were speaking as Italian. Most of them looked at me with what appeared to be a mixture of curiosity and suspicion. As with almost everything involving Roman officialdom, my quest for information seemed to drag on interminably, and if I were not a foreigner with a title and ample funds, I suspect I would not have received any information at all.

It required several trips, a return visit to Waterfield's assistant, intervention from the office of the Commissioner, and the exchange of a certain amount of money, but at last I was offered the name of a retired inspector, a man named Valenti. He agreed to speak with me after he reviewed the records.

On the day I arrived, Valenti waved me into a tiny alcove where he squeezed his big frame between a table and the wall behind him hung with portraits of Garibaldi and Victor Emmanuel.

He was a big, gruff character, and not friendly. He was also difficult to understand. I'm reasonably sure that I caught the import if not the nuance of sentences overflowing with what I recognised as strikingly vulgar expressions.

"Yes, I remember," he told me. "In 1854, I was still junior agent. Not in charge of investigation. Not present when first officers arrived. Called in after. When I entered the apartment, mousy old man lying on the floor. Pictures of naked boys on the walls. Obviously one of these foreign sodomites infesting Rome. Now, because of this 'accident,' one less of them.

"The sodomite—um, victim—" This quick correction made me wonder if Valenti thought I might be another foreign sodomite— "was tied up, naked, lying on the floor in a pool of blood. Beside a bench in the middle of the room. There was a big piece of ivory shoved in the bugger's food hole. Several teeth knocked out. Blood everywhere. Already turning black and sticky. Probably died by suffocation.

I was appalled by the scene Valenti described and his manner of describing it. Newton at the British Museum had told me that the ivory was implicated in Gottlieb's murder, but I never imagined that it could have been the murder instrument.

"His bumhole also sticky with blood. Must have been big object shoved up there, too. Quantities of blood. Covered entire rug. Seeping into the floorboards. Bugs already at work."

Valenti related the details with perfect composure as if this were something a policeman in Rome would see every day. Maybe, I thought, Gottlieb's death was only one of many equally bizarre and gruesome deaths he would have encountered in a long career.

Valenti continued. "We thought at first robbery. Neighbours said boys often came to German's flat. Probably for filthy acts paid by sodomite. That day neighbours saw two boys. One seen before. The other spoke German. Eventually found that boy—an Austrian. Admitted he visited the old man earlier that day. Said sodomite paid him to do disgusting things. Claimed he knew nothing about murder. We could not prove anything against the Austrian. Never found the other boy.

"The German sodomite had been in bad way. Paying for protection. Either Mafia or Camorra. Maybe both. He sold sculpture stolen from museums in Reggio Calabria and Palermo, cemeteries, even churches. Can you imagine? Churches! Holy Mother of God!

Disgusting! And even worse. Filthy pictures. Naked boys. Didn't deserve to live."

I was only half listening. I kept thinking that it was impossible for my father to have been involved in any of this. He might have known Gottlieb. He could well have purchased pieces from him. But murder? I could not believe that he had anything to do with violence of any kind. But why did he have that piece of ivory?

Valenti shifted in his chair. "He had many enemies. Including a cardinal. Found out that sodomite sold him fakes. Sodomite also blackmailed by boys he paid to bugger him. Had not paid rent for months. Many people wished him harm. My thought—maybe it wasn't robbery. Maybe he wanted to die?

"Never found out what happened. Family members in Hamburg were contacted. Not interested in knowing. Some men arrested later for gross indecency said German liked to be tied up, paddled, and sodomized. We thought maybe the ivory could tell us something. We brought in experts to examine."

"Do you remember what it looked like?"

Valenti looked at me suspiciously. "Yes. Of course. Big curved thing like this," he said, grabbing his member through his trousers. "Covered with filthy pictures."

Now I was sure this ivory was similar if not identical to the one in my father's office.

"We were investigating. Then pressure from a cardinal to stop. No one here is ever eager to make enemies in Church. I was told to forget it."

"Do you know what happened to the ivory?"

He looked at me even more suspiciously but apparently decided it was not his business to question the motives of a well-dressed foreigner. "No idea. Ask a clerk in the police central bureau. They will have record."

Given my experiences with Italian bureaucrats, I suspected that if the ivory were of any value, it would have disappeared long ago. To my surprise, when I appeared at the central office the next day, a clerk found some notes in a big ledger. He said that by law the ivory had to be offered to family members first, but since no one in Hamburg had wanted it, it was offered to a museum in Palermo, but it was again refused. Eventually it was transferred to the Capitoline Museum.

Chapter 18:

A Meeting in the Settignano Foothills

To speak with James Waterfield, an elderly English painter who had lived in Rome in the 1850s, required a trip to his villa outside Florence. On the train I observed the magnificent countryside with its vineyards, small farms, and picturesque towns—Terni, Spoleto, Perugia, Cortona, and Arezzo. From Florence I took another train to the Rovezzano station, where I engaged a carriage to take me to Waterfield's villa, located about ten miles east in the Settignano foothills.

As the carriage rolled along the villa's gravel entrance drive, I caught glimpses of the house, framed by tall cypress trees that lined each side of the drive. It and several nearby outbuildings were set on a series of walled terraces planted with ancient olive trees that cascaded down the hillside to a lush valley floor.

The house appeared to have been a modest farm dwelling that had been expanded and modified over the years. In its present state, it was an informal but still imposing residence rendered in ochre stucco, now weathered and pale, and partly covered with a luxurious growth of wisteria. It was the perfect Englishman's image of an Italian villa. The house in Carlton Hill was obviously intended to evoke just this kind of property, but the result fell far short.

At the front door, I was greeted by a striking Negro dressed in a uniform consisting of tight white trousers tucked into brilliantly polished knee-length boots, an olive-green waistcoat, and a crimson jacket with black and gold trim. The effect was reminiscent of lithographs I had seen of native soldiers serving in the British army in the Cape Colony of Africa. His face was full and jet black, the same colour as his close-cropped hair. Since my experience with Fabrizio, I found myself instantly and unconsciously wondering what the handsome men I encountered might look like without their clothes, what it would feel like to kiss them.

The Negro seemed to read my thoughts and gave me a knowing smile. "Welcome, Lord Barrington. Mr. Waterfield is awaiting you in the drawing room," he said in a deep rumbling baritone.

I could not concentrate on what he was saying but followed him into the house. Our walk through the entrance hall gave me a good chance to examine him from behind, a view at least as striking as the one from the front. He was fairly bursting out of his trousers and jacket. As we entered the drawing room, I didn't at first see Waterfield standing by the door in shadow. He could not have missed my intense scrutiny of his manservant.

He stepped forward and shook my hand. "I see you have met Prometheus," he said with a wry smile. "He makes quite an impression, does he not?"

I could see that Waterfield, although he was quite elderly, stooped, and not in good health, must have been extremely handsome in his prime. He was dressed in a dark brown velvet smoking jacket and slippers and held a long-stemmed wooden pipe. He moved slowly and carefully, leaning heavily on his walking stick.

"Thank you, Prometheus," he said to the Negro. Then, turning to me, "I gather from your note that you have seen that cockscomb Walter Bury. I hope you will discount anything that insolent youngster might have told you about me." With that, he started to cough violently. Then, through his coughing, "I'm surprised that old maid is still alive. But maybe 'alive' was never quite the word for her." Another "humph" and chortle followed by a further fit of coughing.

His manner of speaking was in complete contrast to the elegant surroundings, and I was taken aback by his words about Bury. I wondered if Waterfield had had an affair with him when both were younger.

"You must excuse my coughing," Waterfield said. "A slight indisposition," and added something like "humph."

He seemed to speak only in short bursts, but even in his clipped phrases he managed to make himself understood—and to shock by his lack of inhibition. To my description of my father's death, his only comment was: "Good old Joseph. Lusty to the end. Glad to hear."

I was delighted to find one person who might be able to tell me something about my father in Rome. I was eager to hear more, but before I could say another word, he grabbed my arm and started walking, slowly and painfully, into the villa, muttering words which may have been condolences.

We walked slowly through the house. The walls were covered in a dark green and brown paper with equally dark drapes, mostly closed and cascading heavily onto the floor. All the furniture seemed to be ancient and made of ebony with art objects of all descriptions, ancient and modern, crowded together on tables and chests of drawers. As we walked, he described some of the paintings, which occupied almost every available vertical surface.

I grew impatient. Although Waterfield had a splendid collection, it was not the object of my trip. And his pace was painfully slow. However, I became aware that he was apparently confining his commentary to pieces of art that he imagined might be of interest to me in my quest to understand my father and his time in Rome.

He passed over most objects in silence, including his own paintings of leopards, panthers and other large cats. In my opinion, they were quite well done but somewhat conventional. In the library he stopped in front of an elaborate gilt frame and pulled back the red velvet cloth that had been attached to keep out what little light filtered into the room. I could tell at a glance it was a drawing by Michelangelo, a magnificent sketch in *encre de chine* of a young man from his knees to his neck in a pose that mirrored that of the Belvedere Torso.

I remarked on the similarity. He replied, "Yes, right you are. Michelangelo loved that torso. And why not? Majestic legs, shoulders, musculature. Beautiful. Only one problem. I have never understood. The great Italian master of all things masculine. Why such small male equipment? I myself would have made these parts much larger." This last sentence seemed to have been too much for him. The chortle was cut short by another "humph" and a fit of coughing.

After he had recovered, he continued, "I apologise if I shock. I am old and impatient. I will save you time by getting directly to the point. I believe that art must deal with all aspects of mankind. Including the so-called baser passions. Baser passions! Such nonsense! In my opinion a passion for beauty in any guise is noble. Michelangelo is often called 'divine.' I agree. But to my mind his divinity included more than a little of the so-called baser passions. Which brings me to my point. I understand that you have made inquiries about Jean-Louis Fortin."

Waterfield led me to a beautifully panelled alcove. On the back wall was a painting I immediately recognised as Fortin's. The caption identified it as *Jesus and the Disciple He Loved Best*. Presumably this was the Apostle John, although there were no identifying marks in the painting itself. Jesus was shown as a slim young man with a mournful look on his olive-coloured face, bearded, and with long curly hair, instantly recognisable from innumerable engravings by various artists through the centuries. John, on the other hand, with his well-formed body generously filling out a thin shirt and tight trousers, was an ephebe of great beauty. He was seated next to Jesus on a low bench resting his head on Jesus' shoulder in an achingly intimate manner.

As with his other paintings, Fortin's rendering of the scene looked like something that might be observed in any European city today. As I looked closer, I suspected the model for St. John was the one Fortin used for the St. Philip I had seen in the journal in de Roquelaure's office.

The painting sent the same shiver through me the other Fortins had. However, my thoughts were interrupted when I felt warm breath on the back of my neck and suddenly became aware that

Waterfield had been standing immediately behind me. "Delicious, is he not? Obvious why our Lord loved him."

I stepped abruptly to the side and said the first thing that came to mind. "Did you know Fortin?"

Waterfield subsided heavily into a chair along the wall and made a noise that sounded like a chuckle. "Did I know Fortin? My dear boy! I may be the only man alive who can tell you the full story of M. Fortin in Rome." I waited impatiently for him to catch his breath and speak again.

"Fortin—we called him Everhard or just Hard. Behind his back, of course. He had an enormous appetite for the pleasures of life. He also had enormous talent. But alas, an inflated sense of his own genius. The paintings he did in Rome. Very much admired. I remember the sensation his Sebastian created at the Salon in Paris. Purchased by the French State. An enormous honour for a young artist. I assume that you have seen it?"

"Yes, I saw it while—"

Waterfield was already speaking before I had finished. "None of this was enough for Everhard. He told everyone he was the new Raphael. Then, when the critics didn't give him the unlimited adulation he craved, he vowed revenge."

Waterfield shifted painfully in his chair. "He did research. Started painting canvases in the manner of Raphael. Careful to use only old panels, pigments and oils available in Raphael's day.

"Took these paintings to the best authorities of the day. Claimed they had been found in the apartment of a recently deceased relative. Told them he thought they might be from the Renaissance. But he mentioned only second- and third-rate painters.

"He was delighted when most of these learned men proclaimed them to be masterpieces, late works by Raphael. He could have simply used their endorsement as proof of his skill. But not Everhard. He had a need for praise and a lust for money. He said nothing and started to produce and sell more of them."

I leaned forward to hear every word.

"For several years no one suspected. It was only by accident he was found out. He sold a *Sacra Conversazione*, attributed by him to Raphael, to a dealer in Berlin. However, the dealer later paid a visit to Everhard's studio. He found an identical, almost completed *Sacra Conversazione* on an easel. Fortin had forgotten to hide it. The dealer then contacted several other prominent collectors. He soon learned that there were a number *Conversazioni* in collections across Europe.

"Fortin was an enormous talent. Eventually he even learned to cast in bronze to create small pieces of what he claimed were Roman copies of Greek sculpture. He and a German man named Johann Gottlieb sold the 'antiquities' quietly to gullible collectors. Have you heard of Gottlieb?"

"Yes, I know—"

"The most astonishing thing, though—none of these collectors took the matter to the authorities. In some cases, they didn't want to reveal their own gullibility. In other cases, they didn't want to diminish the value of their investment. I believe quite a few have even found their way into major museums in Europe and America."

"Have you seen any of these so-called Raphaels?" I asked.

"Indeed, I have." After a pause, in a stage whisper, "Don't tell anyone I said this, but I actually prefer the Fortin Raphaels. I don't care if he painted them in our own century. The quality of the art alone should determine its value. Not the character or reputation of the artist or the date of the work. Between you and me, I have never really liked Raphael. Too many insipid Virgins smiling at simpering babies. The Fortin Raphaels are better. And, in my opinion, his saints are better still. Humph!"

Waterfield turned away to cover his mouth with his hand as he coughed and wheezed. Then, gesturing toward the Fortin on the wall, "I bought this one from Everhard himself. He quoted a high price. I pleaded with him that I was just a young artist. He countered with a small reduction. I had to live mostly on bread and soup for the month that followed." After a big sigh, "But what is important after all? *Ars longa, vita brevis,* n'est-ce pas? I certainly never regretted it. I only wish I had been able to buy more.

"Fortin's young saints make us feel the divine beauty as reflected in the bodies of men. And in men making love with men as a reflection of Divine Love, for example what we can imagine when we see this painting of Jesus and his lover John."

I turned. Did Waterfield really believe this? Or was he just an old man enamoured of handsome boys who was trying to shock me? I could not tell by his expression. "Do you really think Fortin created these paintings on a religious impulse?"

Waterfield's breath had become ragged. "Does the motive really matter?" he rasped. "Certainly, Fortin's paintings have the power to arouse certain individuals in a purely physical way. But why not? I don't see any contradiction between human passion and divine love. Christianity needs to rid itself of its damaging dogmas. It needs to embrace the marvellous example set for us by the ancient Greeks, and by Jesus and his disciples."

"I have heard that Fortin destroyed many of these images of saints and other early works."

"That is what he wanted people to think. At some point toward the end of his stay in Rome, Everhard claimed that he had undergone some kind of religious conversion. He said he had become a follower of Father Castiglione. One of the most controversial priests in Rome. A latter-day Savonarola. Castiglione claimed to be following the stringent dictates of the early Church. He denounced almost everything pleasurable in life.

"Of course, he later showed himself to be a terrible hypocrite. He had a fondness for young girls, and he fell into complete disgrace. But before this spectacular fall, he had quite a following. Everhard told everyone that Castiglione had convinced him his early paintings were sinful and would consign his soul to eternal damnation if he didn't repent, destroy them, and use his talents in the service of the Church."

"And you believe that this conversion never happened?"

"I very much doubt it. I think Everhard wanted official, public recognition. He was hardly likely to get it from the young boy saints he modelled after Roman *bardassas*. My guess is that he just sold all the remaining paintings to private collectors. With a little sleuthing, you could probably find them scattered throughout Europe."

My first reaction was disappointment. If Fortin was really as amoral as Waterfield suggested, would I want to study his career and write about him? Almost as quickly I decided the story was so interesting it should be told. I could decide later what moral might be drawn from it.

Waterfield rose to his feet, and I followed him as he shuffled back through the hushed house. We emerged from the dimly lit rooms of the villa to step onto the flagstone-paved patio dappled by sunlight filtering through the ancient olive trees. In the middle of the terrace, a bronze statue of a surprisingly mature Eros, blindfolded, struck a suggestive contrapposto pose, about to loose an arrow from his bow. Although it was a warm day, Waterfield called for a servant to bring him a blanket.

Tea was served on an elaborate wrought iron table by yet another of Waterfield's attractive young servants, this one apparently Arabian and dressed in flowing blue pantaloons, with an embroidered, heavily padded waistcoat and a red fez. With the tea and biscuits were tiny sandwiches of watercress and partridge as well as a kind of bread pudding that, Waterfield informed me, was called a dolce Firenze.

As I picked up one of the cups, I ventured, "The uniforms of your staff are quite distinctive."

Staring off into space, he said in a voice so low that I could barely hear, "I believe that boys are the greatest works of art. God's greatest creation." Before I could say anything, he continued, "I'm extremely pleased that I have been able to collect them. I love to have them on display along with my other works of art." Then with a great sigh, "I'm too old now. I was a votary of Priapus in my youth. Now I cannot do anything more than look at these young Ganymedes. I envy you that you can still enjoy them more fully."

My face turned bright red.

"Oh, I'm afraid I have spoken out of turn, Lord Barrington. I am so sorry. I am an old man and not always careful in what I say." He gave no indication that he was either embarrassed or sorry or careless with what he said. I thought that he had not heard or had forgotten my question, but without missing a beat, he added "Yes, I design the uniforms for my little seraglio. I have them made by a clever seamstress in the village of Settignano."

He started coughing violently. The Arabian boy hurried back. Waterfield said in a choked voice, "I am very sorry, Lord Barrington. You will have to excuse me. I'm afraid I will need to retire now."

As the boy helped Waterfield out of his chair, Prometheus hurried out of the house. He wished me a safe return to Rome, showed me to the waiting carriage, then returned to help carry Waterfield into the villa.

Hours later, sitting in the rail car, I was distraught that Waterfield had told me almost nothing about my father. As far as I knew, he was the only man alive who might have known him well in Rome, and given Waterfield's precarious health, I was worried I might be unable to speak with him again.

Chapter 19:

Subterfuge at the Capitoline Museum

Back in Rome, I went for a second time to try to see the ivory the police had told me that they had deposited at the Capitoline Museum.

On my first visit, weeks earlier, the keeper, a nervous elderly gentleman who identified himself as Egidio Barzoni, had denied that the ivory was in the collection. I protested and insisted on seeing the director. Given my experience with Roman bureaucracy, I was not surprised to learn that he was out of the office for a month. The assistant director was also out.

When I was finally able to see the assistant director, he accompanied me to a tiny office at the back of the building where an ancient clerk confirmed that the museum did, indeed, own the ivory. The assistant director told me to return to Barzoni and, if there were any further trouble, to contact him. Of course, Barzoni was out.

On my final visit, as I stood in the great oval piazza with the statue of Marcus Aurelius at its centre, I was reminded of the grandeur of Rome. However, standing in front of the museum, I was more than ever aware of the diminished glory of its present state. I made my way back to Barzoni's office.

He was obviously quite unhappy to see me again. He spoke slowly and distinctly as if I were a child. "Yes, I remember now. We do have that ivory. It was transferred from the municipal authorities. Probably from one of the workshops in Asia Minor. Of course, it is also possible that it is a clever forgery. It is difficult to tell. The subject matter is repulsive, so we don't allow the public to view it. Is there anything else I can do for you?"

"It is very important for me to see this piece," I responded. "It was used in a murder, and my father may have had some connection."

"I am sorry, but we keep that piece locked up. It is inaccessible."

"The assistant director of the museum told me I could see it. I am now asking you to obey his direction." I had learned that when my English politeness failed to bring the desired results, it was useful to resort to more forceful language.

Barzoni gave one of those typical Italian shrugs and unleashed a torrent of invective. I understood only a fraction, but it went something like this, "The museum should never have accepted this infernal piece. It is an abomination. Men fornicating with boys. Like animals rutting." Barzoni was almost shouting. "It should be destroyed! Such things interest only those with criminal perversions. I hope one day I will prevail, and they will all be swept into a fiery blaze. Our Lord certainly would not want me to show this offense to everything we hold dear to a foreigner with who-knows-what intentions."

I was extremely angry but managed to say in my most icy voice, in English, "I suspect our Lord has more important business on his mind than considering whether you should show certain objects in your collection. In the meantime, I will see this piece no matter how much time and energy it takes even if it means having you discharged." I have no idea how many words Barzoni might have understood, but he clearly recognised the tone of my voice. Still, he just gave another dismissive shrug.

Burning with indignation, I left Barzoni's office intending to go directly to the assistant director. Out in the corridor, I stopped and thought about what I had just done. Making threats was not how I had been brought up. But then I reflected that this was righteous anger, and it was a good sign that I allowed myself to display it. My outburst at the gallery in Paris, when I confronted the artist Fortin, was perhaps not an aberration after all. I was becoming more assertive. I was proud, but also afraid this behaviour might become a habit as it was with a number of older men I had met.

I was dismayed when the director's secretary informed me that all the men in the office had once again departed and would not be back for several days. I decided I had spent enough time on this fruitless quest and was walking back to the entrance when I noticed a young man in the corridor. I could tell by his smock that he was an employee of the museum, presumably someone who dealt with routine maintenance. He was watching me with curiosity, and when I looked back, he didn't divert his gaze. By now I had learned something about this kind of unspoken communication.

I walked directly up to him. He didn't seem at all surprised. Because his Italian was quite halting, we communicated in a mixture of English, Italian, and hand signals. I could decipher the fact that he was Greek and had arrived in Italy with his family only a few years before. I suggested that we should talk outside the museum. Once again, he did not seem at all surprised by this request. He named a café around the corner and indicated on his hands 10 minutes.

I went to the café, ordered a coffee, and waited. Within a few minutes he appeared, sat down, and gave me a conspiratorial smile. He had taken off the smock and in the full sunlight it was apparent that he was both younger and more handsome than I had realised. "Bruno," he said, pointing to himself.

He managed to make it clear that he was prepared to come to my hotel that evening. I shook my head and tried to explain that he had misunderstood and what I needed was his help at the museum. I indicated to him that I wanted to see an object in a locked storeroom. He didn't seem to understand so I asked the waiter to bring me a pencil and paper. I drew an image of the ivory to the best of my ability. He smiled broadly and made a gesture with his hands at the front of his trousers to indicate that he understood.

Bruno then made a motion as if he were using a key to open a door, pointed to himself and me, and nodded. Everything suggested he was used to providing all kinds of services at the museum and gaining entry to a locked room was something he had done before. He wrote some numbers on the paper sitting between us that I should come to the museum at two in the afternoon two days hence. He tried to tell me where we would meet. When I didn't understand, he took the pencil and did a surprisingly competent sketch of the monumental figure of Mars in the central gallery.

He stood up. "Anche questo serra in Albergo?"

I shook my head no. He looked disappointed. For a moment I wondered if there would be any harm in engaging him for that service as well, but I quickly decided it was not a good idea to mix business with pleasure. I had remained faithful to Fabrizio to that point and saw no reason to mar my record. As I focused back on Bruno, I saw that his thumb and forefinger indicated that it was time to transfer some scudi.

I arrived as instructed on the appointed day and stood for a while pretending to admire the artifacts in the gallery. Italians have a more flexible sense of time than we English, but even so, I started to worry that Bruno would not appear. At almost the same moment, I saw him enter the gallery. He didn't greet me or even look directly in my direction but walked directly toward the adjoining gallery. Just before entering, he turned and with a slight motion of his head, indicated me to follow.

We walked through several galleries and down two sets of stairs to a dim corridor. He stopped at an unmarked door, pulled a key from his smock, and unlocked it. Inside was a small room entirely lined with shelves. Each shelf was filled with artifacts, each artifact with a small handwritten number on a piece of paper attached to it with glue or with a string. The objects appeared to be sorted by subject matter. He pointed to a section of a lower shelf entirely devoted to phallic objects. Picking up a grotesquely large carved wood phallus he grinned and made obscene gestures indicating how one might use it.

I saw the ivory and pointed to it. Bruno picked it up and handed it to me.

Even a first glance confirmed that it was almost identical to the one I had seen at the house on Carlton Hill. However, the two central figures were not the same. At first, I was vastly relieved.

Perhaps there were many nearly identical ivories, and the similarity with the one my father had was coincidental. However, a moment's reflection made me conclude this was unlikely. Given the immense skill and labour involved, I doubted many of these pieces had ever been made.

As I continued to examine the piece, I was fascinated once again by its smooth rippling surface and its lustrous, almost translucent quality. Although the individual figures of boys and men were small, they were rendered with exquisite care, and the figures in the central medallion were startlingly life-like.

A slight scuffling made me aware again of Bruno. He was watching me intently and smiling. I handed the ivory back to him. However, instead of putting it back, he moved it back and forth in front of his open mouth, at the same time pushing his cheek out with his tongue. He broke out in laughter and put it back. I turned to leave but Bruno caught my hand, turned me back toward him, and kissed me.

I was suddenly highly aroused. We were deep in the bowels of the museum in a tiny, locked room. I looked at Bruno. He had his hands in the pockets of his smock and was looking downward instead of at me as if waiting for me to decide what would happen next.

I suddenly felt like my body had been invaded by someone else and was acting on its own. I grabbed his arm, pulled him roughly toward me and kissed him hard on the mouth. After a minute, I pushed his head down, and in a movement that seemed almost instinctive, he fell to his knees and started pulling down my trousers and drawers. With a start I realized that I was treating Bruno exactly the way Fabrizio had done with me.

Thinking about Fabrizio gave me a shiver of guilt, but I recalled how little he had written and how noncommittal his notes had been. For all I knew, he was doing something similar at that very moment. It increased my desire. I felt a surge of power, heightened by some desire to punish Fabrizio by playing the man to this attractive boy.

I was thrilled by the way Bruno relished the rough treatment I was giving him. After each time I pushed his head down he would gag, pull away for a brief moment then return to the task with renewed enthusiasm. Everything around me blurred. The electricity coursing through my body was the only thing that mattered. Bruno indicated he would like me to turn him around and penetrate him. I was eager to do that, but it was already too late. I was starting to buck wildly, and within moments I was shooting my seed into his mouth.

Everything had happened so quickly. Bruno stood up, licking his lips and smiling broadly. Then he kissed me on the mouth. I could taste my own spending. As I backed away, I marvelled at how young he looked and how adorable when he smiled. I thought that I should do something to reciprocate, but he was already moving to the door. I caught his arm again and pressed into his hand all the coins I had. He smiled and kissed me again before hurrying into the corridor.

I stood in the storeroom for a few minutes, stunned. I thought again about Fabrizio. My first impulse was satisfaction that I had broken the spell I had been under. I no longer needed Fabrizio. I could be my own man. But almost immediately afterwards I realized that I was mistaken. The image of Bruno faded and that of Fabrizio took his place.

Did I feel guilty about what I had done? After a few minutes of churning thoughts, I decided I had broken no promises and had no reason to feel guilty. I also had a sense that this experience opened up entirely new and unexpected perspectives on my future interaction with Fabrizio. I was now a different person, and if there was any future for us, we would need to start again.

I exited the small room, pulling the door shut after me. Instead of returning to my hotel, I paid a visit to the British Academy. I wanted to examine again the portrait of Gottlieb by Fortin I had seen in de Roquelaure's office in the Louvre. I had a vague memory that I wished to confirm.

I found the Academy on a narrow street near the church of

Santa Maria della Concezione. I requested the volume of the *Gazette des Beaux-Arts* with the reproduction of *The Antiquarian*. When it came, I opened it to the page I remembered. There it was. On the shelf to the left of Gottlieb's head was a pair of carved ivories exactly like the one I had seen at the House on Carlton Hill and the one I had just seen in the Capitoline Museum. They were the most prominent objects on the shelves. He must have been quite proud of them. It was impossible to make out all the detail, but on closer inspection, I could tell the central figures of Gottlieb's ivories were probably the same as the ones I just saw at the Museum. They were definitely different from the ones on Carlton Hill. I was relieved but still puzzled.

Back at my hotel, I found a letter from Fabrizio. It was the first communication that I had had from him in several weeks. He recounted some of the things he had done since he had last written, the arrival of new artifacts in the gallery, several dinners he had attended. And then, in the last lines, this piece of news: "By the way, I thought you might be interested to know that I have made some inquiries about a possible trip to New York this fall to explore business opportunities, such as we briefly discussed before you left. I have the steamship timetables, and a gallery owner there has sent me the names of several hotels he recommends. I was hoping that you might be interested in accompanying me."

My heart skipped a beat. This trip to New York was the entire reason for the letter. It was as close to an apology as I was likely to get from that proud and stubborn man. And it was probably as close as he could bring himself to acknowledge the depth of the emotional attachment we had formed. This letter, coming so soon after my experience with Bruno, renewed the turmoil in my mind. I was overwhelmed with a desire to return to Paris, confront Fabrizio, demand that he answer all the questions I had. First, however, I wanted to revisit Waterfield if I could and see if I could find Contessa P.

Chapter 20:

Return to Florence

A few weeks later I was relieved to receive a note from Waterfield saying that he had somewhat recovered and that I would be welcome to call. Several days after the arrival of the letter I found myself once again sitting on the patio opposite him. I was finally able to ask him about my father.

"I had been in Rome for a year when your father came to that ancient city on the Tiber. I met him at the salon of the Contessa P. Have you heard of her?"

"Yes, I have heard something from Mr. Bury. Do you …"

"That bloody Bury again! But never mind. As I said, I believe that I met your father at the salon of the Contessa. She was a great friend of many artists, architects and musicians. I believe we met at a small soirée at her apartment to hear the famous castrato Giovanni Battista Velluti. He had created a sensation in Venice the year before in the role of Armando in Meyerbeer's *Il Crociato in Egitto*."

With that, Waterfield stopped and mopped his forehead with a pale green silk handkerchief. "He was the last of his kind. Expired a few years later. A tragedy, in my opinion. The era of the sublime castrati, if I can put it so, killed off in the name of humanity and so-called progress. Our nineteenth-century progress can go to the devil as far as I am concerned. But I am digressing. You were here to learn what you could about your father, and I was speaking of the Contessa."

I nodded and waited. "The Contessa was the brightest star in the firmament of ladies who were the ornaments of Roman society in that era and the ones who hosted the most artistic of the salons. Her drawing room was notorious for attracting both the most eminent and the most notorious of the day, often, of course, one and the same. I have heard that she had something of a scandalous past, including at least one husband, a wealthy Polish count, and many lovers of various ages, genders and nationalities. She must have had extraordinary powers of seduction, because it was clear to me that a high percentage of the men were by nature more interested in other men than in women, if you catch my meaning. She would be quite old by now, but I believe that she is still alive. You should try to speak with her."

"I will certainly try to do that," but, now really anxious to manoeuvre the conversation back to the main reason for my journey, "What can you tell me about my father?"

"Ginger—we called him Ginger. I remember him as a quiet, serious young man. Well-spoken and popular with all the foreigners in the city. He was not what I would call handsome but attractive enough, particularly when he smiled, and invariably very well dressed. Unlike most of us, he always seemed to have money which he spent freely. Some of my friends resented him for that, but he was also quite generous."

"How close were you?" I surprised myself with my boldness. "If I'm not being too intrusive."

To my surprise, he made no reply. Were they friends who had fallen out? Had they been lovers? Rivals perhaps? To break the silence, I asked, "Can you tell me anything about his desire to become an artist?"

"Have you heard about the Académie Ganymède?"

"No, I have not."

"There was a notorious institution in London called the White Swan Club. On Vere Street. Men and boys. Young men to be more accurate. It was raided decades ago. After the scandal that followed, a number of the members left England for the Continent. Some of them found their way to Rome and founded a club there similar in nature to the one in London. They called it the Académie Ganymède. This was a reference, as I'm sure you know, to the beautiful Trojan boy of Greek myth. Zeus transformed himself into a giant eagle to carry him up to Olympus as his lover.

"The story has been completely obscured by euphemisms. You may have heard some of these at university. Suggestions that the boy was merely some kind of domestic servant. Ridiculous! What was young Ganymede supposed to be doing the rest of his day? Or worse, that his flight to Olympus was about his ascent to spiritual awakening. Ha!" More sputtering and coughing.

"Membership at the club waxed and waned. However, each successive scandal in Britain replenished the roster. Admittance was difficult. A limit of fifty members. Nomination by three existing members. Then approval by the entire membership. A single negative vote was fatal. The club was expensive. One hundred guineas at the outset. Plus, an annual subscription fee. I was lucky. One of the gentlemen who sponsored me paid for my membership. Of course, I was an attractive young man all those years ago. If I do say so myself. I think that even your father would not have argued otherwise even if he preferred somewhat younger men. Humph!" I tried to imagine Waterfield and my father as young men.

"We had a small suite of rented rooms. Near the All Saints' Anglican Church. The rooms were maintained by a young man lodged in a chamber behind the public rooms. He was, I think, in the employ of a member of the Vatican office, one Archbishop M.

"The club had brilliant gatherings. Some of the leading lights of European and American arts and letters. I remember meeting the American journalist Charles Warren Stoddard with his friend Francis David Millet, the artist. There were even a few women. Tribades of course. I became friendly with the American sculptress Anne Whitney. She was with her companion, a Miss Manning from Boston who was, I believe, a painter."

"Thank you. The Archbishop. Is he still alive? Do you know . . ." I started to say but I never finished the sentence.

"Yes, the Archbishop is frail but still alive. You might wish to see him. But where was I? Members would present papers. Read from their work. Show recent paintings or pieces of sculpture. My paintings were very well received, if I do say so myself. I make no great claim for them. Still people do tell me my animals capture something of the glory of God's creation."

I found this a surprising comment from such a profane old man. I murmured something that I hoped would sound vaguely affirmative.

"The club also sponsored sessions for sketching from models. They were invariably scheduled on Sunday mornings. At the same hour as the service at All Saints." At that, Waterfield made a noise that I can only describe as a cackle, but it quickly turned into another fit of coughing. When he recovered somewhat: "I went frequently to these events. Ginger—your father—also went frequently."

"Do you remember anything about his work? Was he talented?"

" His work was far from brilliant. In fact, to be charitable I would say—" Waterfield abruptly stopped.

"Please continue."

"My opinion is of no importance. To return to the drawing sessions. There would be one, two, or three boys on a low platform. They would start fully dressed. Often in outlandish costumes—as a guardsman or midshipman or an American savage. Then, in a series of poses, each more provocative than the last, gradually strip down to posing straps. Or to nothing at all.

"Toward the end of the session the model was encouraged to bring himself to orgasm. If more than one, the boys usually pantomimed sodomitical acts. Or actually performed them. Most of the men would remain to chat with the models. Perhaps take them back to their lodgings. I assume that Ginger did, but he was very discreet, and I never saw him with a boy."

"Please go on."

"These boys were often quite sweet. During the break between poses, they would walk around the various easels in whatever costume they had been wearing, if any. They would look at the sketches and exchange pleasantries with the artists. Sometimes, comment on the work. Often their commentary was more—what shall I say—penetrating than that of the club members themselves, if you will excuse the expression. Humph!

"I'm almost certain that most of the boys were *bardassas*. I suspect many of them had no interest in this line of work or in being intimate with men. Only interested in the money. Boys here in Italy need to mature quickly. To survive, many must do things they find distasteful.

"I myself always preferred members of the military and guards of the papal states. Especially the Swiss Guard. The guardsmen are invariably handsome specimens, don't you agree? Of course, their striking red, yellow and blue gala uniforms—designed by Michelangelo, did you know?—can make even the more homely ones look tempting. But what was my point?"

I shifted uneasily in my seat, hoping Waterfield would bring the conversation back to my father. "Oh, yes, I remember now. Economic necessity. Here in Italy the guardsmen are never paid sufficiently. As long as there is no scandal, their superiors look the other way if they contract for some additional work. Modelling at the club was similar. It paid little but was a good way to meet men for more lucrative private sessions."

"But all this is such a long time ago now. And the world has so much changed. I have so much changed. You tell me that Ginger is gone. So are most of my friends." He paused for a deep sigh.

I finally had the chance to pose a question that I had wanted to ask since he started talking about the Académie Ganymède. "By any chance do you remember this particular boy?" I showed him the sketches by Fortin.

Waterfield's face brightened noticeably. "Yes! I certainly do. The boy who became Fortin's Sebastian, no? His name was Jacopo. He was probably the favourite boy of most club members. Reputedly the most beautiful boy in Rome. But also—I have heard. I can't personally confirm—the most wicked. I went specifically to sessions when I knew he would be posing. He was not a large boy, but in face and body there was an uncanny resemblance to a classic Greek statue. Curly dark hair and dark eyes that seemed to penetrate deep into you. Penetration! Yes! Humph humph!

"His body was flawless. A particularly magnificent arse. Like two perfect melons with that mysterious dark cleft between them. I often wondered . . . Where was I? Oh, yes, a perfectly shaped *membrum virile* as well. When he started to stroke, almost everyone stopped sketching and just stared. He seemed to pay no attention. Lost in his own thoughts. Which made him seem even more unattainable and desirable. I later heard that he was also the most intelligent and presentable of the boys. Friends of mine were even willing to have him accompany them in public, to dinner or the theatre."

The image I had of Jacopo in my mind's eye was becoming more concrete. I became aware, with some feeling of guilt, that my quest for information about my father and Fortin had now become caught up with an increasing interest in Jacopo.

Waterfield picked up one of the sketches. "That face and body, not to mention that other particularly delectable part. Indelibly inscribed in my memory. I wonder where he is now. Unfortunately, these boys from poor families often have lamentably short life spans. They get married, get fat and die young."

"I had heard," I said, "that there might be some connection between the men and boys at the Académie and the murder of that man Gottlieb you mentioned earlier."

"Gottlieb was an undistinguished little man. Elderly, unattractive face and bad teeth, poor vision. Ironic in a so-called connoisseur, no? He had a passion for classical art and Italian boys. Not necessarily in that order. At least in his early career he was quite successful selling antiquities. Apparently, many forgeries. His murder was an enormous scandal. There were, of course, uncanny echoes of the murder of Johann Winckelmann in Trieste in the last century. I assume you know about Winckelmann and his murder?"

"Yes, I know something about Winckelmann. The great scholar of classical art."

"Then you know that Winckelmann was a firm believer that most of the great art of antiquity was founded on a profound appreciation of the beauty of the male body. I remember an anecdote recounted by Antonio Canova. The renowned Italian sculptor of classical purity. One day Canova found Winckelmann with his trousers down to his ankles mounted atop a beautiful boy. Winckelmann explained that he was trying to enter the minds of the ancient Greek artists. Or words to that effect. Delicious, no? I think that Canova . . ."

I was starting to get impatient with Waterfield's digressions. For once, I was willing to interrupt him, "According to Pater, Winckelmann's murderer was someone named Arcangeli, who stole some medals. But Arcangeli clearly was not a stranger to Winckelmann. Do you think that was true with the Gottlieb murder as well?"

"Yes, most of my friends believe that Gottlieb was killed by someone who knew him. When the murder was announced, it threw a certain segment of Roman society into a panic. Many of the men from northern Europe left Rome. Including much of the membership of the Académie Ganymède. I believe your father also departed about the same time, although I am sure that he had nothing to do with the murder."

Waterfield had not stopped talking. "I was not as worried as some, but soon thereafter I came here to Florence. Eventually to this old farmhouse, which, as you see, I have converted into a comfortable dwelling. As you have noticed, there is an ample supply of boys. For very little money, they are willing to take care of this ancient house. And my increasingly ancient body."

"What happened to the club?" I asked.

"Since the Gottlieb affair, some former members have returned to Italy. I have resumed my association with them. However, as far as I know, no attempt was made to re-establish the club. Too much scrutiny by the authorities these days. They are now suspicious even of men who had been living peacefully in their midst for years. Today, you cannot pick up a newspaper without seeing some new scandal. Change seems to be happening faster and faster, and none of it good."

I tried several times to obtain further information about my father, but Waterfield seemed to get lost in long digressions, and I heard little further of interest to me in the minutes that remained before he announced that it was time for him to retire.

On the train from Florence back to Rome I reflected that I had learned more from Waterfield than from anyone else in Paris or Rome, but I was still far from understanding how my father had the sketches and the ivory or how he might have been connected with the murder of Gottlieb. It appeared that the Contessa P and the Archbishop M were my last chances to learn more.

Chapter 21:

A Venerable Roman Lady

As soon as I returned to Rome, I tried to see the Archbishop M. However, I was told by members of his household that he was too ill to receive visitors and that I should inquire again in several weeks.

I was also disappointed in my attempt to meet the Contessa P. I wrote to everyone I knew who might direct me to her and provide a letter of introduction, but she seemed to have disappeared from society. Only Walter Bury seemed to know anything. In his note he asked me to pay him another visit.

At his lodgings, this time without his young assistant, after some interminable preliminaries, Bury finally addressed my question about the Contessa. "She lived on the northern end of the Corso. Perhaps she still does." That was all the useful information that Bury seemed to have, but that didn't stop him from continuing to talk for a painfully long time. "Very eccentric. Her favourite colour at the time was pink. Pink walls, pink furniture, pink clothes. Even a brace of poodles with hair dyed pink. A most ghastly colour choice, one would think. But the Contessa somehow carried it off."

Bury went on in that manner, shifting from the Contessa to other women he had known in his younger years and to his work as an architect in London and to a discussion of the new pastor at the Anglican Church in Rome, but I was no longer listening. I squirmed in my seat until I could finally break free.

I was starting to despair of finding anything further about my father or Jacopo, but as I lay awake one night unable to sleep, it occurred to me that something Walter Bury had told me, that the Contessa kept several pink poodles, might be useful in finding her.

It was madness and extremely undignified, but I was so eager to speak with her that, on a hunch, I made several trips up to the northern end of the Corso in the morning and the early evening—the likely times when residents or their servants might walk their dogs—with the idea that I could somehow solicit information that might lead me to the Contessa.

My plan was to try to identify the breed of dog an individual was walking and pretend to have a similar pet back in England. I was aware that the odds were exceedingly slim that I would find out anything useful, but I was now so involved in my search that I proceeded anyway.

On my third or fourth trip, approaching total strangers, mostly domestic servants walking their employers' dogs, I found many of them willing to engage me in pleasantries about matters canine. When I finally asked if they happened to know anything about a Contessa P who lived on the street, most of them clearly assumed I was engaged in some kind of nefarious activity and hurried away. But just as I was ready to abandon once and for all this hapless adventure, I came across a young woman walking a whippet.

She was clearly a servant girl, and from what I could gather from her manner, she probably assumed I was more interested in her than in her dog. I confess that I was willing to encourage her a little in this harmless little deception if it made her more amenable to chatting. After only a few minutes conversation about the dog, the girl became noticeably flirtatious, telling me her name was Anna Maria and starting to ask me surprisingly direct questions about who I was, was I married and my reason for being in Rome.

I had not prepared for this kind of interrogation. Without stopping to think through a response, I said, "My father asked me to find a woman, Contessa P, who used to live on this street. She was an old friend of my father's. He is near death, and he asked me to try to find her to give her an important message.

While I was still trying to decide whether what I had said was even remotely plausible and to fabricate something further in case it was not, immediately, and to my great surprise, she replied,

"Yes, I know who that is. I have never actually seen the Contessa, but I know that she lives there," pointing to the windows on the piano nobile of a building almost opposite where we were standing. "I know Elena, one of the Contessa's servant girls. She walks the Contessa's poodles."

I was briefly elated, but then Anna Maria added, "I am not sure she would see you. Elena says she never leaves the apartment and never has anyone visit except her doctor and her confessor." I could tell Anna Maria was obviously keen on finding an occasion to see me again. "If you give me your card with the name of your father and the hotel where you are staying, I will ask Elena to give it to the Contessa. If you meet me here in two days, I will probably have an answer for you."

I did as I was requested and, much to my surprise, found both Anna Maria and Elena waiting for me with the whippet and four poodles—white not pink and clipped in such a way that they were almost unrecognisable as members of the canine species. After several minutes of conversation, it was clear to me that Elena had not given my card to the Contessa, but she told me that she would for a small consideration. Two days later a note from the Contessa arrived at my hotel.

When I arrived at her apartment the following Sunday, I was ushered into her drawing room by a young serving girl. The room was barely navigable because of the profusion of furniture, bookshelves, musical instruments, and works of art.

The Contessa was sitting on an ancient settee covered in a faded pink brocade and gestured to me to sit on an even more delicate Louis XV side chair covered in the same fabric. Although it made a fearful creaking, I succeeded in safely settling myself onto it. The Contessa rang a little ceramic bell to ask a servant girl to bring us tea.

She was an elderly lady, obviously fragile, but sitting erect and fully alert. She must have been quite beautiful in her prime. Dressed in pale pink with her white hair done up with ribbons and an elaborate preparation of her face, she reminded me of the delicate paintings on porcelain used on brooches and lockets in the previous century.

We chatted for a few minutes about myself and my trip to Rome. Eventually the subject turned to my father. "Elena told me about your father being near death, Lord Barrington. I'm so sorry to hear. She said you were carrying a message from him."

I squirmed uncomfortably in my chair. "I'm ashamed to admit that I fabricated that story to try to convince you to see me. My father passed away last year, and I have no message from him. I'm so sorry for the clumsy and inexcusable deception."

To my great relief, instead of being angry, she laughed heartily with a surprisingly deep infectious laugh, but then abruptly stopped. "I'm sorry. So wrong of me to laugh after you have delivered this sad news. I am sorry to hear about your father. Joseph was a charming man. I was delighted to have known him.

She continued, "I should apologize in turn. I am not nearly the recluse that my staff and friends make me out to be, but I have found that rumours to that effect are useful in allowing me to see only those individuals I really wish to see. But did you really play detective on the sidewalks of the Corso to find me?" and with that she burst into laughter once again.

I told her about my desire to learn more about my father and my research into the early work of Fortin. I said nothing about the erotic artifacts in his collection or the murder of Gottlieb.

"I knew Joseph, of course," she said. "He was a distinguished visitor to Rome, and I believe I am only pointing out an objective fact when I say that my salon was among the most brilliant in Rome in those years. It would have been unthinkable for him not to have come. My collection of distinguished foreigners was unrivalled, and he was here at a wonderful era in the history of this city." She stood up. "Please follow me."

Her body may have been frail, but her mind and her memory seemed quite undiminished as we walked slowly through her rooms. "This is the antique pianoforte that Liszt played for my guests when he visited during a concert tour of Italy. This Russian enamelled figurine was a gift of the composer Tchaikovsky. Here is a set of books inscribed to me by Alexandre Dumas Fils, this a beautiful Venetian scene by Guardi given to me by Prince Petrov—or at least a man who claimed to be Petrov. . ." After pointing out many other tokens of esteem from the men who attended her gatherings, she stopped at a side table and pointed to a small, elaborately framed grey wash landscape on a miniature easel. "And here is something that your father gave to me. It is a preliminary sketch for a painting of ruins in Palestine by one of his friends, another frequent visitor here, an English artist named Arundel."

In the ensuing conversation the Contessa hinted at several points in the conversation that the invitation she extended to some of her visitors involved more than a visit to her drawing room.

When we had been seated again, she poured the tea into ridiculously small porcelain cups and handed me a correspondingly tiny plate with several elaborate but miniscule chocolate confections.

"A charming man, your father," she began again, "and welcome in all the best houses. He immediately drew everyone in my circle to him. We became rather well acquainted when he first arrived. Very well, indeed," she said and then did something with her face that looked distinctly like a wink, but I could not tell for sure because her hands and face were constantly making small involuntary motions. I wondered whether she and my father had been lovers, but of course, I could never have asked. But then she volunteered, "before his, um, interests moved in an entirely different direction."

I was so surprised at the boldness of her implication that I almost dropped my cup. However, I could not think of anything to reply so I asked, "Can you tell me anything about what my father did here in Rome?"

"He was a true gentleman," she said. "He was studying art, of course, but he never showed me any of his work. He was always beautifully dressed. I remember that he had suits that he brought from London. They were beautifully tailored. They were also much too warm for our Roman summers, but he seemed to feel that he had to maintain his image. He developed quite a circle of friends here in a remarkably short time. Many of them were artists. I believe that he met many of them at my salon."

I asked her whether she knew Fortin. She replied in the affirmative but said she remembered only that he had a somewhat clouded reputation. She knew a good deal about the Gottlieb murder but nothing I had not already learned. Then I ventured a question I was almost sure she could not answer. "Do you, by any chance, know anything about a boy named Jacopo who was one of Fortin's models?"

To my great surprise she broke into a hearty laugh and answered immediately. "Yes, I do remember young Jacopo. He was well known at the time as the most beautiful boy in Rome. At two or three of my gatherings, Archbishop M brought him along. Everyone was astonished that His Grace would be seen in public with a boy who was known to be a *bardassa*, but the Archbishop was a true libertine, and it was said that he was protected by one of the most powerful cardinals in the Church.

"In his prime Maurizio, the Archbishop, reportedly loved men and women, boys and girls. I can personally testify to the truth of only one of these one categories." Once again there was that quick eye movement and suppression of a slight smile. It hardly seemed possible for such words to come from the mouth of this elegant, elderly lady. Clearly, whatever else she might have lost over the years, it didn't include her candour.

"My dear boy. Do I shock you?" Again, the throaty laugh. "I believe that your father was also scandalized by some of the things I said. Englishmen, in my experience, seem to be easily shocked."

I smiled but did not reply.

"To return to young Jacopo. To everyone's surprise, the *bardassa* proved to be more of a gentleman than most of the titled men who came to my house. I think everyone assumed that it would only be fair that anyone the Creator had allowed to be so beautiful would also be ignorant or ill-tempered. But the boy was as charming and well-spoken as he was beautiful, and he seemed able to converse at ease with the eminent authors, musicians and artists who frequented my salons. I have always wondered what happened to that young Adonis."

With that the Contessa stopped and fingered the pearls around her neck. "But you have not told me much about what happened to Joseph. I know that he returned to England and was married. You told me that he had two children, yourself and your sister. And you said that he took over management of the family bank and made a success of that. I am pleased to hear this. But you didn't tell me any of the important things. Did he love your mother? Was he happy? Did he love you?"

It seemed, once again, like remarkably intrusive questions to ask anyone only a few minutes after meeting, but upon reflection I decided that at her age she felt she could disregard the customary proprieties. I decided to answer as truthfully as I knew. "I am sure he loved my mother in his way, and I have no doubt that he loved me, although he never really knew how to show it."

"Did he give up on boys after he married?"

I was now truly scandalized, but I was also relieved. I could think of no reason not to tell her about the house in Carlton Hill, the ivory I found there and its possible connection with the murder of Gottlieb.

"Yes, I had heard something about all this," she said.

"You did? How is that possible?" I stammered.

She just smiled. "You are so much like Joseph. Are you in love?"

This time the Contessa had exceeded all bounds. I was about to make up an excuse to take my leave, but once again I seemed unable to escape the pull of her personality so I replied, "I don't know for sure, but I think I might have been. Maybe I still am." Then, gathering up all my courage. "Someone I met in Paris. But I don't see that there can be any future in it."

"I somehow guessed that was the case. I am sure that, whatever happens, he is lucky to have known you."

I was dumbstruck to hear her use the masculine pronoun. My initial reaction was annoyance that she was probing so deeply into things I had never discussed with anyone. And consternation that she seemed to be able to read my mind. However, after several moments of further reflection, I decided, yet again, that there was no reason for me to hold anything back, particularly since the Contessa somehow seemed to know exactly what I was thinking anyway.

"Thank you," is all I said, but I realised a moment later that with my tacit admission of the truth of her assumptions, I had finally revealed to another person a fundamental truth about myself. I was surprised to feel no guilt or regret but a wave of relief that spread over me.

As I was leaving, the Contessa said, "I am still owed favours by many individuals in the city. In memory of your father, whose friendship I still cherish, I will be happy to help his charming son in any way I can. I am quite curious myself to learn what you discover about your father's time in Rome, so please call on me for anything."

Chapter 22:

At the Archbishop's

"There is one more person I should like to visit," I told the Contessa on a subsequent visit. "The Archbishop M apparently knew my father and many of the Englishmen in the colony here. You told me he also knew Jacopo. Unfortunately, his private secretary informed me that any visit was highly unlikely given the state of his health."

"I doubt that he really is ill," she replied, "any more than I am. I suspect his secretary uses that excuse the same way I do. He will certainly see me," she said with that inscrutable twist of her mouth. "Let me see what I can do."

One week later I received an elaborate card inviting me, in Latin, to an audience. The Archbishop's palazzo was a superb structure near the Piazza del Teatro di Pompeo. Judging from the robust proportions and sculptural decoration, I guessed it must have been constructed in the seventeenth century at the height of the Italian exuberance. The heart of the building was a courtyard ringed by an arcade and surmounted by two stories of regular arched openings, each framed with an elaborate sculptural surround. I followed a member of the Archbishop's staff up a broad stone staircase lined by enormous family portraits. I recognized at least two recent popes.

I was ushered into a lofty library. The long walls were lined from floor to ceiling with books accessible by a series of balconies. On one short wall was an enormous portrait of Pius IX, probably painted decades earlier on the occasion of his election and hung while there was still so much hope for his papacy. Below it hung a smaller portrait of what I assumed was the Archbishop himself, sitting majestically on a vast golden chair.

I was directed to the centre of the room where several throne-like chairs upholstered in deep red velvet and surmounted by elaborate carved crests sat on an oriental carpet. After a few minutes wait, the sound of slippers shuffling along the stone floor echoed in the great room alerting me to the arrival of the Archbishop. Turning around, I saw him enter by an inconspicuous door in one corner of the room. From the splendour of the room, the image in the painting, and the remarkable stories I had heard about his passion for life, I expected a large, robust man in elaborate robes.

What I saw instead was a diminutive figure who must have been at least eighty years old in a simple black robe relieved only by a white clerical collar and a heavy chain around his neck with a substantial gold cross. When he sat, the large chair dwarfed his figure. He looked fragile and tired, but his eyes, behind thick eyeglasses, were bright and alert.

He motioned for me to sit across from him and apologised for the difficulty I had had in obtaining an audience with him. We talked briefly about my trip, the differences in the weather between London and Rome, and about some of the people I had visited. When I turned the conversation to my father's death and my search for information about his life, it was clear that the Archbishop was already well informed.

"Yes, I know about the things you want to ask me, Lord Barrington. I should say at the outset that I knew your father but not well. I'm truly sorry to hear of his demise. I knew Joseph because of my position at the Vatican. I was in charge of supervising the restoration and re-installation of sculpture in the Chiaramonte Museum. In this capacity, I met many men interested in antique art. Most of them, like your father, were also keenly interested in the kind of beauty appreciated so fully by the ancient Greeks."

The Archbishop's allusion emboldened me to ask about the sketching sessions at the Académie Ganymède.

"I was a patron of that club, although, because I was devoid of talent, I rarely went to the sessions. Watching the evident joy these meetings brought, I was sorry our Heavenly Father never endowed me with this talent. I was, however, able to lend one of my personal assistants to the club to help manage its affairs.

"I think the club did a great deal of good. It was an excellent meeting place for creative men, particularly from abroad. It was undeniably good for the artistic life of the city. Many of the most inspired spirits of the day regularly visited and met like-minded individuals there. It also provided the chance for many boys from poor families to make some money and to interact with men who were in a position to help them. I believe that for gentlemen with talent or beauty, it was the liveliest place in the city, the salon of Anastasia—the Contessa P, that is—excepted, of course."

I merely nodded my head but was astonished at the casual way the Archbishop spoke so lightly of a club that allowed activities clearly antithetical to the teachings of the Church. "I know this club and one or two other organisations have been maligned for certain, um, activities, but I think they were harmless, really, and provided a way for members to meet basic human needs with minimal risk. I was sorry when it ceased to exist."

"I appreciate your candour."

"In the past, I would have only whispered such things to intimate friends, but I knew your father, and I have confidence in the discretion of English gentlemen. And, of course, I have come to the point in life where I'm unlikely to face any negative consequences for anything I say. Still, for everyone's sake, anything I tell you needs to be held in strictest confidence."

"Of course, Your Grace. I'm only here to better understand the life of my father."

"I assume that your father was a member of the Church of England."

"My father was quite active in the Church after he returned to England. I assume he was an Anglican congregant here as well. However, I don't know how much of a believer he was."

"And yourself?"

"For several years while at university, I had the idea that I might find myself in your church. I'm afraid I was more seduced by the music and pageantry than the doctrine."

"Most interesting. I confess that it was somewhat the same for me. Of course, I was brought up in the Church, but it was my love of sacred art that kept me in it. It allowed me to advance to the highest levels in the Vatican, even when it must have been apparent to everyone who knew me that I had little appetite for doctrine—or chastity or piety!

"Personally, I don't believe that there is any sound basis for the negative attitude about love between men in Holy Scripture. I could cite the various verses and explain why they have been misinterpreted, but I don't wish to detain you. Moreover, if buggery is a vice, I have always maintained that a little vice can only make virtue the more attractive." At that he smiled. "But, of course, I keep these thoughts to myself."

"Of course."

"But enough of that. I will be quite frank. I think that the Académie Ganymède was a good way for men—mostly men of letters, architects, painters, and sculptors—to meet boys. Much better than the notorious taverns and other establishments. It was also a good thing for the boys. They often came from some of the poorest families. Their only assets were their youth and beauty. They were well paid for their work, and some of the brighter ones used their connections to make permanent advancements in their lives."

This pronouncement brought to mind an image of my father in a robe in his rooms paying a poor Roman boy for his company. This was profoundly unsettling.

"Some of the boys formed strong emotional attachments, and club members were instrumental in furthering their careers, even aiding their families. I think of this as a modern reincarnation of the Greek ideal of *paiderastia*. However, as the Church and general public have become more aware of such activity, it has been increasingly difficult to carry it on. Enough of that. I understand from the Contessa that you have something to show me?"

I had debated whether to bring the sketches from the house of Carlton Hill into the palace of an archbishop, but I now realized nothing was likely to shock this archbishop. I picked up the portfolio and showed him a few of the sheets, telling him that I believed they were of a boy named Jacopo.

A broad smile crossed the Archbishop's face. "Yes, I'm almost certain it is. He was an angel. Breathtakingly beautiful. I offered him a means to escape Trastevere by giving him employment as a groom here at the palace. I regret to say that I lost touch with him. I suppose by now, if he is still alive—the mortality for boys from the poorer quarters being what it is—I imagine he is married, overfed, and much the worse for the wear. It is so sad. 'Où sont les neiges d'antan.' Do you know that expression?"

"A line from a poem by François Villon, is it not?"

"Indeed. In his day, Jacopo was both the most attractive and the most intelligent of the boys from the club. I don't think I ever met any boy with a similar combination of physical beauty and native intelligence.

"What I most clearly remember was a *tableau vivant* he arranged for a party I was giving for my superior, Cardinal J. His idea was to portray Narcissus regarding himself in a pond. He placed a large mirror on the ground in a secluded part of the garden, then obscured the edges with foliage, and sat down beside it, gazing down as if admiring himself in a body of water. As I brought the Cardinal by on the way to dinner just at dusk, the illusion was complete."

He gave a great sigh. "Of course, nothing was the same after the murder of that ridiculous little German fraud, Johann Gottlieb."

I told him several people believed some club members might have had a connection to that murder. "That is ridiculous. Certainly, none of our members would have had anything to do with such a sordid deed. I heard rumours it was the Camorra or a rival clique. I also heard that Gottlieb may have deliberately staged the murder as a dramatic way to end his problems, but I don't think the civil authorities or the Cardinal Vicar ever found out who killed Gottlieb or why. Even if they had, they might have wanted everyone to just forget about the entire affair. That happens frequently here in Rome."

"Many club members, including my father, appear to have departed Rome shortly after."

"Yes, but I'm sure that it was only because the scandal brought heightened scrutiny to anyone who had any connection with Gottlieb. Certainly, your father had nothing to do with it. In any event, I heard no more from him. As for me, Cardinal J sent me briefly to Naples to secure some busts for the museum. As soon as the scandal died down, he brought me back and protected me.

"Working in the Vatican museums was a perfect career for me. Painters and sculptors can reveal things that cannot be fully conveyed in any other way. For example, the glory of the human body. If Man was made in God's image, I cannot see how it is wrong to celebrate this beauty. I refuse to be apologetic about that."

With that pronouncement, our audience came to an abrupt end. He stood up and turned to walk away, but before the left the room, he pulled out a leather-bound volume from a massive secretary bookshelf and leafed through it until he found the page he was looking for. He took a piece of paper and wrote on it the single name, Ambrogio, and the name of a street in Trastevere.

"This is someone who might be able to tell you more. If I remember correctly, Ambrogio and Jacopo were both raised in Trastevere and both modeled at the club. I believe that they were great friends. There is a good chance Ambrogio knew your father. I was, um, in fairly close contact with him for several years after the murder, but I have not heard from him or about him for some years.

"I have continued to make some small donations to his mother, so I assume she must still live at this address. Even if Ambrogio no longer lives with her, she will undoubtedly know where to find him. If you do find him, I would be grateful for a report on what he is doing now. He was a very charming lad."

The Archbishop's blatant disregard of some important doctrines of the Church was something I could excuse, particularly given my own rejection of the same teachings. And he did have a point about how activities frowned on by the church might help poor boys pull themselves out of terrible poverty. But I was disturbed by the clear implication that men in his circle had used their position to their own advantage at the expense of those boys. As I returned from the palace, the doggerel about the Arsebishop of Clogher came into my head, and I had to laugh.

Chapter 23:

Ambrogio from Trastevere

It seemed unlikely Ambrogio would still live at the address given to me by the archbishop, but I went the next morning to the Via della Pellicia in Trastevere. The squalor was even worse than the slums in the East End of London. Hordes of ill-nourished children in ragged clothes raced through the narrow streets, dodging great piles of refuse. Young girls and painted women made obscene gestures inviting me to step inside doorways with them. Old men sat on the piles of garbage and drank wine.

A priest was able to direct me to an ancient, foul-smelling building where, on the fourth floor, an elderly, stooped woman came to the door in an apron with a cloth tied around her head. The apartment behind her was dark and smelled strongly of garlic. She was wary at first, but when I mentioned the Archbishop's name, she straightened up, crossed herself, and brightened. "Ambrogio is my son. The Archbishop took a great interest in his future. He has been very generous."

When I asked how to find her son, she replied immediately, "You should be able to find Ambrogio in the cobbler shop near Regina Coeli convent."

It took some time to locate the place, a dirty small shop on the ground floor of a decrepit building. The street was almost impassable because of the activity spilling out of the open workshops lining both sides. The noise coming from them was deafening.

When I reached the cobbler's, the proprietor looked at me suspiciously but called over a sturdy man in bulky dark trousers, unbuttoned shirt, and a leather apron. "What yer want from me?" Ambrogio demanded.

"I want to talk to you about a boy named Jacopo. I think you knew him."

"Maybe I do. Maybe I don't. How yer find me?"

"The Archbishop M told me how to find your mother, and your mother told me I would find you here."

"The Archbishop? You talk to the Archbishop?"

"Yes."

"You must be very important."

"Not really."

"You speak with my mother? She knows nothing about my business with Archbishop. I hope you tell her nothing. What did yer tell her?"

"Only that that the Archbishop told me where to find your mother's house. That is all."

"Why yer want to know about Jacopo?"

"I'm searching for information about my father, who recently died."

"Sorry, I am, Sir," Ambrogio said mechanically. He softened a little but remained skeptical. "Yer father a gentleman like yerself? He knows Jacopo?"

"Yes, he apparently met him here in Rome when you and he were young men."

After looking around to be sure that our conversation could not be overheard: "I do know Jacopo when we are young. I do not like talk about those days. But yer a gentleman and not from here. I can maybe give yer information. If worth something to yer?"

He spoke in a dialect with terrible grammar, and his voice was almost drowned out by the cacophony of the street.

"Yes, I am quite prepared to reward you for any information that will help."

"Not talk here."

We agreed to meet the following Sunday at the Caffè Napoli near my hotel.

When he arrived, Ambrogio looked like a different person. He was wearing a pair of light brown trousers, white shirt, tan waistcoat, and black coat. His hair was slicked back. He almost looked like a gentleman if you didn't examine too closely the condition of his clothes or his fingernails. Although the café was far from elegant, he clearly felt uneasy and acted in an overly polite and formal manner. I should have suggested a tavern closer to his home with a more familiar clientele.

"Would you like something to eat or drink?"

"Just a beer, thank yer, Sir," he said, but after it arrived, he apparently decided that as long as he was at a café with a gentleman, he might as well take full advantage.

"Would not mind some *crostini di fegatini* if not too much trouble, Sir."

"None at all." I ordered some red wine for myself. After the waiter brought my wine and his *crostini*, I told him about my search for information about my father and his time in Rome. "My father spent time at a place called the Académie Ganymède. The Archbishop thought that my father might have met Jacopo there. Maybe you as well. Do you remember an Englishman named Stapleton?" I asked.

"No, I dunno. Many Englishmen. Most old. And rich. All the same, all pale, fat."

"My father would have been thin, and he would only have been ten years older than you at the time."

"Excuse me, please, Sir, for what I say. Maybe yer father is not old then, but most of them English seem old to me. I never know most names." Crumbs from the *crostini* fell from his mouth, making him even more embarrassed than he already was.

I continued. "The Archbishop M. thinks you might have known Jacopo since you were boys."

He smiled ruefully. "Yes. Jacopo a friend. We grow up around the corner from each other. My mother and his mother, friends. We play together when we are young boys. I get to know him better when we are older. We both go to that club of them foreign sodomites. Maybe I best not say words like that to gentleman."

"No, it is perfectly fine. I know something about Jacopo and the club and want to know anything more you can tell me."

"Jacopo and I are favourites with them old men. Jacopo more than me. He is so handsome. Neither of us want nothing to do with them fat, ugly, old men. And what we do is a sin. A terrible sin. But we need the money. They pay."

I saw deep hurt in his eyes. "What did they do to you?"

"You know. What rich old sodomites like to do with boys. A few boys, they like it, but most of us hate it and do it only for money. I find later the money they give us is not much. It just seems like it then. I think some boys, they make much more money than me. Jacopo makes much money."

"Can you tell me about the sketching club?"

"They make pictures of us. They dress me up as Russian sailor, Chinese emperor. Every few minutes I take off more clothes. At end of hour, they always want me to put on little show. You know. Either by myself or with other boys. Or sometimes other boy puts his thing in my mouth or up my . . . you know. Maybe bad to say this."

"No, I'm not offended. Go on."

"If I close my eyes, I can imagine I am with girl. Some boys are pretty. Jacopo is pretty. It almost feels good, like with girl. But then I open my eyes. All them old men staring at me. And I know is a terrible sin."

"It must have been unpleasant. But go on, please."

"There are parties. Sometimes they take off all our clothes and paint our bodies. Make me all gold or look like marble statue. I stand on pedestal in dining room holding heavy metal thing with candles. Not supposed to move no matter what club members do. Some of them come by, pinch nipples, slap me behind, stroke me, even, um, stick a finger in me. Disgusting.

"After party I am expected to go home with any man what asks. I can say no, but then I know I am not invited back. I only get little money from the club. More when I go with them. I pretend to make love to their ugly fat bodies and wrinkled skin.

"They treat me like I am servant, slave. Some men want to slap or take a cane to me. I sometimes let them slap a little, but I never let them do what some other boys allow. There are some men what want me to take a whip to them. I do, but I hate to hurt anyone. It is all terrible!"

"Did Jacopo feel the same way?"

"Jacopo is real good at hiding what he thinks. When he is with them, he looks happy. He smiles and laughs and talks with everyone. They all love him. But sometimes when we are alone, and he has too much to drink—all of us drink too much—he is angry. He says it is unfair. Hates that men can tell him what to do just because they are rich, and he is poor.

"I understand why he says this. He is real handsome, much more than any of us. And he has good manners and fancy clothes men buy him. He is very smart. He speaks languages, reads books, teaches himself. I see him talking to priests and professors. About art and music and books and things. They seem happy to talk to him. Like they are talking to a gentleman. I can never do that. I guess that is why I never get as angry as he does. I figure it is just my life."

Ambrogio was sitting back in his chair, looking up at the ceiling. I waited for him to resume.

"I only see how angry he is a few times. Once I am with him when we are at house of an old man. Very rich but old and feeble. He wants us to tie him up and whip him. Jacopo willing to do that. So, I just watch. Jacopo tells him get naked, slaps him hard when he fumbles with clothing. Then he ties man's hands behind his back and pushes him to floor. Ties his ankles. Connects rope to wrists and to his—you know—between his legs.

"Then this old man says something rude to Jacopo. I do not remember what. Jacopo seem to become different person. He starts yelling at man. Calls him *puttana* and dirty sodomite and piece of filth. He starts hitting harder. The old man is bleeding, screaming for Jacopo to stop. Finally, I think I need to stop Jacopo. He is really hurting the man. I don't want trouble."

"What happened?"

"The man is real angry, but nothing he can do. Not going to police, for sure. He gets dressed. Pays us. We leave. I don't see him again. He never causes problem. What if I not there? What will Jacopo do then?"

"Do you know what happened to Jacopo?"

"No. There was murder of old German. Suddenly many foreigners leave Rome. When foreigners leave, most of us boys are afraid. Afraid we are accused. We stay out of sight."

"The man who was murdered was named Gottlieb. Is there a chance that Jacopo knew him?"

"It is possible. He know all them old foreigners."

"How did the murder affect you?"

"When foreigners leave, none of us boys know what to do. We have no work. Terrible time for me. Many friends and relatives hear about scandal. They afraid I am involved. They avoid me. They call me all kinds of bad names.

"My family is real ashamed. My father finds a family willing to accept me as son-in-law. Makes me marry the daughter. So, I marry Marta. I never really like her. I know she does not like me. She leaves me after few months and goes back to her parents. Since then, I am with several women, but I am not the same since foreigners pay me to do sinful things. They corrupt me. Now my health is no good. My life is no good. I am afraid I go to Hell."

I was burning with indignation. When I had heard the stories in Paris and London about the way men used their money and power to find boys for their use, I just imagined it was the way of the world. For a moment I had even told myself Archbishop M was right, that it was the best alternative for many of the boys. But, sitting across from Ambrogio, I was shocked by my own naïveté.

Ambrogio went on almost to himself. "I always wonder if Jacopo finds a way to live like he wants. I ask him once if he regrets sinful acts. He laughs. He says he has no belief in sin. Rich people can worry about sin, he says. I tell him that is terrible blasphemy, but he does not listen. He says that if God makes the world the way it is, He makes a terrible mistake.

"He says he does not care what he will do. He will have money and eat in restaurants and buy warm clothes and not let people tell him what to do. I never feel that way. But Jacopo is different. Jacopo always good to me. I love Jacopo."

"So, you don't know what happened to Jacopo?"

"No. I don't know what Jacopo does. I only know that he does not come back to his house."

"Do you know what happened to his mother or any brothers or sisters he had?"

"I think one brother and sister maybe alive. They leave Rome many years ago. I think that his mother is alive but not sure where she is."

As we rose to leave, and I saw how defeated he looked, I felt terribly sorry for Ambrogio. I knew it was a meaningless gesture, but I took all the coins in my purse and gave them to him. It was very little for me but probably a significant sum for him. I could see him calculate how much before putting them into his pocket. He sat for a long time, trying to make up his mind about something.

Then he looked up and said, "I hear rumour. That Jacopo goes to Paris. After the murder of that German."

The realisation hit me like a thunderbolt. I knew at that moment that after Gottlieb's murder, Jacopo travelled from Rome to Paris. And reinvented himself as Fabrizio.

It made sense. The model in the sketches from the house on Carlton Hill was Fabrizio. The painting of St. Sebastian in the Louvre was Fabrizio. The model for the boy on the ivory was Fabrizio. And if Fabrizio was Jacopo, it meant that he lied when he said he came to Paris in 1853, before the murder. And that lie suggested strongly he had something to do with the murder.

This realisation answered several questions that had troubled me. For example, why no one in Paris knew much about his past. Everything he had told me—and presumably everyone else—was part of an effort to keep anyone from connecting him to Rome at the time of the murder.

I asked Ambrogio, "Why are you only telling me this now instead of earlier when I asked you what happened to Jacopo after Gottlieb's murder?"

"I am afraid you think Jacopo involved. I am sure he has nothing to do with murder."

I returned to the hotel and immediately summoned Walters. "Walters, I admire your discretion and your desire to protect the memory of my father, but I have two important questions, and I need direct answers. The truth. While he was here in Rome, did my father know an Italian boy named Jacopo?"

"I promised your father I would not tell anyone about certain parts of his life. Just as I would tell no one about yours."

I didn't have time to consider the implications of that last remark. "I appreciate that, but this is my father we are talking about. I have a right to know. You don't need to tell me anything, just confirm this one thing that I believe I already know. I just found out that my father met a boy named Jacopo here in Rome. You don't even need to say yes or no. Just nod your head one way or the other. I'm sorry to press you, but I need to know. Is it true?"

Walters nodded his head in assent. He looked pained.

"Thank you. You have helped me a great deal. I do have one more question. It should be easier because it is not related to my father. Do you remember a murder of an old German man named Gottlieb?"

"Yes, I remember it well. It happened the day before we departed for Paris."

Immediately after he said this, Walters' expression changed. He must have realised that he should not have linked the two events.

Suddenly I was impatient to be back in Paris. I could not imagine continuing on to Athens and the rest of my itinerary. I was determined to find out the truth. Why did Fabrizio leave Rome?

What connection did he have to the murder? And how was my father involved in any of this?

Except for the hotel staff, I didn't tell anyone I was leaving. I telegraphed Fabrizio that I was coming back to Paris and would like to see him in six days. I planned to arrive two days before that. I cabled the Meurice and reserved a room. I decided I would be better off without Walters and sent him back to London with most of our luggage. He seemed to be relieved.

Before leaving, I cabled Griswold about something that now puzzled me.

Chapter 24:

Return to Paris

I was so agitated I barely paid attention to the journey. I sat in my seat and stared straight ahead. How was it possible that Fabrizio—this successful, married gallery dealer who knew so much about classical art, spoke so elegantly, and frequented the best houses in Paris—had grown up a poor boy in Trastevere? Or had any connection with the sordid Gottlieb affair? Something serious had clearly caused him to flee Rome. Could I believe anything he said about his past? And what about my father? Had he engaged the services of Fabrizio—Jacopo—as a young *bardassa*? The thought revolted me.

I was even more perturbed by what Fabrizio's lies indicated about his feelings for me. My Uncle Rupert said I was too trusting, too ready to believe people, especially the ones I wanted to believe. I was now much less ready to trust anyone, Fabrizio least of all.

Even if all my fears were unfounded, if he had nothing to do with the murder and had come to love me while I was with him in Paris, would he feel the same way now? I was still a boy when I first met him. I had learned a great deal since then.

I was a different person from the one who left London less than one year ago. At that time, I had little idea what I wanted to do with my life. By the time of my departure from Rome I had published a half dozen articles that had commanded respectful attention. I had embarked on a career.

And I had learned a great deal about myself. Before meeting Fabrizio, I had never known what love might feel like. With Fabrizio, I experienced both the exhilaration of finding what I thought could be love and the desperation of losing it. I was no longer the naïve and pliable individual I had been. I was surer of myself, more confident in dealing with people, more wary about what others wanted from me, and less willing to bend to their will.

Even my appearance had changed. I had gained a little weight. It made me look more mature. I had also learned to dress in a style bolder in cut and hue. Above all, there was my beard. To please Fabrizio, I had intended to return clean-shaven. But after the recent revelations, I changed my mind. If Fabrizio wished to resume our friendship, he would need to accept me as I was.

When I arrived in Paris, there was a letter from Griswold waiting for me at the hotel.

"My Dear Robert, I trust that you are having a most enjoyable and rewarding sojourn on the Continent. I heard from Rupert that you learned a good deal about your father's early life, and it appears from reports that I have heard that you have learned more on the Continent.

"You asked me in your cable what your father had instructed me to do with the personal items he left in the house on Carlton Hill. In fact, his first idea had been for me to remove any evidence of his time on the Continent or his activity in that house. I confess that, at first, I was pleased. I was never comfortable with certain aspects of his life. We didn't talk about any of that, but you saw with your own eyes the evidence at the house.

"I destroyed much of the correspondence. However, in the last years before his death, I could see your father wavering about certain artifacts, particularly the antique pieces. Many years ago, he thought that he would give them anonymously to the British Museum during his lifetime. He knew the keeper there. But as time went on, he seemed to change his mind when he saw how interested you were in art.

"I also suspected that his thinking might have changed about how much he wanted you to know about his life. He finally admitted to me one night—and please excuse me for saying this—that you might appreciate the artifacts in the London house the same way he did. And if they were not to your taste, you could do as he had intended and donate them to the museum."

I was thunderstruck. Was I the very last person in my family and entire circle of acquaintances to understand the truth about myself? How could I have been so blind?

The letter continued, "I am reasonably sure I did the right thing by leaving almost all the artifacts in the house. I should confess that I might not have followed his wishes on one point. At the time of his death, he may have wanted me to destroy the sketches that you and I examined in the portfolio. He was never completely clear about it. I personally could not understand why these sketches would be more objectionable than the other objects. Furthermore, they were the work of a significant artist, and because of that, I assumed that they might have considerable interest to you and, perhaps, to posterity.

I certainly hope that your father, looking down from heaven, is not too angry with me if this action of mine violated his trust, and I pray that you yourself will agree that I did the right thing. With that one possible exception, I believe I have been strictly faithful to every item in your father's instruction.

"If there is anything further that I can do for you, please let me know. Please advise on your expected arrival back in London. Everyone here looks forward to your safe return. Respectfully yours, Griswold."

I smiled. Good old faithful Griswold. He clearly knew something about what my father did in Paris and Rome, but it was also obvious that there was quite a bit Griswold did not know.

The morning after my return, I went to the Louvre. I wanted to look again at the Fortin painting and compare the image with what I remembered of Fabrizio's appearance. Standing in front of the painting, I paid close attention to some of the tell-tale details, the kind of thing an artist makes little effort to edit or idealize—the shape of the ears or configuration of the nostrils, for example.

The more I looked, the more I was certain that the painting, the sketches, and one of the figures on the ivory all used Jacopo as the model. There was no longer even a shadow of doubt in my mind that Jacopo in Rome had become Fabrizio in Paris and that almost everything Fabrizio had told me about his past was a lie. I was unable to sleep that night.

I arrived in Fabrizio's gallery late the next afternoon, as I had cabled him I would. When I arrived, he seemed guarded. He did not kiss me or even shake my hand. His cold behaviour made me nervous. I looked to see if the ring was on his finger—the ring with the cameo of Antinous that was the mate to the one he had given me. It was not. Did he notice I had removed my own ring?

Despite all my misgivings, I couldn't help but notice how wonderful he looked. I was struck again by the regularity of his features, his superb bearing, the cut of his clothes.

I wanted to ask him all the questions I had, but I was afraid of what he might say. There was no reason to rush, I reasoned. I needed to be rested and clear-headed when the time came. Despite all my fears, I ached to be together with him, kissing and lying in bed. If I was never to see him again, I could at least enjoy one last encounter. I put the questions aside.

Assuming I had just arrived in Paris, Fabrizio asked if I wanted to take a bath after my long trip. I said I would. He started to run the water and then proposed doing something that, for a few minutes, took my mind completely off my discoveries in Rome. He suggested shaving my body, something he had done in the past.

I felt torn. On the one hand, I wanted to preserve my dignity in case I learned the worst about his time in Rome. On the other, despite my brief encounter with Bruno, Fabrizio was the only man I had been truly intimate with. I was eager to feel and smell and touch him again.

I stripped off my clothes and stood facing him as so often in the past with me naked and him fully clothed. We appraised each other. Fabrizio was even more beautiful than Jacopo. Jacopo had been a sublime boy, a true Ganymede who would have tempted any of the gods. As he had grown into manhood, he had lost none of that beauty but had gained size and strength and a firmness of features. Even in his clothes I could make out the muscular arms and legs, the powerful body, the sense of tightly controlled energy. And the bulge in his trousers.

Once again, I could not dispel the idea that I had never met anyone as handsome. Was that really possible, or was I just incapable of judging? Was it possible, despite all my newfound wariness, that my feelings of gratitude for the way I had bloomed and come into my own since meeting him, blinded me to any kind of objective evaluation, even now?

Fabrizio told me to lie down on the bathroom tiles so he could remove the hair on my legs, chest and arms. He did so in a mechanical way with no effort at affection. I was grateful that he made no effort to shave my beard. He had obviously noticed it but had said nothing.

Then he told me to get onto my hands and knees, and I felt him lathering my buttocks and reaching between my legs to apply the cool cream to my scrotum. The feel of his hands and the slippery cream in the crack in my arse and my member was bringing me to an involuntary full stand. I felt just the way I had when Fabrizio first shaved me. It was at once intensely humiliating, as though it was making me a young boy again, and at the same time wildly exciting.

Even if the feeling was the same, I knew that I was no longer the same person. I was not a passive participant in what we were doing. I was choosing to submit to Fabrizio but fully prepared to take matters into my own hands at any moment.

After he finished, Fabrizio watched me climb into the bath, then told me he needed to leave the apartment for a couple of hours. I bathed, dressed, and made myself comfortable.

When Fabrizio returned, he was agitated and even more distant. We had dinner as usual. I could hardly concentrate on eating. Both of us were ill at ease and neither ate much. I was not sure whether my state of mind was caused by anxiety about the questions I had to ask him or excitement about what I knew we would do after dinner. He told me about his daughters and the latest gossip in Paris. I told him about my time in Rome, circumventing any mention of anything connected to what I learned about him.

Anxious as I was, I tingled with anticipation, knowing full well it could be our last time. I had no idea what would happen after I confronted him. I hoped there would be some simple explanation, but I had a strong premonition I would not like what I would hear.

After dinner I went into the chamber, took off my clothes, and laid face down on the bed with my eyes closed, waiting for Fabrizio to come into the room, hoping he would kiss, caress, and ultimately penetrate me. I heard him walk over to the bed. I felt him grab my right arm and straddle my body. Then he grabbed my left arm, pulled my hands together behind my back and cuffed them together.

Without saying a word, he pulled me to my feet and dragged me, still cuffed, down to the basement. We had played out this scenario many times before, so I struggled a little, but Fabrizio was much rougher than usual and still with no trace of affection. I grew increasingly concerned. When we reached the Pit, he fastened me face down to the padded bench, then abruptly left the room.

Chapter 25:

Back in the Pit

Paris, rue de Seine, 21 May 1879

I am tightly bound to the bench. In front of me is an ivory. It is identical to the one I saw in Rome. The figures on the medallion are not the ones from Carlton Hill. They are the same ones on the ivory used to murder Gottlieb.

Why does Fabrizio have this ivory? Why did he put it in front of me? To see if I know anything about it? If Fabrizio thinks I learned about the murder in Rome, is he afraid I will go to the police? Does he plan to use this ivory on me the same way the one in Rome was used on Gottlieb?

It isn't cold down here, but I cannot stop shivering. I am terrified. I am no longer sure of anything. What if Fabrizio does intend to harm me? Other than the hotel desk clerk, no family or friends know I am in Paris.

The room is utterly isolated. No one can hear anything that happens down here. Except Queen Victoria, the cat. Fabrizio left the door at the top stairs open, and she is scratching at the lower door now. Does she know I am here? Why am I thinking about that bloody cat at a time like this?

Part Two:

Fabrizio's Story

Prologue:

At the Top of the Stairs

I am standing at the top of the stairs. Paralyzed by anxiety.

You can understand my dilemma. I have no idea how much Robert knows. What if he suspects that I had some part in the murder of Gottlieb? What if he tells someone? It could destroy my life.

At the very least I could be taken in by the police and questioned. The truth about my past would inevitably come out. This could be devastating to my reputation. I might even be jailed. My wife and daughters could end up living in poverty and disgrace the rest of their lives.

If I find he knows too much, what are my choices? I could stop him from ever leaving this building. I have never done anything like that. But I've never faced a situation like this.

Or I could run. I already did that once and could do it again. Erase this life, forget him, start over somewhere else. Maybe in the Americas.

Or maybe I should be the one who will never leave the building.

What do you want to know? Did I kill Gottlieb? Do I love Robert? The answers are not so simple.

I will try to answer them by telling you honestly what happened. As honestly as I can after so many years trying to obscure the truth, even to myself.

Chapter 1:

Carlo

You know I grew up in Rome and that my name was Jacopo. We were poor. Mama, my four brothers and I, and our one sister, Isabella, lived in three rooms on the Via del Moro near the church of Santa Maria in Trastevere.

Our surname was DeLuca, but that was from my mother. I never knew my father, though he may have been one of several men whose visits were brief, vivid, occasionally generous, and sometimes violent.

I was neglected and bullied because I was small. Worse, many people said I was pretty. That alone would have made me a target. It didn't help that I was quick to learn to read and write. That was not a valued skill in the Via del Moro.

Fortunately, my mother saw my gift for learning as a way for me to rise above my station. My oldest brother, Vigo, had also wanted to rise. He tried a career in the military, joining the Palatine Guard, but he was killed in a brawl with several other officers. So, Mama sought a different path for me.

My school, about five minute walk from our home, was run by the De La Salle Brothers. My instructors liked me and suggested that I might have a career in the Church. At their urging, Mama allowed me to continue in school longer than any of my brothers. As laughable as it now sounds, for a few years I thought I might become a priest.

My oldest living brother was Carlo. Five years older than me, by the time of my later childhood he had become a man while I was still a boy. The girls called him "Horse," a nickname I didn't understand at the time. He pretended to dislike it, but I could tell that he was actually pleased.

He and I shared a bed. It was narrow, in a tiny room without windows, but it was the centre of my world. I loved to lie on my side and have him hold me from behind. It made me feel safe and protected. He looked after me.

Many of the boys at school called me vulgar names and shoved me around. I'm certain they would have done worse except they knew Carlo would come after them. Carlo taught me how to box and wrestle and urged me to develop my body.

He asked a blacksmith, a distant relative named Lodovico, for some horseshoes, tied them together, and showed me how to use them to develop my arms. We ran most days along the riverbank, which he said was good for my legs and lungs. He told me girls loved strong men with muscles. And, he added with a wink, those girls would keep me exercised at night.

In warm weather, we would wrestle together on vacant land by the river. He would occasionally let me pin him down to give me some sense of accomplishment. I loved the exciting feeling coursing through my body when I straddled Carlo, held his arms over his head, and had him under my control. After he told me it was not right for me to kiss him on the mouth, I would bend down and kiss him on both cheeks. I loved Carlo with all my heart.

Of course, everyone else loved him too. Mama and the men who lived with her favoured him over all the rest of us. Every girl in the neighbourhood flirted with him.

When Carlo was twelve, he started to work for Lodovico. It was hard, dirty work. Lodovico was always on the verge of throwing him out, but I doubt he ever would have followed through. When Carlo wanted to charm, no one could refuse him anything.

He eventually acquired friends who were a bad influence. At first, they would only take a little food from shops and street vendors, but eventually their thefts became more serious. He was reluctant to include me in their activities, but eventually he let me act as lookout. They were constantly on the verge of getting into real trouble, but for a number of years nothing serious happened.

Mama adored Carlo but was worried about him. She was happy enough with the money and jewelry he brought home, but she didn't want to know how he got them.

My mother always seemed worn out. No matter how hard she worked, it was never enough to provide adequate food and clothing for us. Still, I know she loved me. She was proud of my book learning. During the few minutes she had to herself, she loved to hear me read from a battered old Bible, or else a small book of poetry by Leopardi. I have no idea how that book came into the house. I suspect one of my brothers stole it. I preferred the Leopardi even though there was much I didn't understand.

My mother was not devout, but she wanted her children to have a Catholic upbringing. She would take my sister and the younger and more pliable boys to Mass. I was the only one who liked to go. I loved to stand near the fountain in the piazza in front of the church and watch the jets of water splash from the heads of wolves.

The church filled one side of the piazza. I was proud that our church was such an ancient building. It had been founded by Callixtus I on the spot where a spring of oil had miraculously appeared at the time of Christ's birth. Marvellous mosaic decoration covered the façade. The Virgin occupied the place of honour at the top where she sat with the Christ Child on her lap. Below her were saints and apostles and two popes. I loved to hear stories about the saints. When I was quite young, I wondered if I could become a saint one day. As you will learn, I actually did—in a way.

Inside the church was a magic world. There was the golden, coffered ceiling, the light streaming from the windows high on the wall, the mosaics behind the altar, and, above all, the organ. When I knew the organist would be practicing, I would come and sit in the nave to feel the power of the great instrument, the soaring treble line and rumbling thunder of the bass that shook the entire building.

During Mass, the priests in their splendid robes led the way to the altar followed by altar boys holding aloft banners and swinging thuribles. I wanted to be one of the choir boys and wear the red robe and white surplice, but my mother would not hear of it. She said she loved the Church but could not trust the priests.

I had some idea what she meant. My friends had told me about priests who performed unnatural acts. I was not sure what an unnatural act was, although I learned that if you did one you would go to Hell. Soon after, a boy at school told me about a monsignor who was found behind the barracks of the Swiss Guard sodomizing a guardsman. I must have looked confused because the boy grabbed me, spun me around, and acted out the role of the priest. That gave me a general idea even if I didn't fully understand the mechanics of it yet.

Holy Week was a high point in the year. We all went to see the procession of the penitents. A baldacchino bearing an image of Christ in agony on the cross was carried through the streets by robed men. Other men carried heavy crosses on their shoulders. Or removed their shirts and flagellated themselves. I was repelled and fascinated.

As I grew older, my life in the church and at school became increasingly separate from my life on the streets with Carlo. My brother had found new employment. He would go to a tavern near the Vatican owned by a man named Vespaziano where he would meet what he called his patrons, many of them church officials from the Vatican and foreign visitors to the papal court. For a small fee—which he split with the owner—he would go upstairs with them. I was not allowed to follow, but I soon had a good idea what went on.

Carlo clearly disliked what he had to do with the men at the tavern, but it was easier than the work at the blacksmith shop and paid much better. Certainly, his work there never stopped him from confirming his nickname among the girls in the neighborhood every chance he got.

Many of Carlo's patrons were men from Germany. These

Germans seemed to love Italian *bardassi*. While I sat downstairs waiting for Carlo, they would tell me, in heavily accented Italian, about the boys around the papal barracks and on the Spanish Steps. Also, the boys in Naples, who, they said, were easier to find and less expensive than those in Rome. And the gondoliers of Venice and the *femminielli* in the Imbrecciata of Naples.

One day Carlo told me that these men suffered from the *vizio allemano*. I laughed at Carlo's use of such a fancy phrase. I later learned that there were similar terms in most of the languages spoken in Europe: *l'amour francais, il vizio Inglese, die französische Krankheit,* and so on. Everywhere in Europe, it appeared, people wanted to believe that this terrible sin was an importation from somewhere else.

I soon learned that northern Europeans had a notion that we Italians, particularly those from the south, were closer than the British or the Germans to a state of nature and had been corrupted by centuries of Oriental influence. Another of their theories was that the warmer climate and the hotter sun encouraged unnatural appetites.

Carlo told me he would rather do business with foreigners than Italians. He said it was safer to deal with foreigners, particularly affluent ones, because the Cardinal Vicar, the official charged with protecting public morality, was likely to overlook their activities. This was also true for priests who were usually good customers. And bishops, archbishops, and cardinals were the best. They paid well and rarely caused a problem.

Mama knew something about Carlo's life at the tavern and was not happy. However, I think she secretly hoped one of the men might take him under his wing and find him a respectable job as a valet or a secretary, maybe even help secure a suitable husband for my sister, Isabella.

Carlo appeared to be a particular favourite of Eugen, a German man who was younger than most of the foreigners. He was the son of a wealthy banker from Rostock. Quite handsome, in a stern northern European way, with penetrating blue eyes and wavy blond hair, he was always elegantly attired in suits of fine grey wool.

Eugen actually came to our rooms once and met my mother and the man she was living with at the time. They were tongue-tied in the presence of such an elegant foreign gentleman, but Mama was thrilled with the small presents he had brought for her.

Eugen also bought fine clothes for my brother so he could take him to fancy restaurants. He also coached him on how to behave in polite society. He even took me along once or twice. My brother was uncomfortable in these places. Strangely enough, though, I felt more at ease with Eugen and other older foreigners than I did with boys my own age.

Through Eugen, I met several gentlemen, mostly English and German, who told me stories about the world outside our parish. I asked them about Berlin and London, art and books. I started to pick up foreign words and tried to read as many books as I could find. I devoured the ones in Italian. With the ones in German, French or English, I would laboriously try to figure out the meaning of the words. My favourite book was French. A battered copy of Balzac's *Pere Goriot*. I spent hours trying to decipher enough of it to learn about Paris.

One day Eugen took Carlo on a short trip to Capri where Eugen had many friends, mostly older German men. Eugen apparently claimed my brother was a distant cousin in the Italian branch of his family. Of course, none of Eugen's friends or the boys working in their houses believed him. I never understood why, but the trip did not go well, and we never saw Eugen again.

Carlo had other business ventures as well. He enlisted my help in one of them. Along with one or two other friends, we would walk up to the piazza in front of St. Peter's on feast days when it was crowded. One of us would go up to men or women who were obviously visitors and pretend to sell them, for a few scudi, a small pendant with an image of the great church. As soon as their attention was diverted, Carlos or one of the others would crowd in behind them, grab a bag or wallet and disappear into the crowd. We would yell and run after them, pretending to chase the criminals.

Other days Carlo would arrange a meeting at a local tavern with a wealthy married man. As soon as they were upstairs with their clothes off, he would grab their wrists and tie them behind their backs. One of his friends would burst through the door wearing the closest approximation he could fashion of a policeman's outfit. The man would invariably be terrified and surrender whatever money he had and promise to pay more as soon as he returned to his rooms or hotel. My brother and his friend would accompany him to collect.

Carlo started to make a great deal of money, and things seemed to be going well. He bought clothes and gifts for Mama and was very attentive to her. He even went to Mass with us once or twice, and he claimed he went to confession. I cannot imagine what he would have told the priest. Or maybe I can. In my experience, nothing seemed to shock the priests.

In the months that followed, we saw Carlo less and less, and late one night he was found lying on the sidewalk near our building in a pool of blood with a knife in his back. He survived in agony for a few days, then died. The police did a hasty investigation. They arrested someone, but it was never clear who was responsible.

Chapter 2:

Vespaziano

Did I grieve? Did I pursue justice? Did I find the killer and wreak my vengeance? There was no time for grief or vengeance. I was getting older, and I needed to find a way out of poverty and out of my neighborhood.

When I was fifteen, I left school and, like my brother before me, started working for Lodovico at his shop. I hated it as much as my brother had and was even less skilled. It only provided a trickle of income to the family, but it had one benefit that soon proved to be very important in my career. It did a great deal to build my muscles and fill out my frame.

Lodovico was a terrible master, unskilled and brutal, also stupid and determined to stay that way. I could take the work and the abuse. I had grown tough. But the work did nothing to satisfy my growing ambition to make something of myself. After several months, I went to see Vespaziano.

He seemed surprised to see me. He told me I seemed too innocent. I told him I was already older than some of the boys working there, and I knew what went on upstairs at the tavern. Reluctantly he agreed to consider me. He asked me to undress and walk around the room. I was excited, but I instinctively put my hands in front of my genitals.

He pulled them away and ran his hands up and down my back, my chest, my legs, and began to play with my privates. I started to show a full stand and pushed his hand away. He slapped me, pulled his cock out of his trousers and told me to put it in my mouth. After he spent, he told me he believed I was ready to work.

He then launched into what sounded like a set speech. "You

are entering an ancient and august profession, young Jacopo. You will be privy to secrets of an art that has been passed down from generation to generation. It is more than an occupation. It is a calling. It involves beauty and the giving of pleasure, which are divine gifts."

He asked Giovanni Battista, a *bardassa* a little older than myself who had been working at the tavern for several years, to take me upstairs.

"I was very young when I started. I had no choice," Giovanni Battista explained. "Mama was sick, and we needed money. At first, I worked mostly outdoors on the streets, especially around the Colosseum. There was always activity there at night, particularly in the arcades and inner spaces.

"But it was dangerous. After I was badly beaten a few times by violent men or the police or older boys who didn't want the competition, I knew I had to find something safer. I was happy when a boy I knew told me about this tavern. He also told me how everyone here would burn in Hell. Because I was already in Hell, I figured it could not be any worse, so I came over that very day.

"I have been happy here. I think you will like it, too. You are already older and bigger than me and much more handsome. You should do well. It takes a while to learn all the tricks you need to know in this business. You have to learn what guests—that's what we call them—want even when they don't know themselves or are too embarrassed to say. You have to be clever."

"What do most men want?" I asked.

Giovanni Battista was proud of his sophistication. "In most cases the gentlemen who want a romp with young fellows like us only want the active role. They want us to gamahuche their swollen knobs and then sodomize us.

"Some men actually want me to whip or sodomize them. I think that is pathetic. No fully grown man should allow himself to be penetrated. But we need to do what they ask no matter how silly. Just yesterday I had an old Nancy boy—he must have been at least forty, but we use 'boy' for any man who is on the bot-tom—who insisted on remaining in his pink silk stockings and top hat the whole time I striped his bare bum with a birch switch while he frigged himself. There was even a gentleman who thought that my Mister Pego was insufficient and required two of us to stretch his hole. 'Chicken on a double spit,' he called it."

When Giovanni Battista took me upstairs, I found a warren of tiny rooms with peeling wallpaper. Each room had a metal bed, a small chest of drawers, a basin for water and a framed picture, usually of the Virgin and Christ Child or one of the saints. Since there was little else to look at, in the weeks that followed I spent a good deal of time studying those prints wondering what the Holy Family would have thought about the activities in the room. It was my introduction to the work of Raphael, Andrea del Sarto, Guido Reni and other Italian masters. I would later be startled when I saw the actual paintings. Because I had become so used to the faded lithographs, the canvases in museums seemed garish.

I had met a number of the men who had come regularly to the tavern to go upstairs with my brother. They had chosen Carlo because he was big and strong and unafraid to be aggressive with them. Without having to ask, he knew which men wanted him to order them around, treat them roughly, make them beg. In my first months, these men never asked for my services.

However, I worked hard on developing my body and learned to became more confident. I also learned that "guests" would pay more money when I told them I preferred women and was just at the tavern to make money. Soon, some of them wanted to reverse roles and play the boy with me. That seemed awkward at first, but I soon found I preferred it.

My favourite customer in those months was an officer of the guard named Ettore, a handsome man of perhaps thirty whose wife brought him to the tavern. As he walked through the door in his uniform, he looked very manly, as though he could command a battalion. After he and his wife and three or four of us boys had arrived in a room upstairs, his wife would say that Ettore had been naughty and needed to be punished.

On a typical day we might order him to take off his clothes, get on his hands and knees on the floor and crawl like a dog to gamahuche one of us after another. After that, we might order him to crawl up on the bed and position himself so one of us could enter him from the front and another from behind. Eventually we would flip him onto his back and each of us spend all over his chest and face. Ettore remained at full stand from start to finish, but we never let him spend or clean up before putting his uniform back on. Meanwhile his wife would sit quietly on a chair watching. We always had a good laugh after they left.

One of the most frequent visitors to the tavern was a priest who thought that the ordinary clothes he wore to the tavern hid the fact that he had a high position in the Vatican. One day, when one of his favourite boys was not available, Vespaziano suggested he go upstairs with me.

The man was hesitant. He asked whether I had ever tied up a guest. I wanted the money, so I lied and said that I had. I don't think he believed me, but he went upstairs with me anyway. When I obviously had no idea what to do, he was annoyed but said he would teach me.

I loved how I felt once he was bound. I could do anything I wanted. I tried slapping his arse, pulling his balls, and pinching his nipples. And not gently. This must have hurt, and he squirmed and moaned, but he didn't protest. When I finished, he paid me well. On his third visit, he said he loved me.

I doubted that love played any role in our interactions, but he came back regularly every week or two to ask for more. With him I learned to expand my repertoire. The more inventive I became in abusing and humiliating him, the happier he seemed. Vespaziano was pleased. Many of our customers were Vatican clerics, and they paid well.

I was grateful to that old priest. With him I finally discovered how much I loved the feeling of power that came with being in control. It pushed from my mind all the anxieties I had when I was younger and felt I never had control over anything. The feeling of being the one in control was intoxicating.

Chapter 3:

Ganymede

One day the old priest brought with him a man who, from the way everyone in the tavern treated him, was obviously an important person. This, despite the fact that he was dressed, like the priest, in old and ragged clothes.

When we went upstairs, he didn't want to undress completely. He said he was too modest to be seen naked and just wanted to talk. This was fine with me. He appeared to be satisfied with his experience and returned the week following. During this second visit he became bolder and asked me to take off all my clothes and sit on his lap so he could kiss and caress me. This continued for several weeks.

I didn't find this man attractive, but I looked forward to his visits because he was kind and attentive. He would ask my opinion about art or music. He said that I was even more handsome than my brother Carlo and that I reminded him of Antinous, the young Bithynian lover of the Roman Emperor Hadrian. He told me stories about boys from Greek and Roman mythology. I was particularly interested in the story of Zeus and Ganymede. I pictured Zeus as a powerful figure with a massive chest and arms, a large severe face, and a great black beard. The idea must have come from engravings I had seen. I pictured Ganymede as a beautiful boy with dark hair and eyes and a slight but nicely formed body.

Like me. I imagined Zeus transforming himself into a huge eagle to swoop down from the heavens and carry me back to his bed on Mount Olympus, where he would transform back into a god. There he would take me into his arms and make passionate love to me, although I was never clear exactly what kind of lovemaking I expected from the father of all gods.

This customer explained to me that he was particularly attracted to young boys like me who were, he said, at the peak of perfection for only a few years, like a rare tropical flower that would last only a day or two before it wilted. For that reason, he loved mythological figures like Hyacinth who, at the height of his beauty, was turned into a flower, so he never grew old.

After he had worked himself into an excited state, he would ask me to lie on the bed and frig myself for him. He would scoop up the seed with the fingers of his left hand and put it in his mouth, then use his right hand to finger himself to climax. After that he would hurriedly dress, press money into my hand, and depart.

After a month or two, I learned that he was Archbishop M, one of the most powerful figures in the Vatican. Eventually he sent an emissary to ask me if I would consent to be part of his household in his palazzo.

I later learned that my consent was not really needed. The Archbishop had already paid Vespaziano a considerable sum to have me move into the palace. I was installed in a tiny room in the stable wing. Officially I was supposed to be a groom, but the only things I had ever mounted were men at the tavern. I knew nothing about horses and was never expected to.

At first the Archbishop called for me frequently. I mostly did what we had done at the tavern. He explained that if he removed all his clothes in my presence, he might be unable to stop himself from wanting to commit a *peccatum contra naturam*. I was not sure I understood where he drew the line on what constituted a *peccatum*, but I had no objection. I believe that in later years he was less strict in his interpretation and was known to commit every kind of sin with women and with men.

Another one of my duties was helping at his entertainments. He loved to stage banquets in the manner of the ancient Romans. Guests would come dressed in togas and recline on sofas lined along the outer edge of a large room while the food was served by pretty young boys.

For a while, I was his favourite. He liked me to dress in a gauzy silk toga that, he said, made me resemble a marble figure of Ganymede that occupied the center of a pond at his villa in Tivoli. Dressed in sandals and the ridiculously short toga, I would greet the guests and perform small tasks like slicing fruit or pouring wine. He told me boys like me were works of art that he liked to display.

Later, when the Archbishop started to require my presence less often, I was at first slightly offended but soon decided that the arrangement suited me perfectly. It left me with time for myself. I spent as much of this time as I could in the Archbishop's library. The librarian was an old priest named Father Gregorio. He had been engaged by the Archbishop's father who was the one who had amassed the hundreds of books in the collection, each bound in leather and embossed with the family crest.

Gregorio was always happy to see me because hardly anyone else in the Archbishop's household ever came to the library. Most of the domestic staff were ignorant and could not read, and the Archbishop, his family members, and the sycophants surrounding him had no interest. Gregorio taught me about the ancient Greeks and Romans, classic and modern literature, and painting and sculpture.

He also advised me on which of the Archbishop's books I should read. I studied carefully the volumes in Italian, and with Father Gregorio worked my way through books in French, English and German. Above all, I loved the books with pictures— engravings or etchings—of paintings and sculpture.

Every now and then the Archbishop would have me accompany him on a social call. On several occasions we attended the Thursday afternoon salon of a grand lady, the Contessa P. She was a beautiful woman who dressed in flowing silk gowns and glittering jewels. Accompanied by a brace of poodles, she swirled through her rooms, engaging everyone in conversation.

Gregorio was jealous. He told me that her gatherings attracted some of the most eminent writers, artists and musicians from across Europe. Chopin, Berlioz, Ingres, Meissonier, Thorvaldsen had all come to pay their respects.

There were always a few younger men in the room. I envied the way they seemed perfectly comfortable with their place in life and appeared to know exactly how to calibrate their response to each guest. I imagined them walking into a box at the opera or a seat at the racetrack in their coats, top hats, and kid gloves. I desperately wanted to be like them and vowed that one day I would find a way to do so.

It was clear that my expected role at these salons was to stand silently at the Archbishop's side. He would introduce me to the other guests, pat my head as if I were a puppy, and look gratified when they complimented him on my appearance. I said nothing unless I was asked a direct question. In those cases, if a conversation resulted, the Archbishop's friends appeared amazed that I could talk about books or the opera. They sometimes reacted as though they had just met a dog trained to speak in classical Greek.

The Archbishop found it all amusing. The Contessa, for her part, always treated me with respect and took it upon herself to pull me aside, supply me with gossip about the guests, and introduce me to as many of them as possible. Through her, I met and spoke with some of the most eminent figures of the day. The Archbishop's library and the Contessa's salons provided the most important education of my early years.

Soon some of the Contessa's guests started asking the Archbishop if they could "borrow" me for parties or private sessions. He seemed happy to oblige. I suspected he liked doing this because it was such an inexpensive way for him to give a present.

I became the favourite boy for a circle of church officials, military officers, artists, musicians and writers. Many of them belonged to something they called the Académie Ganymède. I learned that it was modelled on a similar organisation in London that disbanded after a big scandal. The club in Rome was apparently protected by a high church official. I think it might have been my Archbishop, although he apparently didn't wish to be publicly associated with what went on there.

The club had a suite of rooms near the Anglican church called the Granary Chapel. Many members of the club, instead of going to church on Sunday morning, met in the club for sketching from live models.

The men, mostly artists or architects but also amateur painters, would sit on high stools in front of easels. There would be a model, sometimes two, on a low dais in front who would pose in various positions for about an hour. I probably did this at least twenty times over the course of two years.

When they started, the models would usually be wearing a few pieces of clothing, for example a Roman toga or a military uniform.

In the usual routine, after ten minutes or so a bell would ring, and the boy or pair of boys would be instructed to assume the next position which almost always meant removing some piece of clothing. By halfway through the session, they were almost always naked or wearing only some small accessory: a cap, a chain around the neck, an ankle bracelet, or a metal belt that locked around their genitals. They might be instructed to imitate the poses of famous pieces of sculpture.

With a few minutes left in the session, a man at the back of the room would give a triple bell signal. The idea was for the model to frig himself and try to climax exactly on the hour. This didn't always happen, but some of the boys were very talented, and when it did happen, the artists jumped to their feet, cheered, and surged toward to the dais to press coins into the hands of the triumphant boy. Following the session there was no prohibition against club members setting up private appointments and taking one of the boys back to their lodgings. In fact, that might have been the chief reason for the club.

I won't pretend to be modest. I was clearly the most popular of the boys, and I rarely went directly home. The club itself paid me, but the private sessions were considerably more lucrative. Some of the men would also give me presents, often clothes that they wanted me to wear to accompany them to a restaurant or the theatre. I learned how to act in their company and sometimes even enjoyed the role.

Occasionally, the man who had me accompany him back to his hotel or lodgings would introduce me to his friends, saying I was a distant relative from Naples or Modena. I could tell that most of them knew I was nothing of the kind. To my amazement, though, an increasing number of them pretended to believe him and engage me in conversation, particularly after I had I invented amusing anecdotes about my fictional life. I worked diligently to learn enough about events of the day and currently fashionable painters or musicians to join in conversation on the occasions when my companion seemed to be comfortable with my doing so.

I felt a certain amount of conflict within myself. In many ways I was happy. Of course I was pleased to be out of Vespaziano's shabby tavern. I was happy that I could help my family. My younger brothers, Gaetano and Paolo, who still lived at home, were too young to do much work so what little I brought home helped keep the wolf from the door.

And I was also happy with the money and trinkets distinguished older men gave me and being able to share, however briefly, their luxurious life. And I won't deny that I liked being admired and the centre of their attention.

But it was never enough. I was gratified that these men thought my face and figure handsome, but this was just about my appearance, something God had given me. I hated the fact that I was nothing but a diversion for them, that I had to please them and do whatever they told me.

A good deal of the physical contact was disgusting. Some of the things they wanted me to do I found repulsive. Some liked to insult me and call me names like *culatone* or *puttana,* or they would ask me to leave as soon as they had spent with no word of thanks.

It particularly infuriated me when I was expected to pleasure young men barely older than myself. I was at least as intelligent and agreeable as any of them, and I was almost always more handsome. Why should they have all the advantages in life, while I was only a plaything, one they could order about or discard at will?

I developed a fierce determination to create a new life for my-self no matter what I had to do to reach that goal. Fortunately, despite the handicap of my birth, I had advantages not shared by most boys. I was lucky enough to be attractive to some highly influential men, and I was intelligent enough to learn from them how to advance myself.

I knew that these men were the best means I had to protect my family and secure my future. For this reason, I pretended I liked what I was doing and used every opportunity afforded me to learn from them. I knew there was an urgency. I would not be young forever, and as soon as I ceased to be their Ganymede, I would fall out of favour and be banished from their world. I needed to find the man who could help me escape the life I had been born into and fashion a new one.

You may call that heartless. I call it surviving.

And, fortunately for me, the man I sought was about to enter my life.

Chapter 4:

Joseph

After a modelling session at the Académie, a young Englishman who said his name was Jeramiah invited me and August, an Austrian boy who was modelling with me that day, to come back to his rooms at the Hotel d'Angleterre in the Via Bocca di Leone.

He did a series of drawings of us in various poses, trying to make us look like pieces of ancient Greek sculpture. The first time he motioned for me to come over to look at his sketches, I burst out laughing. He blushed furiously and asked me what I found so funny. I told him that I was laughing at the way he had had us pose naked but in his sketches he had covered our genitalia with fig leaves. He said he was trying to imitate the sculptures he had seen in the Vatican.

When he invited me back alone the following week, he admitted he preferred sculpture or drawings with a little bit of drapery or a fig leaf. He said it helped draw the eye to the "body's most interesting parts." Thereafter I devised all manner of amusing ways to hide my "interesting parts" during our sessions. However, as soon as Jeremiah walked over to inspect my pose more carefully, my arousal undid my preparations.

I soon learned that his real name was not Jeremiah but Joseph and that he was the son of a British viscount. Joseph's Italian was not very good, and my English was not yet fluent, so it took me a while to understood that he was traveling on the Continent to try his hand at painting. He was taking lessons from a French artist but needed to decide if he wanted to continue or return to run his family's business, a bank in England.

On the fourth or fifth visit, it seemed he wanted to sketch me in the usual way, but every few minutes he walked over and paced around me examining me from every angle, occasionally moving my arms or head back and forth.

I had a good idea by then of what men wanted but couldn't bring themselves to ask. I reached up, drew his head down to mine, and kissed him hard on the lips. He quickly pulled back but, after a minute, tentatively returned the kiss. We hugged, me naked and him still fully dressed, both of us obviously aroused. After only a minute or two he pulled back again, apologizing profusely, saying that he could not do any further sketching that day. But he made me promise to come back the next day.

When I did, any pretence of life drawing was completely abandoned. I took the lead. I had Joseph sit in a chair in the drawing room, fully dressed. I walked around the room, slowly removing my clothing one piece at a time. Then I pulled him to his feet and started to strip him, stopping after each piece of clothing for extended kissing.

When I got down to his shirt and drawers, he tried to stop me. I brushed his hand aside and pulled his drawers down to his ankles. He grabbed my wrist and, without removing his drawers, hobbled into the chamber, pushed me onto the bed, and closed the shutters and drapes.

The room was completely dark. Even though he had seen me naked and fully erect many times, and he knew I could feel his cock throbbing against me when I sat on his lap, he was embarrassed to be seen naked. He never got comfortable in full light.

I have a vivid memory of that day. Only the occasional shaft of light entered the dim interior of that corner room. It played over the floral pattern of the rug, the subdued fern pattern in the wallpaper, the tangle of fresh white sheets on the bed. It was quiet and cool.

I got down on my knees and demonstrated for him the reason generations of his countrymen had ventured south. He appreciated my skills and soon tried returning them, but he was remarkably untutored in the art and never really learned to appreciate it.

At first, Joseph was just another customer. But there was something about him that was different from the others. He was considerate, concerned that our time together satisfied me as well as him. He treated me more like a friend than someone he had hired.

I started to enjoy our time together. I almost suggested I come to him even if no money changed hands. At the last moment, I decided against. I was highly skilled at my craft and deserved to be paid. Besides, Joseph obviously had a considerable amount of money. I was still poor—successful at my trade, but in comparison with him, poor.

I also felt strangely protective of him. Although he was ten years older than I, and he had travelled extensively and had more schooling, I was experienced in ways Joseph was not. At times it could almost feel like I was the senior partner.

I usually knew at once if I was attracted to someone. After an initial encounter, that feeling would rarely change, and almost never for the better. With Joseph, for the first time in my experience, my physical attraction started only after I learned to like him as a person and continued to grow as I got to know him better.

His face was not unpleasant, with blue eyes, light brown hair, and fair skin with the slightest hint of freckles, but there was nothing distinctive about it. He refused to grow a moustache or beard because, he said, his facial hair was too sparse, and it made him look immature. To me, the lack of facial hair called attention to his weak chin and the pallor of his complexion. I, on the other hand, was eager to grow a beard so I would look older and more imposing, but Joseph was adamant that I remain a clean-shaven youth.

Joseph's body, on the other hand, was well-proportioned. I suppose that after the flabby older men I had become accustomed to, I was pleasantly surprised by how firm it felt when I held him. How soft his skin was when I caressed it. I particularly liked the fine soft hair on the nape of his neck and his arse cheeks. I liked to plant kisses on those cheeks. That embarrassed him, and he would invariably pull my head back up to his face.

The more I grew to like him, the more exciting our lovemaking became, and the more comfortable he became with me. After we fully explored the French technique, Joseph asked if I could introduce him to the Greek way. He said I should demonstrate on him, since I was more experienced. I was quite skilled in this art; nevertheless, Joseph didn't enjoy it.

He loved the idea, though, and thereafter almost always wanted to use that technique but with him always on top. I would have much preferred the other way around, making him play the boy, maybe tying him up before pushing my cock into his mouth and up his arse, but he wanted to stay in control. Perhaps he felt that it was demeaning for him, as the partner who was older and of higher social status, to allow himself to be put in what he considered the subordinate position.

I was so happy to be with him and making money in such an easy and enjoyable way that I was willing to do whatever he wanted. And Joseph, over the next weeks became much more confident in private and in public. I liked to think that I played some significant part in that transformation.

Eventually Joseph moved out of the hotel into a set of rooms he rented around the corner from the Spanish Steps, and I started spending most nights with him there. The Archbishop didn't seem to notice or care.

On certain rare visits, I encountered his valet, a dour man named Walters. His reaction was impenetrable. He was invariably correct in his behaviour, but there was certainly no warmth there. I was shocked that Joseph didn't seem to care what Walters thought, even on one occasion when Walters accidentally glimpsed the two of us in bed.

When Joseph saw I was interested in art and architecture, and that I had learned how to behave like a young gentleman in public, he started to take me with him to restaurants, galleries, and museums.

He encouraged me to continue my reading in English, French, and German. Even Latin. In return, I helped Joseph with his Italian. I tried hard to obliterate my Trastevere accent and manner of speaking. They were hardly suitable for the class of company we were keeping.

After a while Joseph insisted on speaking to me only in Italian in private with me answering only in English. He said it was the best way for both of us to learn. In bed at night, though, he allowed that we could let our bodies speak the "universal language."

We both started to pick up words, expressions, and mannerisms from the other. For example, he liked to make fun of the way I said "delicious," a word that I used often. He would mimic me, saying "de leesh us," drawing out the second syllable to comic effect. But he said it so many times he started using it unconsciously, even when he was talking to a friend. I noticed myself using certain English words, like "consummate" or "extraordinary." They sounded appropriate when Joseph said them. When I did, they came off as pompous.

Joseph was interested in Greek and Roman sculpture and paintings that he felt captured the classical spirit. He encouraged me to read passages from the *History of the Art of Antiquity* by the noted German authority, Johann Joachim Winckelmann.

I remember the day he took me to the Cortile del Belvedere in the Vatican to meet with one of the men who helped manage the collections there. He was a German named Hasenpflug or Hasenhirst or some such thing. He was about the same age as Joseph. I think that the trip was partly to show me some of the sculpture we had been reading about, but I also had the impression he wanted to show me off.

From all indications, the friend was suitably impressed. Joseph had me stand next to a life-size bronze figure of Antinous. The statue and I were about the same height and build. Hasenpflug— or whatever his name—hovered around me, moving the position of my legs or taking my left arm and putting it across Antinous' shoulders, then around his waist. He walked around and around comparing me, feature by feature, to the piece of sculpture and making favourable comments.

Then he asked me to kiss the statue's lips. Both Joseph and I protested, but after looking around to be sure that no one was looking, I did press my mouth briefly against the lips of that beautiful bronze boy. Despite the slightly acrid metallic taste, I found the act arousing, particularly when I slipped my hand down his back to where his arse cheeks started to part.

Just then a well-dressed couple and their two children walked around the corner. All three of us suddenly turned away and pretended to look at display cases elsewhere in the room, but I think the parents sensed that they had interrupted something not meant for them to see. The wife hurried her brood past.

I believe that Joseph was as happy with the day as I was. At very least, as we rode in the carriage back in the Spanish Steps, I could tell that Joseph was eager to be alone back in our chamber.

I remember that day for another reason. It was the first time I saw the Apollo Belvedere, the Laocoön, and the Belvedere Torso. I was particularly impressed by the torso. Joseph told me Michelangelo was asked to complete the figure but declined. I felt that was the right decision. I loved the piece exactly as it was. That spectacular body with the enormous chest and massive splayed thighs, putting his genitalia on full display just above head height, made me tingle all over.

Surprisingly, the fact that part of his cock had been knocked off seemed only to make the effect more potent. Perhaps it was a little like those fig leaves. It made me fill in the full picture in my mind.

By this time, I already fancied myself quite the critic. Several times when I was expounding on a subject I saw Joseph trying to suppress a smile. I wondered if I had become a project for him, an experiment to see if he could make a young gentleman out of a *bardassa* from Trastevere. I became determined to learn enough to hold my own in any conversation about art.

Joseph also took me around to Rome's art galleries. Before he met me, he had started buying paintings and small pieces of sculpture to ship back to England. When he saw how excited I was to go with him, he increased the frequency of his visits to the galleries. He was mostly interested in small bronze and marble pieces. He would keep them for several weeks before sending them on, arranging them on tables and desks, picking them up, turning them in his hands, caressing them. He typically arranged them with their faces to the wall. He explained this was to minimize distracting allegorical elements such as tools, farm implements and pieces of athletic equipment. I think he simply found their backsides more attractive.

We spent hours going from shop to shop deciding whether to buy this Apollo or that Adonis or Antinous. It was a kind of game. The shopkeepers invariably claimed the wares in their shops were very rare original works of antiquity. Joseph frequently seemed sceptical of their authenticity, but as long as the pieces were well executed and the prices reasonable, he was not greatly concerned when and where they had been made.

I learned to identify which works were antique and largely intact, which extensively restored, and which were recently manufactured—*nello stile antico*, as Joseph would say when trying to impress me with his grasp of Italian. He said he considered all of them authentic, either authentic antique pieces or authentic nineteenth-century fakes or forgeries. The only thing that was inauthentic, he told me, was any effort to pass off a recently created item as a genuine work of antiquity.

I was proud when he started asking for my advice, and I helped him negotiate prices with the shopkeepers. It was a task he thoroughly disliked. I had no trouble driving hard bargains on his behalf.

Joseph eventually sent Walters back to England. I think he felt I would be more comfortable without him in the same suite of rooms. I believe Walters was hurt by this decision, but of course he said nothing. At that point Joseph started telling people he met that I was his *valet-de-place*, which, by then, after I had learned to fit into his world, seemed plausible enough.

I was grateful to Joseph and was becoming quite comfortable being with him even if I often felt awkward switching between my new life and my old one when I visited family or saw friends from my childhood.

I felt this division in my life most acutely the day Joseph and I paid a visit to my mother. Joseph had suggested it. I, in turn, asked Mama. I had previously told her that I had met Joseph and had started to work as his assistant. She didn't press me further about my duties, but I am sure she knew that there was more I wasn't saying. She was obviously nervous about the visit.

When we entered the old neighbourhood, it was Holy Week. I had forgotten it was upon us. As a boy, the constant pageantry had thrilled me, but this time I was apprehensive. In Joseph's company, the familiar streets seemed dirtier and shabbier than when I returned alone. The procession of the penitents, once exciting, now seemed vulgar and excessive. I worried about Joseph's reaction to my family. I worried he might think less of me, seeing the world I grew up in. I hoped he would give me credit for using my wits to escape.

When we reached my old apartment, neither Mama nor Alphonso, her current boyfriend, had any idea what to say. But I needn't have worried. Joseph was at ease, polite and sweet with my mother. He gave her some small gifts he had brought—a silk scarf and a few bits of jewellery. She nodded her thanks but said nothing. Joseph was even deferential to Alphonso (which must have confused the poor man).

After a few polite final words—Joseph's in perfect Italian, Mama's in our local dialect—just as we reached the door, she said, "Jaco," and gestured to me.

Mama had not called me by that name since I was a boy. I looked to Joseph. "I'll wait in the street," he said. He smiled, nodded to Mama and Alphonso, and left.

Mama told Alphonso to leave as well, which he did with obvious relief.

Then she had me sit beside her.

"Your Giuseppe seems a fine young man."

I beamed. "He is, Mama."

"And these are fine gifts." She fingered the scarf and jewellery. "But I cannot keep them. I cannot have them in the house."

I was baffled. "But why? They are yours. We bought them for you."

"Jaco." She looked at me with deep sorrow. "These are the same gifts Carlo and his young man brought on their visit." She placed them in my lap. "I cannot have them. I cannot have a third dead son."

I stood. The gifts fell to the floor. "They are yours. You don't need to keep them. Give them to someone else, but please don't ask me to take them back. It would be an insult to Joseph.

"And Mama. Please don't worry about me. I have done nothing wrong and have never been in trouble. I have no intention of dying. Joseph is helping me to live."

I left all that behind me as I met Joseph in the street. He let me show him places from my childhood, starting with my old parish church, Santa Maria in Trastevere, where I had been taken so often as a child. I was pleased to be able to explain some of its history and point out the major features. And I was proud that when we opened up the Baedeker I had brought from Joseph's apartment, it confirmed what I had told him.

A bit later we took a cab up the Janiculum Hill to see the Acqua Paola, the Tempietto by Bramante in the courtyard at San Pietro in Montorio, and the spectacular panorama from the piazza in front of that church. From that vantage point, we had a view across the entire city from the dome of St. Peter's to the north to the open fields beyond the walls to the south.

The sun was about to set. The light through the dusty atmosphere made the vista look like a painting by Tiepolo. Being with Joseph in the neighbourhood where I was born, dressed in a handsome English wool suit Joseph had bought me in anticipation of our visit, I felt the old ties loosen and dissolve, replaced by a deeper contentment than any I had ever known before.

Some fundamental change had taken place. I was no longer constantly aware that he was a British lord and I a poor rented boy. I felt more confident. I believed that, one way or another, it would be possible for me to live the kind of life lived by Joseph and others in his circle of friends.

I was certain Joseph liked me, but it was still possible he liked me primarily because he was lonely, and that, at least for the moment, I satisfied some basic needs. I wondered if I was like one of the pieces of sculpture he was buying—an object to be acquired, admired, shown to friends. For my part, I realized that despite my very warm feelings toward him, I didn't know how much of it was simply due to the way he had rescued me from my former life and had shown me a new and better one.

My old friends were convinced our arrangement was strictly trade, a mutually beneficial but temporary arrangement, nothing more. And they warned me that I needed to act quickly to take advantage of my situation. Foreign men inevitably lost interest in Roman boys, they said, and they never remained in Rome for long.

At this point you may think they were right, that I was a fool to believe that I was anything to Joseph but a diversion, an acquisition, a project, one that he could promptly abandon. But we are far from the end of the story.

Chapter 5:

Fortin

One afternoon Joseph took me to the studio of Jean-Louis Fortin, a French painter, on the Via Margutta. I knew that this street had housed many artists, particularly Americans and Englishmen. He had inherited the studio as well as the apartment at the front of the building from his father. The elder Fortin, also a painter, had been quite successful in his prime. According to Joseph the younger Fortin was an astute businessman as well as a fine artist and already making a name for himself.

Fortin greeted us at the door in his shirtsleeves. He and Joseph greeted each other warmly. As he shook my hand, he seemed to examine me intently. He was a young man, perhaps a few years older than Joseph, with sparkling dark eyes and an alluring smile.

To reach the studio, Fortin led us through the front apartment where he lived with his wife, Marta and a young son named Narcisse. At the back of the building, the studio, overlooking the garden, was a large, double-height space. The windows that almost completely filled the back wall were partly shaded by a white muslin cloth, letting in a cool, even light.

Fortin was eager to tell us about a series of paintings he had recently started. He explained that his conceit for the series was to portray apostles and martyrs as they appeared in their youth. He showed us a handful of finished paintings propped up against the back wall and a large portfolio of sketches.

Joseph laughed. "I see you continue to have certain, um, qualifications for the boys you hire to pose for you. Your young saints all look quite similar and all alarmingly handsome."

"Actually, all this work was done using only two models, but I have tried to give them different poses and attributes. I don't expect many people will see enough of these pictures to notice that Ambrose looks a good deal like Alphonsus or Jerome like John of the Cross."

"Quite efficient, but I must say," Joseph continued, "that none of these boys show much indication that they are destined to become vessels of God's will."

"Do you suppose most boys who eventually become saints have any sense of their destiny?" I could not tell whether Fortin was being serious or facetious. "Surely most looked and acted like ordinary boys, and, as you no doubt have experienced yourself, boys are no strangers to impure thoughts and untoward deeds."

"I imagine you have more firsthand knowledge of this than I, so I suppose what you say is true," Joseph said. It was now clear from their banter that the two men were close friends accustomed to joking between themselves, "but these boys are hardly ordinary. They look like the Roman *bardassi* you would find on the Spanish Steps today."

"If you say so, Joseph. I believe you are the expert in that department." Both men laughed.

By the way Joseph kept going back to look at certain sketches, I could tell that he would soon ask me to return to negotiate prices.

After we had thoroughly examined the young saints, Fortin called for tea, biscuits, and marrons glacés. Then, several minutes into a desultory conversation about the Paris Salon, Fortin abruptly turned to Joseph and said: "Your young Jacopo is exactly my vision of St. Sebastian as a boy. I have planned Sebastian as the crowning glory of my series. Would you be willing to lend him for sittings?"

Fortin looked surprised when Joseph turned and asked me if I would be amenable. I was deeply flattered by Fortin's offer and curious to learn more about how painters worked. As an additional inducement, Fortin proposed a handsome fee.

I tried to hide my enthusiasm, but I don't think I fooled anyone. They both knew I was eager to do it. In the carriage on the way home I pressed Joseph, "Did you say anything before today to Fortin about my modelling for him?"

"Yes, I confess I did."

"How did he know I would be right for St. Sebastian?"

"I hope you will not be angry at me, but I showed him one or two sketches I did of you."

I tried to look angry, but I was actually pleased. I would be posing for a real artist. "I am not angry," I eventually said.

"Good. I'm relieved." He pulled down the shade on his side of the carriage and kissed me on the top of my head. "I think you could learn a good deal from the experience." I pulled his head down and started kissing him on the lips. He responded eagerly. When we arrived at Joseph's building, we straightened our clothes before leaving the carriage and climbed the stairs as quickly as we could.

Fortin used me as a model for a number of large religious scenes, sometimes as a man in a crowd and sometimes as the main figure. Fortin could transform me into a Roman centurion witnessing one of Christ's miracles or a Hebrew youth being tutored in a synagogue. I posed in the nude, but in the paintings, Fortin would add a wool cloak, uniform or suit of armour as appropriate.

In the case of the Hebrew youth, he used my body but used the head of a different boy whose face Fortin thought looked more Semitic.

"I do these canvases because I need the money," he told me, "but my real interest is my collection of saints. They are in high demand by patrons. For some of them I choose my own subject matter. In other cases men commission me to paint specific figures with detailed instructions about poses and costume. I have made four particularly, um, evocative paintings for a German count in Dresden who calls himself Pansy."

I was fascinated. It was tiring holding a spear or sceptre for long periods of time, and the heat in an animal skin coat was stifling, but I was thrilled with this introduction into the life of an artist.

During the entire time I posed for him, Fortin chattered away, mostly in French but partly in Italian with some Latin phrases sprinkled throughout. It was mindless chatter, but it aided in my study of foreign languages, and I could see how the gossip about other artists, much of it malicious, might be useful to me.

Eventually Fortin started the St. Sebastian. By then I knew the history of art well enough to know how Sebastian's martyrdom had been treated by numerous artists in the past. The idea of a young man tied to a stake pierced by arrows afforded a good many dramatic possibilities. In many cases, it was quite obviously an excuse to show off a minimally clothed young man.

I had studied one of these, in my opinion the best painting of the subject, Guido Reni's, in a pale print on the wall of a bedroom at Vespaziano's tavern. I remembered wondering if the contorted position of Sebastian's body and his facial expression showed extreme pain or erotic passion. Or perhaps both?

I was curious to see how Fortin envisioned the young Sebastian. He started by asking me to take off my clothes, climb onto a table draped with a thick turkey carpet and sit with my arms wrapped around my knees. He sketched me from every imaginable angle.

A few weeks later I saw Fortin's first attempt to develop the composition of the painting. The drawing showed me in profile sitting on a rock on the top of a hill with several sheep around me. This grouping was set against a mountain range with a distant view of the sea. Unlike the other apostles and martyrs, Sebastian would remain completely nude although with genitalia hidden behind the forward leg. When he finished the painting, he called it "The young St. Sebastian praying near his home in Gallia Narbonensis."

After he finished the painting Fortin gave some of his sketches of me as a gift to Joseph. Included in this set was the final sketch, the one he used to construct the canvas. Fortin added an inscription and his signature. Joseph was very pleased. He took the sketches out frequently to show his friends.

Most considered them an excellent likeness of me, but the idea that they represented St. Sebastian struck them, as it had me, as somewhat ridiculous. This did nothing to diminish their enthusiasm for the painting when they finally saw it, however.

Fortin sent the finished painting to Paris the following year to the annual Salon. From all accounts, it created quite a stir. Joseph read me some of the reviews. Some were critical, suggesting that the painting was just a glorification of sensuality. Others were extremely positive. These reviews said almost nothing about the bow or arrows or the martyrdom. Instead, they praised the composition and brushwork, and there was a great deal about the curve of Sebastian's back, the position of his head, the resemblance to various pieces of Greek sculpture.

But above all, there was much nonsense about how the youthful figure radiated innocence and spirituality. There were even claims that paintings like this could invigorate Christian art and Christianity itself.

Joseph and I laughed at these reviews. I certainly was not radiating any innocence or spirituality during those long, boring days. The only thing I actually remember thinking during the sessions was a series of lewd fantasies about Fortin, what he would look like without his clothes, what he would want to do in bed. At first, I worried that my cock would crow and swell and become visible beneath my forward leg.

In fact, that did happen. Fortin walked over to look more closely, but he didn't touch me. I was perhaps a little offended. Fortin must have sensed what I was thinking because he said, "I would dearly love to acquaint myself more intimately with the young Sebastian, but I promised Joseph."

"What did you promise?"

"I said I would return young Sebastian to him as innocent and untouched as when he arrived."

"I'm neither innocent nor untouched," I said, becoming red in the face. "And I don't need Joseph to protect me."

"Don't be angry with him or me, young Jacopo. You should

feel lucky you found each other. I would be grateful if I found a young saint half as beautiful as you. Heaven knows I spend much of my time looking."

"And what about your wife and child?"

"Marta and I have never spoken about it, but I believe she understands."

When I got home, I confronted Joseph.

"Did you tell Fortin not to touch me?"

"I did. I'm sorry if it offends you, but at least for the time being I would like to keep you all for myself. I was alarmed when Fortin told me about the twelve models he used for a big historical picture of Jesus driving out the money changers from the Temple. He told me he had 'consummated' eight of them."

Joseph's comment about keeping me for himself made me feel guilty about the way I was keeping company with other men. I vowed to give up that activity although not immediately. For the moment, though, we both just laughed.

Fortin attended the opening at the Salon in Paris. "It was a triumph. Sebastian drew so many visitors that it was difficult to see the canvas. All the papers commented on it. It caused a certain amount of scandal from a few critics, but most loved it."

I wondered how many of the critics who wrote positive reviews were primarily interested in the young male flesh on display but were afraid to say a single word that might betray that interest. And was it that interest that motivated the official in one of the government ministries who purchased the canvas for the French state? In any case, it was installed in the Luxembourg Palace but later transferred to the Louvre ensuring its place in history.

Over time I learned a good deal more about Fortin. Before I met him, he had been the subject of a major scandal involving forgeries he had passed off as long-lost Raphaels. To the amazement of his detractors, Fortin not only survived the scandal but was even more successful with his young saints and martyrs. He soon had more orders than he could possibly fulfil, so he started hiring young apprentices to paint the backgrounds and, eventually, entire paintings that he would merely sign.

His success further fired his ambition and his desire for public recognition. Just before he returned to Paris, he told everyone that he had had some kind of religious conversion and renounced all his previous work. Gossip had it that the conversion sprang from a bad case of the clap he contracted from a Sicilian boy, but I believe the conversion never happened, that it was simply a way to reinvent himself once again. After moving to Paris, defying yet again all predictions, he managed to obtain at least a dozen major commissions from the Parisian archdiocese for murals in big new suburban churches and was named a member the French Academy.

Myself, I became quite busy. I realize I told you I intended to stop providing personal services to select gentlemen. I confess that, despite my firm intention to do so, the business was becoming just too lucrative. It was also increasingly enjoyable.

It was thrilling to order a wealthy, well-dressed older gentleman, the kind who, under other circumstances might have derided me as a *bardassa*, to strip, get on his hands and knees, crawl over to me and beg me to sodomize him. I learned what a powerful aphrodisiac humiliation could be, both to the humiliated and the one devising the humiliation.

I had another motivation for continuing my trade. I was particularly happy when gentlemen would show me their art collections. I didn't know exactly what my next career would be, but I knew it would involve art in some way, and I believed the information I was gleaning would be useful. After all, I was already sixteen and not getting any younger.

None of the other men compared with Joseph. He was closer to my age than most of them. Also, although he gave every indication he greatly enjoyed our physical interaction, he seemed genuinely to care about me and my future. For example, he said he was concerned about my soul. He suggested I attend church with him at All Saints' Anglican, but I always declined.

As we spent more time together, we started to tell people that I was his personal assistant. We even talked about leaving together and taking up residence in Paris or London.

Although Joseph understood my need for independence, as time went on, he became less comfortable with my spending the night away from him. One day he overheard someone call me a *bardassa*, and that settled it for him. At the very least, he told me, he wanted me to leave the Archbishop's palace.

He offered to rent a small apartment for me. However, in the end, we decided that it would be more convenient if I moved into his set of rooms by the Spanish Steps. It would be consistent with our claim that I was his personal assistant. He promised that I could have my own room and come and go freely.

He did ask me to pledge that I would be entirely faithful to him. I told him I would, but I knew, even as I was saying it, that I couldn't comply completely. I tried to meet him halfway, though. I kept my old customers, but I mostly stopped acquiring new ones.

I told Joseph none of this. I told myself I didn't want to hurt him, that things he didn't know would have little effect on him. And I reasoned that having a little money and some relationships of my own made me more confident and therefore made my relationship with him more secure.

So, I packed up my few things and moved into a small maid's room at the rear of the suite he occupied, accessible by a separate stairway from the interior courtyard. We started to go out together more often but often did so in the company of his friend Miss Edwards—Polly, he called her—a woman he knew from childhood, and Polly's younger companion, a French girl named Clarice. To casual acquaintances, it would appear that Joseph was with Miss Edwards and I with Clarice. Of course, few of Joseph's friends were deceived.

Those months with Joseph in Rome were the most fulfilling in my life to that point. Would you call that love? I would not. Not then. I was happy to be with Joseph. He was always sweet and affectionate. He would, for example, sometimes walk up behind me in the middle of the day, spin me around, start kissing and pulling my clothes off. I particularly enjoyed the times when we would lie together on the bed after we had both spent and talk about art or music or plans for the future.

Still, it was clear that he needed to take the lead in almost everything we did. For example he just assumed he would determine what we would do in our lovemaking. His repertoire was quite small and unvarying, and it almost always ended with him penetrating me.

I followed his lead. It felt right, mostly, given that he was older, still physically bigger, and he had a much higher position in society. But there were times when I was not satisfied. I had more experience than he, and I would have loved the emotional charge that came with being the one on top.

Growing up, I had always felt obliged to do whatever I was told. In my family, decisions were made, if not by my mother, then by an uncle or my brother Carlo. At the tavern, I had to do what the customers wanted. Even when that involved my dominating them, it was on their orders. So, I suppose I was a little disappointed that Joseph rarely let me take the lead.

And, truth be told, as satisfying as all our lovemaking was, at times I craved something more aggressive and raw, the kind of thing I experienced with certain other gentlemen.

Before I forget, let me mention one other odd thing about Joseph. As often as not, a minute or two after spending, he would be asleep. I loved the minutes that followed, the way his breathing became calm and regular, and the sheet above his chest moved rhythmically up and down. Then, almost exactly ten minutes later, he would suddenly wake and start talking, sometimes finishing a sentence, as if he had been awake the entire time.

Chapter 6:

Gottlieb

After I moved into Joseph's apartment, I was more careful with my time away from him. I didn't want him to hear rumours or for there to be any trouble. For a while, no problem arose. When it did, it came from an unlikely quarter.

Through the painter Fortin, I met a German scholar and dealer in antiquities named Johann Gottlieb. The antique sculptures in Fortin's studio had mostly come from Gottlieb, and Gottlieb often commissioned Fortin to make paintings or sculpture that he could sell as antique or Renaissance pieces.

I first encountered Gottlieb quite by chance at Fortin's studio. Gottlieb asked if I could serve as his assistant. I suspected what kind of services he had in mind, so I refused and said nothing to Joseph. But he was persistent and kept returning to the studio on days he knew I'd be there. When he realised how much I had learned about antique art, he offered me a job assisting him in research, writing descriptions of the objects to be sold, and packing them for shipment. I agreed.

I loved going to his apartment with its view down to the piazza in front of the church of the Gesù. I figured the arrangement with Gottlieb was safe because he was old and feeble. Mostly he just liked to look at boys the way he liked to look at sculpture or drawings. He seemed to prefer drawings because they were always available while the boys were unpredictable and difficult to control.

Eventually he did ask me to find attractive boys he could undress and fondle. He sometimes asked them to tie him up and take a whip or cane to him. That would lead to his frigging himself furiously. In my mind, all of this was quite innocent. I hardly ever let him touch me, and he promised he would say nothing to Joseph.

He was a silly old goat, slow and fussy, and with his stooped appearance, thick spectacles, and greasy unkempt hair, quite unattractive. However, he gave me free access to his small but excellent library and assisted me in my study of Greek and Roman history and art.

"The ancients are the basis for our civilisation, mein junger Jacopo," he would say.

"The fountainhead of sodomy and pederasty," I would reply.

"I don't like that word 'sodomy.' It was the elders teaching the young. Art, literature, science. Plato, Socrates, Alcibiades."

"Of course. Just like the men today who meet boys at the Colosseum." My flippant tone annoyed Gottlieb, but he learned not to take offense.

I was awed by his knowledge at first, but over time I saw he was not as wise as he thought. He was often fooled by the forgeries his southern Italian contacts sold him. Of course, it is possible he knew they were fakes but figured his customers would not know or perhaps even care.

The trouble began when Gottlieb bought a spectacular ivory, reputedly Roman but possibly a recent forgery, from a Corsican with a dubious past. The ivory was tubular and slightly tapered, like an elephant's tusk, hollow on the inside. I suppose it was nominally a drinking cup, but it was probably intended to be mostly decorative. It sat in a little bronze saddle affixed to a marble base. You could lift the ivory off the saddle to examine the images carved on its surface.

At first glance, it looked like many other antique *objets de vertu*. Two central figures, a young man and a bearded one, stood facing each other in a central cartouche carved in high relief. The older handing a *kylix* to the younger, a typical love offering. However, on closer inspection, the figures in low relief encircling the cartouche were highly erotic scenes of nude youths wrestling, engaged in sporting events, and older men courting and coupling with them. With its tubular shape and bulbous head, it was easy to imagine how the object might have been used to substitute for the male member.

It was difficult to resist caressing the ivory. It had a pale cream colour delicately traced with darker veins. I loved to run my hands over the coupling men and boys, imagining the heat the ivory's irregular surface would generate as it slid in and out of one of the boys. I wondered what it would feel like to put it in my mouth, to lick the slick surface, or feel the head pushing against the back of my throat. Or inserted into my arse. I confess I tried all these things more than once when Gottlieb was out of the apartment.

Gottlieb was intensely proud of this ivory. He didn't want to sell it. If anyone asked, he quoted a price so exorbitant he was sure it would discourage anyone.

I frequently saw Fortin at Gottlieb's. Both were members of the Académie Ganymède and attended the salons of Contessa P. One day Gottlieb asked Fortin to do a portrait of him in his study. In the picture, the ivory—actually a pair of them, since Fortin included a mirror image of it—occupied a prominent place on the shelves behind his desk. Gottlieb displayed the finished portrait prominently on the wall beside them.

So many customers asked about the ivory that Gottlieb decided to let life imitate art. He asked Fortin to make another piece, identical but in mirror image. Gottlieb took the original to a Corsican craftsman who specialized in replicas. When I told Joseph that Gottlieb was having a replica made, he immediately said he would pay to have a second replica made, this one with an image of the two of us in the medallion. We posed for Fortin so that he could make a detailed cartoon that he gave to the Corsican.

When the two new ivories arrived, Gottlieb notified Joseph, who picked up the piece he commissioned without telling me. Presumably he intended to present it to me on my next birthday or some other occasion. But in the circumstances that soon followed, it was forgotten and was shipped back to London along with many other things Joseph left behind when he departed from Rome.

The two ivories that Gottlieb now had were amazingly similar to each other. Gottlieb himself appears to have forgotten which was the antique and which the copy. He didn't seem to care.

Then, to Gottlieb's great surprise, a wealthy English marquess, another member of the Académie Ganymède, met his outrageous price. Gottlieb was thrilled, particularly since he now had two pieces, could sell one, keep one, and could commission more if needed. The marquess placed his piece on a mantel in the bedroom of the suite of rooms he kept on the Piazza di Spagna, where it was much admired by visitors. He promised to pay in a fortnight after inspection by an advisor he consulted on his purchases of art.

Gottlieb was also immensely relieved. His business had been slow, and the marquess's purchase would finally allow him to repay a pressing debt to the Corsican. He even commissioned some new "antiquities."

Unfortunately for Gottlieb, the advisor, a professor from Hamburg, pronounced the ivory a forgery. The collector brought it back to Gottlieb, berated him, and threatened to tell everyone he knew that Gottlieb was a fraud.

In the meantime, the Corsican was now pressing hard for his money. He warned that if the money was not forthcoming within the week, he could not vouch for Gottlieb's continued good health.

I was unaware of any of this when I went to visit Gottlieb as usual on a Tuesday afternoon. No sooner had I entered his rooms than Gottlieb started accusing me of stealing some of his antique coins. He was in a rage and called me a thief, a *puttana,* and many other insulting names.

I became furious. To be sure, I had taken a few coins, but I knew they were not valuable. "I have taken nothing, you silly old man!" I shouted and walked out the door of his apartment, slamming it behind me.

After only a minute Gottlieb came running after me down the

stairs, "Jacopo, please, I'm so sorry. I'm not myself today. I had another visit from the Corsican. Please come back."

"You have insulted me," I shot back over my shoulder as I walked away.

I was not angered so much by the accusation of theft. It was, after all, legitimate. But in his anxiety, Gottlieb had betrayed his belief that I was still just a hired boy. That was no different from the way I had been treated by many men in my earlier life. At that time, I had thought of myself as simply a *bardassa* and had let it pass. But now, after I had learned so much, after Joseph had treated me with such respect, and I had learned to move in the company of accomplished men, I saw myself in a different light.

I was angry. Two days later I came by his rooms early in the morning. I said nothing about the recent incident, pretending I had forgotten and told him about a boy I had recruited for him for that evening. "His name is August. An Austrian. You will be able to converse freely in your native language. I'm sure he will provide you with a most satisfactory experience."

"I don't hire boys for their conversation," Gottlieb said turning away. Then, thinking better of it, he turned back and asked, "Is August attractive?"

"Many men consider him to be at least as attractive as me." This was not quite true. I also didn't add that August was poorly educated, had a wicked temper, and was constantly getting into trouble with the authorities.

"Have you told him what I like?"

"Yes. I believe you will find him experienced in all the appropriate techniques."

I instructed August to arrive at Gottlieb's rooms at ten in the evening and put on a mask before entering. I told him I would meet him at the door but not enter Gottlieb's rooms until after August had tied him up and blindfolded him. I had picked out a few pieces that I thought Gottlieb probably would not miss and that would fetch a little money.

August arrived late and drunk. After he entered, I heard Gottlieb shouting at him and heard him use my name several times. I understood enough German to know that he was calling both of us ugly names. August, in turn, started shouting insults back at him.

August had left the door ajar, so I could watch what was happening. He grabbed Gottlieb, now blindfolded, by his right arm and twisted it sharply behind him.

"Follow my orders now and behave, and I will not hurt you, you miserable old sodomite," he shouted. He gave the arm a vicious tug, which caused Gottlieb to scream, but August put his hand over Gottlieb's mouth and ordered him to undress. I was startled. I had rarely had the audacity to treat customers so roughly, but Gottlieb must not have been offended because he quickly responded, "Yes, Sir," and promptly obeyed.

August pulled out the chair from behind the desk and sat down. Gottlieb, naked and already half hard, was standing hunched over in a pathetic pose in the middle of the room.

"Get down on your knees and crawl over here, you worthless filth."

"Yes, Sir," Gottlieb croaked and crawled as quickly as he could across the threadbare carpet. Seen from behind, Gottlieb looked like a tired old animal that had lost its fur.

Sitting in the chair behind Gottlieb's desk, August turned toward Gottlieb and, with some difficulty, extricated his cock from the tight trousers he was wearing.

"Suck on this, you sick sodomite."

Gottlieb seemed eager to comply. While he was busy, August studied all the objects on Gottlieb's desk and on the shelves behind, interrupting his survey from time to time to slap the side of Gottlieb's face or pull his head forward long enough to make the old man gag. August let him take a single deep breath before pushing him back to his task.

Eventually August stood, went behind Gottlieb, took a length of rope out of the bag he had brought, and quickly fastened Gottlieb's wrists behind him. He then pulled a low bench from the opposite wall into the middle of the room, pulled Gottlieb to his feet, and pushed him face down on the bench so that Gottlieb's arse and genitals hung out on one end and his head on the other.

I had no idea that August was so proficient in this department of the business. Gottlieb didn't seem at all alarmed. He squirmed on the bench and muttered some things in German, but August promptly put a leather gag in his mouth and secured it with a strap. Gottlieb could have easily pulled free or slid off the bench at this point, but he gave no indication he wanted to. August secured him to the bench with additional lengths of rope. Everything was going reasonably well.

I entered the room. I looked down at Gottlieb. I was surprised by how old and flabby he looked, the skin on his arse the colour and texture of dirty potatoes. While he was still blindfolded and immobilized on the bench, August started to go through Gottlieb's desk. He took far more items than I had instructed and put them in the bag he had brought. Then, before I could object, August did something that was not part of our plan.

He grabbed one of the ivories that was sitting on Gottlieb's desk and started to push it into Gottlieb's arse. Gottlieb at first made noises that, through the gag mask, sounded like he wanted August to push harder. However, he soon started writhing on the bench, pulling frantically against the restraints.

"Take the gag out of his mouth and put this in instead," August barked at me as he handed me the second piece of ivory. This was happening so fast that I'm not quite clear what followed. All that I remember is that when he saw a quantity of blood starting to drip onto the floor, August grabbed his bag and fled. I remember thinking that I should untie Gottlieb and see how badly hurt he was, but I knew I was in a dangerous situation. I pulled the ivory from Gottlieb's mouth, put it into my own bag, and ran from the building.

I don't know why I kept the ivory. Perhaps I thought I was removing evidence of my participation. Or maybe I coveted the piece and thought to keep it for myself or sell it. I don't remember.

You may not believe this, but to this day, everything that happened after I walked into Gottlieb's room is a blur, perhaps because I have revised it so many times in my mind to absolve myself of some of the responsibility.

Once outside and safely away from Gottlieb's, I stopped for a moment and realised the gravity of my situation. I was shaking all over. I ran to Joseph's apartment, sprinted up the main staircase, and banged on his door. He appeared in his robe, half asleep. He saw immediately that I was wild with fear. He motioned for me to come in.

"I think Gottlieb has been hurt," I blurted out.

"Gottlieb? Who is Gottlieb? Do you mean Johann Gottlieb, the art dealer?"

"Yes, that old German."

"What do you mean you think he has been hurt?"

"When I was almost at his door, I saw a man running out. He was tied up with blood on the floor."

"Who was on the floor? Gottlieb? Why were you there? Who was running out?"

Joseph seemed concerned but was able to stay calm. That allowed me to compose myself. Though I was still crying, I was able to think. I concocted a plausible story. "I was helping him deliver packages to his customers. When I saw him on the floor and all the blood, I ran."

"Why didn't you call for help?"

"I was afraid people would think I did it."

"Who did you see running from the flat?"

"It was a young man. He had a bag."

"So, it was a robbery?"

"I guess. The desk drawers had been pulled out and the flat was in disorder."

Joseph seemed to believe me. "When you say Gottlieb had been hurt, what did you see? How had he been hurt? How badly?"

"I don't know. When I saw the blood, I just ran."

Joseph was silent for a long time, then he kissed me, told me to calm down, and said we would have to think about what to do next. I was relieved he didn't ask why I was delivering packages for Gottlieb, why I was at his flat so late, what was in the bag I had brought with me.

We talked about going to the police. In the end he agreed that going there could put me in a dangerous position. I never knew if this decision was for my sake or his. If there were any scandal that linked me to the robbery, it might involve him.

Joseph kept asking me if I was sure no one had witnessed my presence in the building. I told him that I was sure no one had ever seen me in the building. That might have been true.

Neither Joseph nor I slept that night. The next morning Joseph went out to see what he could learn. He heard from one of the policemen at the door to Gottlieb's building that the old man had been found dead that morning by his housekeeper. The policeman refused to say anything further.

Joseph returned to the apartment and informed me of Gottlieb's death. Then he went downstairs and told the concierge he would be leaving that day because of pressing business in London. He paid visits to a few friends to tell them the same thing. Next, he packed a single large trunk and arranged to have his remaining things packed and sent either to London or to a hotel in Paris.

I collected my clothes and the few other things I owned and packed them in a chest Joseph had bought me when I moved from the Archbishop's. I was concerned about the ivory. I was afraid to take it with me but even more afraid of leaving it in Joseph's apartment.

I had no idea if the ivory I had was the possible genuine antiquity, or it was the copy. In the end, it didn't matter. It was beautifully executed and highly desirable—at least for a select group of men who wouldn't care about its provenance. At least for the time being, I didn't want anyone to know I had it, so I sewed it into the lining of my travel chest.

By the end of the day, we were on a diligence that Joseph had hired to take us to Civitavecchia, where we boarded an overnight steamer to Marseilles. The next day we travelled by rail to Aix-en-Provence and from there by steamer to Chalon. We stayed the night and took the first train in the morning to Paris.

I had left behind one life. I was starting another. Only two things united them: the ivory and Joseph. And Joseph knew nothing of the ivory.

Chapter 7:

"Fabrizio"

I had never been more than a few miles outside Rome, so the trip
to Paris should have been a great adventure for me. However, I
was so afraid someone would come after me or the customs officials at Marseilles would search my trunk, it barely registered. On
the boat from Civitavecchia to Marseille, I tried as best I could to
sink into a corner of the compartment and make myself inconspicuous. Even between Chalon and Paris I was so unsettled that I
hardly looked out the windows. Neither Joseph nor I said much
during the entire trip.

We arrived at the Embarcadère de Lyon in Paris late in the
morning. On exiting the station, we found ourselves directly
opposite a large prison called Mazas. I was taken aback, but
quickly decided it was a mere coincidence. We took a cab across
the city and checked into the Hôtel Bristol on the Place Vendôme.
Joseph registered as Mister Jeremiah Stewardson from Birmingham with his personal assistant, Fabrizio Croce. I never knew
why he chose that name, but I liked it. At that moment I became
Fabrizio.

During our first week in Paris, Joseph found an apartment near
the hotel just off the Boulevard de la Madeleine. The apartment
had a spacious set of rooms on the second floor with elaborate
parquet floors, and decorative plaster ceilings. Tall, glazed doors
provided access to tiny balconies with wrought iron railings. They
afforded fine views of the bustle on the street below. I had never
before been more than a few miles from my birthplace. This was a
new world.

We came and went without much scrutiny just as we had in
Rome. There was a main staircase just inside the building's outer

door that Joseph used and a service stair in the courtyard for me. We acted as though he occupied the main rooms in front and I the servants' quarters at the back.

We stayed mostly out of sight for a month and then started going out in public occasionally. Joseph reverted to his own name, but we decided I would continue to be Fabrizio Croce. I let my hair grow and started sporting a beard. I wore clothes seen on gentlemen older than myself. I even affected the use of spectacles, although the lenses were only clear glass.

I loved my new look. These small changes made me feel older and more confident. However, Joseph was not happy with them. He said nothing, but it was obvious I now seemed less like a boy and more like a man. I could feel a tension as we tried to reach a new equilibrium.

We manufactured a plausible story that I was the son of a merchant in Rome, that Joseph and I had met by chance in the studio of an artist, and that I was acting as his personal secretary, his protégé who would eventually have his own business.

To forestall any possible association with Gottlieb's death, we explained that we had relocated to Paris well before that event. When there was no indication that anyone had any reason to believe otherwise, our anxiety gradually decreased.

Fortunately, the few people in Paris who had known Joseph in Rome either had not met me or didn't recognise me. Most of Joseph's friends and acquaintances in Paris probably guessed the real nature of my relationship but were sympathetic and not inclined to say anything.

Initially, I was homesick. I missed my family, my friends, and the life Joseph and I had built together in Rome. Shortly after arriving in Paris, I sent a letter to my mother apologizing for my abrupt departure and assuring her that I was alive and safe. I told her that, although I had done nothing wrong, I was afraid if I stayed in Rome I would be falsely linked to Gottlieb's murder.

I asked that she and whoever read her my letter would tell no one I had written. I said I would welcome receiving any news of the family by letter sent to the *poste restante* at the central post office in Paris in care of Émile Dupont, another new name.

I received a letter several weeks later from my brother Gaetano. "Mama cried when I read her your letter. She said you were the fourth of her five sons to disappear from her life. You know that Vigo died while in the Palatine Guard and that Carlo was murdered. What you don't know is that Paolo, has been imprisoned for theft. Now you are in exile Paris. She will also lose me though in a happier way. I have advanced to the novitiate in the Camaldolese order, a branch of the Benedictines, and I will be devoting myself to solitary contemplation at their retreat near Castel Gandolfo.

"Mama's sole consolation is Isabella. Miraculously, she somehow caught the attention of a prosperous merchant visiting from Perugia. A better match than anyone could have imagined. They will soon wed, and Isabella will move to Perugia, but her future husband has frequent business in Rome, so Mama and Isabella will see each other," Gaetano continued.

"I should also alert you to the fact that the police came to our rooms shortly after you left and asked Mama a number of questions. Something about the Gottlieb murder. As you can imagine, she was indignant that they would have any reason to think you were involved. They apparently also questioned a great many other young men in the neighbourhood."

He closed with the new name he would use at the novitiate—Valentino—and said he would pray for me.

For a week or two my anxiety level rose, but when I heard nothing more about the murder I relaxed. I concluded that the police interviews had yielded nothing for me to worry about. I had no idea whether they found August, but I didn't think he would have said anything about me. I was almost certain my name was not on anything in Gottlieb's rooms. As usual, I said nothing to Joseph.

Slowly, I shed my past and became a handsome and promising young Parisian gentleman. My obligations to the past were broken. I was free to rise.

Joseph took private lessons from Tony Robert-Fleury, a distinguished painter well known for his historical scenes. With Joseph's assistance, I found a job at the Drouot auction house. At first, I just packed and unpacked crates and arranged objects for sale. Soon I was doing research on the objects that came in. I loved my time there. Days I sharpened my skills in assessing works at Drouot. Nights I spent with Joseph in the big bed in his corner bedroom with the tall windows and heavy drapes. I was soon happier in Paris than I had ever been in Rome.

When we had the time, Joseph and I would go from gallery to gallery in Paris looking at art. We were particularly attracted to the old shops on the Left Bank near the École des Beaux-Arts. Joseph would buy sculpture and paintings and ship them back to England to add to his collection.

Because I was now earning money at Drouot and had few expenses, I was able to rent a small room of my own at the top of an ancient apartment building near the church of Saint-Merri in the Marais. I spent almost no time there, but it was useful when I wanted to meet friends and customers without disturbing Joseph.

Yes, the answer to your question is yes—I had started to ply my trade again. I was perhaps even more in demand in Paris than in Rome. I had grown in size and strength, and my decision to grow a beard may have added to my appeal. I did the work partly for money but partly because it bolstered my confidence and my circle of acquaintances. Some of the most distinguished Parisian gentlemen came to ask me politely to work my rough magic on them.

The location of my apartment was fortuitous because I grew to love the church of Saint-Merri. Although I felt far from the blinkered teachings of the Church, I had fond memories of Santa Maria in Trastevere and still loved the pageant of the Mass. Seeing the young choir boys always made me stop and reflect. How I had wanted to be one at their age! How innocent they looked! And how far from innocent I had become in so few years.

My job at the auction house allowed me to buy some pieces of my own. I was proud of my small but growing collection and pleased to find that I knew at least as much as many of the dealers. I started reselling some of my artifacts, and, unbeknownst to Joseph, even a few of his. I became quite an expert in distinguishing genuine pieces from later copies and forgeries. I decided I wanted to open a gallery of my own. Joseph thought that this was a worthy goal and encouraged me.

In those days, Joseph and I were everything to each other. Our physical intimacy deepened considerably. Soon after we moved to the apartment, Joseph asked me whether I would object to having a cat. I told him that my relations with cats had never been warm. However, I was grateful that Joseph had asked for my permission and made no objection.

A man named Griswold who worked for his family was coming to Paris with some papers for Joseph to sign. He brought with him one of the kittens from a large feline family that was resident in the stables at his family's country estate.

Griswold arrived at our apartment earlier than expected. Thinking it was Solange, the woman who did our laundry, I opened the door to find a pinched, dour man dressed all in black. He was carrying a cage with a kitten of a particularly hideous shade of orange. The kitten immediately took to Joseph. Both Griswold and the kitten tried their best to ignore my presence.

Joseph promptly named the cat Queen Victoria, as he had three previous cats. I was never sure this was meant as tribute to the British monarch or a joke, but the name suited her. Her Highness immediately assumed she was empress and made it clear that she was not fond of the attention I was receiving from Joseph. Joseph, for his part, doted on the kitten, who quickly became an even more disagreeable cat. She seemed to have a similarly low opinion of me.

One evening, as I was flat on my back, legs in the air, with Joseph vigorously penetrating me, Queen Victoria jumped onto the bed, started hissing, and crept within inches of my head. She smelled strongly of sardines. I was reasonably sure she was about to deploy her claws on my face.

I looked up and saw that Joseph was so preoccupied he was completely oblivious to the cat. Queen Victoria raised one paw, but just then Joseph made a great last thrust, letting out a loud roar and collapsed on top of me, sending Her Highness scrambling off the bed and across the room. Then, as usual, Joseph promptly fell asleep. After that I was careful to make sure to keep the door closed, and the cat and I maintained a state of mutual resentment for the duration of our time together.

Joseph eventually added a new group of friends to his circle, including a number of Englishmen who had fled some scandal across the Channel. For the first time, he told some of them we were lovers. It was remarkable to be welcomed by them openly as his lover and not his servant, although a few made rude advances when Joseph was out of earshot.

These days of peace and happiness were too good to last. One day Joseph told me he was expecting a visit from his younger brother, Rupert. I had heard Joseph talk about Rupert, but as far as I knew, the two had not seen each other since Joseph left for the Continent. I asked if I could meet him. I was not surprised at Joseph's emphatic negative response, but something about Joseph's manner was worrisome.

My premonitions were justified. No sooner had Rupert departed, than Joseph announced he had to move back to London. I pleaded with him to tell me why. He was distraught and would say nothing. I wondered if his parents had somehow heard about me and threatened to cut him off.

I also feared he had tired of me. Maybe I had become too old and was no longer the boy he first encountered. Or perhaps now that I could support myself, the relationship between us had changed. More worrisome was the possibility he had found out that I had not always told him the truth. In any case, he said he had no choice. I told him I understood, but inside I was devastated. How quickly he seemed to turn away from me and from our life together!

I think it was on that day that I first thought I might be in love with Joseph. Before then I had known that I enjoyed our time together, and I greatly admired him, his good nature and his honesty. However, I had always told myself that my primary reason for wanting to be with Joseph was the help he gave me. I never wanted to believe I loved him. I had loved my mother and Carlo, but this was different. I still could not decide. Was I really in love or was this a temporary feeling triggered by the fact that he was leaving me?

In the days that followed, we talked a little about the possibility of reuniting, either permanently or for shorter periods when Joseph would return to Paris, or I would visit London. One evening Joseph took out a matching set of rings, each with a superb cameo portrait at the centre. He put one on my finger and one on his own, saying that they would serve as a memory of our time together. I was overwhelmed. I pulled him tight and covered him with kisses.

There was a tearful farewell on the day that he left. I remember standing with him on the platform of the Gare du Nord. Then he did something I never imagined an English gentleman like him would ever do in public. He leaned over, pulled me into a fierce hug and kissed me full on the lips, paying no attention to the startled looks on the faces of the passengers on the platform near us.

Then, after Joseph had boarded the train, I too did something I had not done in many years. Despite all my efforts to maintain my composure, I felt tears streaming down my face. I brushed them away but soon gave up any effort to conceal my grief. Friends of departing passengers still on the platform stared. I saw them make comments to each other as the train pulled out of the station. I was too distraught to care.

They all eventually left leaving me standing there alone as the train receded in the distance. Were my tears caused by Joseph's departure or because I was once again alone in the world?

I received a telegram from Joseph as soon as he reached London. For a few months we wrote each other frequently. He said he missed me. But I could not stop wondering. Did he really miss me, or was there something else? Had he learned something about me? Or had some trivial thing finally pushed him to decide he no longer wished to continue our relationship?

I had never really known what Joseph was thinking. On the surface he seemed entirely open and forthcoming. And, as far as I could remember, he never actually lied to me. But he also maintained that impenetrable English reserve.

For a few years, we would see each other occasionally when he came to Paris or when I travelled to London, but Joseph always insisted on meeting in a public place where we would encounter no one either of us knew.

I was happy when he bought a house in St John's Wood. I thought we could meet there. It would allow us to rekindle the attachment we had formed Paris. But Joseph was adamant that he had renounced his former life.

Then, at the end of the day on what turned out to be my last visit with Joseph, we were standing outside a restaurant in a remote and decidedly unfashionable part of Camberwell. We were about to say goodbye. At the very last minute, with eyes averted, he told me he was engaged to marry a woman named Emily Tallmadge, the daughter of a British admiral.

He said he was sorry, but he felt he had to break off all contact with me and aspects of his past. When I protested, he grew agitated. When I pressed him, he went further and said he never loved me, that he had just been lonely and wanted the companionship.

I was furious. I was certain he had felt more than that in both Rome and Paris. I could not understand why he would say such a hurtful thing. I was also angry that he had waited until the last minute to give me this news and did so in public on the pavement outside a restaurant. I was so upset I'm not sure what I would have done had not some people walking by stopped to stare.

Without even saying goodbye, I turned and walked to a nearby taxi stand, caught a cab back to the hotel, packed my bags, and took the next train to Paris. On the trip, I remember going through an entire range of emotions, at first mostly anger at Joseph, but increasingly mixed with the nagging suspicion that I had been to blame for not being honest with him.

After my return to Paris, I felt empty. I kept telling myself that, all things considered, my life was still good. After all, I was no longer a *bardassa* in Rome but a promising young gentleman with an apartment, a career at a prominent auction house, and a small circle of friends. Still, on some days the feeling of loss was crushing.

Eventually the ache started to recede. I met and started to court the only daughter of an affluent couple from Caen. Amélie aspired to become a sculptress. She must have been aware that many of my friends were men who preferred the company of men, but she was so eager to be clear of her family that she didn't notice or perhaps didn't care.

She was pretty and sweet. I initially thought her naïve. Only later did I realize she was more aware of everything happening around her than she allowed anyone to suspect. She knew exactly how to steer events in the direction she wished without seeming to direct them at all. We saw each other for several years and developed a friendship although not any degree of intimacy.

I was eager to start an enterprise on my own. Between what I had learned from Gottlieb and what I had picked up in Paris, I knew as much about the market for classical art as anyone in the city. During one of my visits with Amélie at her parents' house, I brought some of the artifacts I had collected and spoke to Amélie's father about my desire to open my own gallery. He was encouraging. One week later, I proposed to Amélie. She was surprised but appeared to be pleased by my sudden willingness to wed.

I soon came to see that her mother was the one I should have spoken to about marrying Amélie and opening my gallery. She made the big decisions in the family, and she was sceptical at first because she could learn so little about my life before Paris. Nevertheless, after seeing how successful I had become in the auction house, how intrigued Amélie's father was with the prospect of a son-in-law with a gallery in Paris, and knowing how much Amélie wanted to be married, she ultimately gave her blessing. She instructed her husband to help set me up in business. The wedding at their church in Caen was one of that city's social highlights of the year.

A generous loan from Amélie's father allowed me to quit my job at Drouot's and make a trip to Naples to see if I could find some of the men who had supplied Gottlieb, and especially the Corsican who was Gottlieb's chief source. I found the Corsican and through him was able to establish sources for the artifacts I wanted to sell. After a few weeks, I was able to send back to Paris several trunks full of artifacts.

I had grown impatient with the prevailing view that genuine antique pieces were valuable and recent work of little value. I had already learned from my experience with Gottlieb that the artists who made the forgeries could produce work that was indistinguishable from genuine antique work even to the expert eye. It made no sense to me that modern work sold for a tiny fraction of the price of antique work, which itself could be a copy or a forgery. If a piece was beautiful, what difference should it make who made it or when? Nevertheless, I was determined to be as honest as was prudent about the provenance of pieces I would sell.

I rented the ground and second floor of a building on the rue de Seine. My gallery was a great success. I was soon selling to men from all over Europe and the Americas. Money from Amélie's family allowed me to secure a large and commodious apartment in the building next door. I joined the kitchen of our family home to a small apartment I had created at the upper level of my gallery by a small passage.

I had some ideas about how to furnish our new home, but Amélie wanted to take the lead. She threw herself into the task with obvious relish, engaging an entire army of decorators and craftsmen. The work went on for months. The shop, on the other hand, was entirely my domain, and I was happy to spend a good deal of my time there.

We also bought a little villa with walls in imitation half-timbering and embellished with spiky wood trim in Houlgate, a town on the Channel that her father was promoting as a resort. At first, Amélie spent most of her time in Paris in the company of a slightly disreputable circle of artists living in garrets in Montparnasse. But after the birth of our two daughters, Eugénie and Sophie, she started to spend less time in Paris and more time in Houlgate.

It was convenient for her because it was near enough to her parents for occasional visits but not too close. It was certainly convenient for me because it allowed me to spend more time on my own and make new acquaintances in Paris.

I was generally content with my life. After the birth of our daughters, Amélie and I were no longer intimate. I suspect she was secretly delighted that so little was expected of her. She developed her own set of friends and enthusiasms. During her time at Houlgate, she spent an increasing amount of time with a young English woman named Alice. Alice was hired as a tutor for our children to perfect their English and polish their manners in preparation for entering society. Alice, plain in appearance but cheerful and good-hearted, soon played a large role in Amélie's life.

This arrangement suited us both. On occasion, Amélie would return to Paris, and we would go out in society, to the opera, the theatre, a ball. We presented ourselves as one of the most attractive and happiest couples in the capital. I loved my daughters. Eugénie, the older, was outgoing and boyish, eager to be outdoors riding horses. Sophie was more reserved and preferred to stay indoors and read. I was always happy when my daughters and I managed to be together, and they seemed to be quite happy with the arrangement that Amélie, Alice, and I had drifted into.

But I never forgot Joseph. For a few years I stayed informed of his activities through individuals we knew in Paris who kept in touch with him. Eventually even this stopped, as Joseph systematically cut off contact with almost all people we had known together in Rome or Paris

Chapter 8:

Liam

One of the few individuals I knew who was still in contact with Joseph was a gallery owner named Jérôme. Joseph and I had met him in Paris where he had been a student at the École des Beaux-Arts. Living in a squalid garret with three other unkempt students, Jérôme at that time was a serious young man, determined to succeed despite the poverty of his family. He was also the first Socialist I encountered.

I was amazed that Joseph seemed sympathetic to some of Jérôme's political ideas. I suppose Joseph, with his family's connections and wealth, could afford to entertain thoughts of levelling society. I was the one who should have been sympathetic. I was the one who had been ill-used by a society that made some men wealthy and powerful, often through no effort of their own, but made the majority of us poor. But I never had time to nurse my grudges. I was too busy rising out of the position society had tried to assign me.

Jérôme eventually gave up on being an artist. And, after he met an affluent, older Scottish gentleman named Hamish, he gave up on Socialism. He and Hamish seemed quite happy together and moved to London. Eventually, at my suggestion, Jérôme opened a gallery on Old Bond Street loosely modelled on my own.

On one of my visits to London, Jérôme confirmed a suspicion I had formed in my mind. He told me that Joseph had resumed his meetings with young working-class men.

"Our friend Joseph seems to have become two different people. When I visit Barrington House, I am shocked to find a man who has become prematurely old. His clothing is monotone with collars so tight they seem to be choking him. But he is recognisably still Joseph Stapleton, Viscount Barrington.

"But at the house in St John's Wood, he seems younger, happier, even a bit silly. On one occasion when I had stopped by of an evening, Joseph was wearing a ridiculous oriental robe and sitting like a Chinaman on a kind of low divan covered in an old damask fabric. On his lap was a boy who actually appeared to be from China."

"Who do you think knows about what happens at St John's Wood?" I asked.

"As far as I can determine, I'm the only one other than Joseph's brother, Rupert. I believe Rupert strongly disapproves but says nothing because Joseph is now the head of the family and the director of the bank. It appears that Joseph has entertained a succession of boys, some of them quite young and often quite rough."

I met one of Joseph's boys on my next trip to London. During a visit to Jérôme's gallery, as I was preparing to leave, a young man, probably about twenty, with long, fashionably unkempt chestnut hair, extremely tight trousers, and a billowing light cotton shirt, entered the gallery. He greeted Jérôme, who did not introduce us, but the young man gave me a bold appraising glance as he walked by. I felt a familiar shiver.

After he had ducked into the back room, Jérôme whispered "His name is Liam. He is the latest "protégé" of our mutual friend. He is living at the house in St John's Wood."

Several minutes later, as the young man was leaving with a set of parcels under his arm, Jérôme introduced us. Liam shook my hand, holding it longer than most people would consider polite and stared directly at me.

From his clothing and accent, I guessed Liam was from London's East End. He told me he wanted to be an artist. I suspected this ambition had been suggested by Joseph. Despite my instant dislike, I could not deny he was handsome. And I was keenly aware of the fire in his eyes.

"Come back with me to look at my work," he said in a peremptory tone.

"Where do you live?"

"My studio is in the house of my friend, Mr. Stewardson. To-day is a good day. Mrs. Farrell, the housekeeper, is normally there, but she is gone to visit her sister." He gave me the address on Carlton Hill.

"Very good," I told him. "You go ahead, and I will probably look in on you later this afternoon." Jérôme, who was standing only a few feet away, could barely contain his amusement.

I felt a mix of curiosity and anger. Why would Joseph abandon me only to consort with a silly boy like Liam? Even as I was thinking this, I realized that Liam reminded me in some ways of myself as I must have looked in Rome. I would never, except at the tavern in Trastevere, have acted as brazenly. But there was a certain similarity in the figure and the facial features, and I could clearly detect in Liam the same driving ambition. It was a little like encountering my younger self. It made sense that Joseph would be attracted.

I confess, though, that my most powerful emotion was a blazing lust. Here was this handsome young man almost challenging me to bend him to my will. I could picture Liam kneeling in front of me, naked, wrists cuffed behind his back, his eyes downcast, willing to follow my every command. And—I'll be honest with you—there was an element of revenge. He was Joseph's boy, but for today, his behaviour all but guaranteed I could make him mine.

After thirty minutes delay—so I would not appear too eager—I took a cab to Carlton Hill. After ringing the doorbell there was a pause long enough for me to start thinking no one was home. But then I heard footsteps. Liam opened the door just a crack and then stood behind it to allow me to enter.

I immediately saw the reason for his caution. He was wearing only the thin cotton shirt he wore at the gallery, rolled up at the sleeves and unbuttoned, and his drawers, short and so sheer they did little to obscure his arousal. The white clothes set off the rosy tint—undoubtedly enhanced by his excited state—that showed through his smooth pale skin. His lips curled in a knowing seductive, smile.

I waited for him to make the first move. Without saying a word, he walked toward the stairs, looking over his shoulder to see if I would follow. Upstairs in a bedroom he took off his shirt. I stood outside in the doorway watching him.

"Would your Mr. Stewardson approve of what you are doing?" I asked.

"Surely not," he replied with a laugh. "I promised I'd not be entertaining visitors here, but he's at his office all the day. Nothing I do here'd have any effect on him. I can be satisfying all his needs in the evening no matter what I am doing in the day. Besides, you know, you are living in Paris; he is living in Birmingham; and you'd likely never be meeting him. Or that I'd ever be seeing you again." He carefully folded his shirt and placed it on a chair.

His composure and cynicism astonished me. I walked into the chamber. He was still in his drawers, fully tented out, standing only a foot away from me and looking straight into my eyes.

I said nothing but leaned down to pull down his drawers. His cock sprang up, almost brushing my face. I stood back up and pushed him hard on his chest. He stumbled back onto the bed. I turned him over so I could render his arse bright red before entering him. He proved to be deliciously submissive and moaned loudly. I promptly clamped my hand over his mouth to muffle his moaning, but he still made a lot of noise, so I took his drawers, stuffed them into his mouth.

I slapped him hard as I continued to penetrate him, and grabbing him by his hair, pulled his head back. He started to writhe wildly and tried to say something. I paid no attention. The combination of lust and revenge was too much, and I increased the pace of my thrusting. Just as I was about to spend, I pulled out of him, turned him over, and shot all over his face.

After I finished, he lay still on the bed, weeping profusely. I was embarrassed and worried I had been too rough with him, so I took him in my arms. He stopped crying and started kissing me all over my face and neck, thanking me, and mumbling endearments. Once I was aware that he was not angry and had actually, at least in retrospect, enjoyed the treatment, I wiped his face with his drawers and gave him kisses in return.

He started to stroke himself, but I told him to stop and ordered him to put the sticky drawers and shirt back on. He was reluctant, but he obeyed. I let him sit on my lap and kiss me for a while longer. He was obviously still quite excited, but I got up, put on my clothes and walked downstairs. He followed in his drawers and shirt.

When we reached the bottom of the stairs, I turned and faced him. He had a devilish look on his heavily flushed face and seemed almost proud to be displaying his dishevelled clothes, wild hair, and tented drawers. He didn't ask for any money, but I gave him some. He examined the coins in his hand and told me he was eager to be "returning to work." However, I pulled out more coins and asked if he would be willing to talk for a few minutes about his Mr. Stewardson.

"I don't think Jeremiah—Mr. Stewardson—would like me to be talking about him," he said. I just kept looking at him. He looked back at the coins in his hand and said, "But I suppose it mightn't hurt, particularly if it's worth a little more to you." I reached into my pocket, pulled out a full crown and put it in his palm.

"Jeremiah is the head of a big company in Birmingham. They are making women's clothes and things," Liam told me. "He's living there with his wife and four children. He says he loves his wife and his family, but he is needing us boys every now and again. He went to a fancy school and then to Oxford and all that, and he speaks real good. He says he was once wanting to be an artist. He has no time for that now. Now he is finding a young artist like myself to help. He calls himself a patron."

"How did you meet Mr. Stewardson?"

"We met at the . . . um, I don't remember. It was over a year ago."

"How often do you see him?"

"Jeremiah has a main office in Birmingham but another one in London. When he comes to London, he usually visits here. Once or twice a week. Sometimes during the day and sometimes after he finishes meetings. But he only stays here overnight with me once or twice a month. Usually on a weekend. Makes a special trip from his home in Birmingham."

"Are you glad to see him when he does come?"

"Well, I'm grateful, of course. I was in a bad way before I meet him. He doesn't mind that I am not comfortable doing everything he wants. And he does not mind that I have a sweetheart, as long as I am not bringing her here. And he has taught me a lot."

"So, you prefer girls to men?"

"Yes, I think that being with men is dirty. And sinful." He opened his mouth to say something more but stopped. "Pardon me. I think I am offending. . ."

After a long awkward pause, I replied, "I'm not offended. But if you prefer girls to men, why did you invite me back here?"

"You looked interesting. And even though you're old, you're still handsome enough. And you looked like you might be generous."

"I suppose I should think you for that compliment?"

Liam seems not to have detected my sarcasm. "I like some men. It all depends."

"Depends on what?"

"Some men can be giving me, you know, things girls cannot."

"Like what?"

"Like what we just did."

"Did you like what I did to you?" Liam looked ill at ease, so I continued. "Does Mr. Stewardson not give you what you need?"

"Usually with Jeremiah it is just kissing and, you know, the usual things. Once he tried to give me orders, tie me up and call me names, but Jeremiah is too small and old to be forceful. So, he wants me to play the man while he plays the boy. I like that better.

I am real good at satisfying men that way. The older men who like to be ordered around and penetrated. What Jeremiah teaches me about satisfying him is good for my business."

"Your 'business'? Does Jeremiah know about your business?"

"No, of course not. I would never tell him. He might turn me out. But it is something I need to do. I don't want to be ungrateful, because I am appreciating everything that Jeremiah does for me. But what he is giving me is not enough. So, I have my other business. You understand?"

I wondered if he was telling me all this to see if I might offer him a more lucrative patronage in Paris.

"You said that Mr. Stewardson taught you things," I asked. "What kind of things? About art?"

"Yes. Now I know what I am looking at when I go to museums."

"What does your Jeremiah do to help you become an artist?"

"He tells me what is good about what I am making and what is bad. He gives me other things also."

We were standing in the drawing room. I looked over at a collection of bronzes on a table. I recognised many of them as pieces that we had bought together in Rome and Paris.

Liam saw me looking at them. "Jeremiah brings back things when he goes to the continent."

"Does he keep other pieces of art here at this house?"

"Yes."

"I would very much like to see them."

He hesitated again, so I dropped another few coins into his hand. He said nothing but led me into a room panelled in dark wood that was obviously set up for use as an office or study. There was a large mahogany desk at the centre.

He opened a drawer in the desk and pulled out a large box filled with velvet pouches. As he opened the largest bag, I almost gasped out loud. It contained the ivory Joseph had asked Gottlieb to make for him, the one Fortin designed after we had posed for him in his studio.

I realized immediately what had happened. Joseph had intended this piece as a present for me, but with our sudden removal to Paris, it was packed up with many of his things and sent to London. Both of us forgot all about it.

But here, almost miraculously, I was holding it in my hand once again. I could feel tears welling up in my eyes. I wondered how I could distract Liam and take the ivory with me. It had been meant for me, after all. But I decided Joseph might notice that it was gone, and my being in the house might come out.

The surprise of the ivory was followed by another. Liam opened a leather portfolio and retrieved some sketches Fortin had made of me in preparation for his St. Sebastian and had later given to Joseph. "I am not supposed to show these to anyone. I can't see how it can hurt to be showing you, though. I think they're real good."

I looked quickly through them and saw the sketch for the St. Sebastian inscribed by Fortin to Joseph. It was a beautiful drawing, but I was mostly struck by how innocent I had looked.

"Did he tell you who the artist was? Who the boy was?" I asked.

"I forget the name of the artist. He told me that these were studies for a famous painting in the big museum in Paris. He didn't say much about the model except that it was a boy he knew in Rome. He says he loved that boy very much and misses him. He says I remind him of that boy. I am not seeing the likeness. I think I am much better looking. What do you think?"

I pretended to study the sketch and told him what he wanted to hear. I was glad I got the sentence out without a problem because I was starting to choke up.

Joseph had loved me. Liam would have had no reason to tell me so if Joseph had not said it. I was happy and grateful and even more resentful than before, all at the same time.

Fortunately, Liam was still talking and noticed nothing. "He said the boy was clever and learned quickly. But otherwise, Jeremiah never wants to talk about him. I wonder about him. He is probably old and fat and married with many children."

"Probably."

"I bet he was just a Roman Mary Ann who was offering himself to old men for money and could not even read or write." Liam studied the sketches for a minute. "Would you like to see some of my drawings?"

"Yes, if I'm not taking too much of your time." Liam gave no indication that he registered the sarcasm.

We went back up to his bedroom, and he pulled a large portfolio from under the bed. It was filled with earnest studies of flowers and vases and dozens of sketches of naked men, the majority of Liam himself.

The drawings were surprisingly well done, and they had the effect of making me hard again. A like effect was clearly visible in Liam's drawers. I toyed with the idea of pushing him back on the bed or maybe onto the floor. But I was curious to see more. There were two or three that he identified as Mrs. Farrell, the housekeeper, completely dressed of course, and many more of one naked girl.

"Did you do these sketches from life?"

"Not most of them. Jeremiah does not want me to have visitors to the house." He blushed. Flustered, he continued, "I do most of these from memory or based on pictures I see, or I am drawing myself and then making the man older or younger or bigger or thinner."

"And the girl?"

"The girl is my sweetheart. Viola. She lives near my family's rooms in Shadwell. Pretty, isn't she?"

The girl looked more plain than pretty, but I made a slight nod of assent. I told him I thought he had promise as an artist. I actually half believed it.

I walked to the front door but just as I reached out to open it, Liam took my arm, pulled me toward him, pressed himself hard against me and gave me a long, deep kiss. "Thank you," he said.

My attitude toward him softened immediately. I realised that what Liam was doing was exactly what I had done. In fact, the similarity embarrassed me.

Does this surprise you? Yes, I assure you, I do know right from wrong. It is just that life isn't that simple. Liam was deceiving Joseph. He was using him to further his career and make a better life for himself. Given what I had done in Rome, I was in no position to throw stones.

And with Liam, as with me, Joseph was getting something in return. Liam provided a way for Joseph to keep his family and still satisfy needs that, if unmet, could have torn his marriage apart. Even if it was founded on falsehood, perhaps his transaction, and my own, years earlier, could be considered an honest trade.

The most important thing I learned that day was that Joseph had loved me. I had been devastated by the way he had cut things off on our last visit. Now, thanks to that silly Liam, I knew what Joseph said to me that last day we were together—that he had never loved me—was not true.

I left London feeling strangely satisfied, as though I had settled some old scores and had gone a long way toward finally closing one chapter in my life.

Chapter 9:

Death of Joseph

Back in Paris, Amélie's increasingly frequent trips to Normandy increased my ability to consort with young men. One day I ventured into the storage space in the basement and decided to convert it into a room in which to properly entertain them.

At first it was just the corner of a dark room with a pallet on the floor and some rope. Gradually I took over the entire space. I added a large platform to serve as a bed, some low padded benches, and other furniture. I installed hooks so I could hang cuffs and other restraining equipment. I used dozens of small candles for light.

My proudest achievement was a heavy old oak chair that I modified with the help of a local craftsman. I used as inspiration an engraving I had seen—a device used in the Spanish Inquisition. I believe my version was a considerable improvement.

First, we cut out a large hole in the centre of the seat. Then we screwed in hooks that could be used to attach leather bands to the arms, legs and high back of the chair. Finally, there was a hinged metal device holding a leather plug that could be adjusted to secure it firmly in the sitter's mouth. I'm sorry you can't see it. I think it is a masterpiece.

The first guests in my Pit were boys I hired, but increasingly I didn't need to pay. Boys who had heard about me volunteered their services. And not just poor working-class boys. To my great surprise, increasingly young men from good, even prominent, families would show up at the front door of my gallery and tell me they wanted a private chat with me about Greek and Roman sculpture. One young man was the son of a duke.

We would progress from a general discussion on the ground

floor to the more specialized art in the Chapel. If I ascertained that the boy was safe and reliable, I might admit him to the chamber at the back of the gallery on the second level. Only if he proved himself there over several visits would I allow him to come with me downstairs to the Pit. These boys almost always returned.

Along with my increased activity in the Pit, my gallery upstairs prospered. I developed a clientele of collectors from across Europe and America including a particularly important set of customers from Boston, New York, and Chicago. They would come by my gallery when they were touring the Continent and often buy great quantities of sculpture and other objects for me to ship back to their homes. They seemed to have an endless supply of money. I considered opening a branch in New York City. I intended to make a trip to explore the possibilities, but the time never seemed right.

Despite the business going well, several developments started to cause me anxiety. One involved my supply of artifacts. These came mostly from the same Corsican who had supplied Gottlieb. I recognised there were criminal elements associated with this man. For a long time, their network didn't extend outside Italy. But at some point, one of their members established himself in Paris. He started demanding payments from me, threatening to do harm to my shop, my family, or myself if I didn't comply. I didn't dare refuse, even when the demands escalated.

Also, one of the boys who had visited me started demanding money in return for maintaining his silence. Nothing I did was illegal here in France as it would have been in Rome or London, but I was afraid he could describe my activities to Amélie and her family. I'm not sure the family would have believed him or taken any action, but I decided not to take the chance. I met all the demands of the Corsican and the blackmailer, but I knew that I was at their mercy. Either of them could raise their demands at will although I supposed that it was in their interest as well as mine to have my business prosper.

Despite the problems, my life was good, and I was pleased

with the course of things. Then, one day in 1878, two momentous things happened. First, there was news from Jérôme. Joseph had died. The news hit me hard. Although I had not seen him for years, I still thought about him all the time, particularly since my encounter with Liam. All the old questions returned. Why had I allowed my pride to let him go so easily? Why had I not told him the entire truth about my past, begged him to stay? Or followed him to London and pleaded with him to find some way for us to be together?

I wanted badly to see him one last time even if only in a casket. I toyed with the idea of asking Jérôme if he would tell Joseph's family that an old friend from Paris wanted to come to the funeral. I quickly decided that that was a bad idea. My time with Joseph had been over twenty years ago, but still it was unwise to do anything now that might cause people to start asking questions. I could not go. I could not see Joseph one last time. I felt terrible.

But then came an event that pushed Joseph's death out of my mind.

Chapter 10:

Robert

A bolt out of the blue. A letter from Joseph's son Robert informed me that he was making a tour of the Continent. He said he had recently arrived in Paris and would like to see me.

How was this possible? Griswold had glimpsed me briefly while Joseph was still in Paris and I know that Joseph's brother Rupert had also visited, but these visits were years ago. Even if they had learned my name, I doubted they would have said anything to Robert or know how to find me. I convinced myself that Robert must have learned about me here in Paris, but I was still worried.

I was tempted to decline to see him, but he obviously had the address of the gallery, so he could just appear at the door. That could have been awkward. Besides, I had an overwhelming curiosity to see Joseph's son. What did he look like? How similar was he to his father? In the end I sent him a note inviting him to come by the gallery the following Tuesday after the close of business hours.

When he appeared at the gallery door, I was stunned. It seemed like I was seeing Joseph as he appeared in Rome, similar in facial features and even mannerisms. For a moment I felt that time was collapsing.

We introduced ourselves and made small talk. Robert said he had obtained my name from that old maid de Roquelaure at the Louvre as a possible source of information about Rome and Paris during the time his father was here. Nothing he told me suggested he knew anything about my past. I was vastly relieved.

However, he also said he was particularly interested in Joseph's connection with the artist Jean-Louis Fortin. He had brought with him some of the sketches he had found in the house in St John's Wood he had inherited from his father. This did cause me some anxiety.

Although I had recently seen these sketches in London on my visit with Liam, seeing them once again in the presence of his son caused a wave of sorrow to wash over me. I felt a sadness that I had lost Joseph. But an even greater sadness that the boy named Jacopo had also disappeared. How young and small and innocent he looked! I was no longer that person. I told Robert I never met his father and had only met Fortin after he had returned to Paris.

I recited for Robert the narrative I had fabricated—that I arrived in Paris in 1853 with my family. Robert seemed satisfied with my account, and we went on to chat about other matters.

I had time to observe Robert as we talked. He was young and full of life. In many ways remarkably like his father. A similar face and body, but also the same initial shyness, and the same candour and enthusiasm once he felt at ease. He, like his father, was no Adonis, but, again like his father, he seemed fresh and open, and when he smiled his face was radiant. I found him, like his father, more attractive than many more conventionally handsome young men.

I kept looking at his lips and wondering what it would be like to kiss them. Although I tried to put it out of my mind, I could not help but wonder what that mouth would look like with a leather gag in it. I believe I was successful keeping my face and voice from betraying my thoughts.

We chatted for some time about the current state of painting and music. I was agreeably surprised by his knowledge of musicians I admired—Berlioz, Meyerbeer, Wagner. And painters— Millet, Bouguereau, Meissonier. And architects—above all Charles Garnier.

As our conversation became easier, I was increasingly conscious of how intently he was looking at me, as though he were trying to peer into my soul. Or, I hoped, he might be mentally undressing me as I had been doing with him. I hoped it was more about my body than my soul. In either case, it was clear a power-ful current was passing between us.

As he left, I invited him to return. He did so the following week, and then again the week after that. By this third visit, I was sure both of us felt a strong mutual attraction. He did not say or do anything overt, but I was hardly a novice in these matters. I was about to reach out and pull him to me.

But I hesitated. I had long ago rejected the teachings of the Church that lovemaking between men was sinful. However, I did wonder about whether I should have qualms about pursuing an intimate relationship with the son of my former lover.

In the end, I decided that, from my point of view, what Joseph and I had done was already condemned by much of society. For the time being, at least, why couldn't I consider this new affront to public morality merely an extension of the previous one?

More troubling was the question about what Robert might think if he ever learned about his father and me. I suspected it might be traumatic for him. But if he never knew about his father and me, that would not be an issue. I was surprised to find I couldn't quite banish this question from my mind, but, as many times before in my life, I decided to leave the issue for later con-sideration.

So it happened that on that third visit I put my hand on his, and the rest seemed to follow quite naturally. Robert kept apologizing for his lack of experience, and I could tell this was his first time with a mature man. But whatever he lacked in technique, he more than made up for in enthusiasm.

It was thrilling. It felt as though I had been given a second chance with Joseph and this time, with me as the dominant part-ner. To hold and kiss him and push him down on my bed sent electricity coursing through my body.

My experience with Joseph convinced me that I needed to be more careful with Robert than Joseph and I had been to keep our association secret. With Joseph I was young and had little to lose. As an affluent foreigner, Joseph was somewhat insulated from any danger of exposure. Now, however, I lived in Paris, had a thriving business, a family, a professional reputation to uphold. I suggested to Robert that we exercise the utmost discretion. He readily agreed.

At first I thought my interest in Robert was mostly physical. But after a while, I began to wonder. Joseph had been the only person outside my family who had ignited powerful emotions in me. While I was with him, I was never sure what those emotions were. I had some idea of the depth of my feeling on the train station as he was leaving Paris but only fully admitted to myself it was love at the time of his death. Now I was having some of the same reactions to Robert, and it was developing more quickly even than it had with Joseph. Was this love as well?

Over the days that followed, my experience with Joseph's son felt uncannily familiar. His speech and facial expressions were similar to Joseph's. He gave off the same clean odour of soap. Sometimes the similarity would hit home with particular force, for example when I first heard Robert exclaim "de leesh us" after a bite of crème brulé, I nearly burst out laughing.

There was one truly startling reminder of Joseph. As soon as Robert spent, he, like his father, he would promptly fall asleep. However, after about 10 minutes he would open his eyes and continue to pursue a thought he had started before dozing off as if no time had elapsed. It was so astonishing and comical a coincidence that I wanted to tell him about it, but, of course, I could not.

Like his father, Robert was very reserved, and his emotions were often as difficult to read. Like his father, he would sometimes sink into frustrating silence. He was invariably polite, rarely raised his voice, took his time making decisions. In short, a perfect English gentleman.

Although there were similarities, there were also differences. Joseph was much bolder and more confident. He assumed from the day we met that he would be the one making all major decisions for us both. This coloured every part of our relationship but especially our lovemaking. After the single instance when I was the one on top, I was expected to play the boy.

Robert, on the other hand, was much less assured, less assertive and more sensitive to the needs and desires of others. Unlike his father, he had an uncanny knack for knowing what would please me. Unlike his father, he loved to try new things. Our lovemaking became even more passionate than it had been with Joseph.

We started in the bedroom, but soon we were making love all over the gallery. One of his favourite spots was the tiny bathroom in the small apartment. Manoeuvring in the large porcelain tub took a great deal of ingenuity and agility, but we managed.

I also used the bathroom to shave his body. It made him look younger, more naked, more vulnerable. And it was clear that the humiliation greatly excited him. I might have let Joseph do this to me, but I could never have imagined doing it to him.

I loved the contrast between the shy, reserved young man that Robert was most of the time and the wildly excited person he became when aroused. He was happy to engage in more aggressive play than Joseph or than almost any of the other boys I had experienced since my days at the tavern in Rome.

When he first saw the Pit, he seemed transfixed. He walked around, slowly examining every piece of rope, strap, or implement. He said nothing, but it was clear he wanted to try them all.

Then, unbidden by me, he took off his clothes and sat in the big oak Inquisition chair. He told me he wanted to feel what it was like to be immobilized and have me treat him the way I had treated other boys. I was surprised. We had never spoken about my other boys. I was relieved that he gave no sign their existence upset him.

I cuffed his arms and legs, blindfolded and gagged him, then impaled him with the plug I ratcheted upward through the hole in the seat.

After squeezing, slapping, and pinching him in strategic spots, I repeatedly brought him close to spending by a vigorous frigging, stopping each time just before he was ready to spend and waited for his arousal to abate. He soon became desperate to spend. Instead, I continued for some time, then untied him and told him to put his clothes back on.

Before standing up, he reached down to frig himself. I slapped his hands away. He reluctantly pulled his drawers back on over his still stiff cock. I loved the way, for the next several days, he seemed frantic to kiss, pull off my clothes, and walk back down into the Pit. I kept refusing, but when I finally consented, Robert was a volcano of passion.

He was fascinated by the padded bench. I had him lie face down on it and secured him with leather straps. I put a leather gag mask over his head and a few plugs on the shelf in front of him to contemplate. He knew that I would use them to relax and stretch him before I penetrated him myself. He quivered with anticipation and tried, through the gag in his mouth, to beg me to take him.

I never hurried. I would stand back and admire my handiwork. A beautiful scene, I always thought, with his smooth young arse exposed and up in the air. I imagined how Fortin might render the image, perhaps in his series on the early lives of saints. I wondered which saint might be assigned to the image given that I recalled none in the Bible put into that particular position.

I was surprised by the powerful paternal feelings I soon developed for Robert. I wanted to lavish affection on him, teach him, protect him. If I said something insensitive, he would usually say nothing but look hurt. Once, he cried. On such occasions I would take him in my arms stroke his hair like I would a puppy. I would tell him I was sorry and would be more careful.

He said things that indicated he thought of me as a kind of father. I did sometimes think of him as my son. It was as confusing as it was exciting that a son would have more wealth and social position than the father. Needless to say, if was even more confusing when that son's father had acted in many ways like a father to me.

The time with Robert was golden. His enthusiasm for exploring the city, experiencing new works of art and writing about them rekindled my own interest. After Joseph left Paris, my intense pleasure in art had, without my being aware, gradually dulled. My life was pleasurable and financially rewarding, but the art I sold became more a means to an end than something important for its own sake.

Spending time with Robert brought me a renewed appreciation. I suddenly recovered some of the awe and excitement I had experienced seeing the Belvedere Torso for the first time or a Guido Reni painting. It was the same kind of excitement I felt seeing a particularly striking young man although I had never lost that kind of appreciation.

Our biggest outing was a two-week vacation at La Rochelle. After having to be so careful in Paris, it was an immense relief to be able to go out together in public to the beach, to the thermal establishments, restaurants, and theatre. Realising that Robert would soon be leaving for Rome, I bought a pair of splendid rings, one of which I gave to Robert and one I kept for myself.

The trip allowed me to deepen my understanding of Robert. I learned that he might not tell me everything he thought, but when he told me something, it was the truth. It also became clear to me he felt no need to impress me or anyone else. I figured both were the result of growing up in a settled and wealthy family. This certainly had not been the case for me. Everything had come at the cost of deceiving others. I reasoned that the lies were justified, but I knew it had taken a toll.

After our return to Paris, Robert made plans to resume his trip starting with the south of France and Rome, then going on to Athens and maybe further afield. Maybe I should have been more concerned with his going to Rome, but I figured it was safe enough. There were few people likely to remember much about me—about Jacopo, that is. Even if they did, I don't think they would tell him much.

But what would happen when Robert returned to Paris? What

if Robert was willing to stay in Paris? We talked about the possibility of introducing him to Amélie. But both Joseph and Robert felt a strong loyalty to their family, even when fleeing temporarily from its obligations. They were expected to return to England, marry and produce an heir. If Robert returned to London, could I open a shop there to be near him?

We also talked about the possibility of meeting regularly in some other place. Robert was keen on visiting and perhaps even living across the Atlantic. I gave some thought to the possibility of opening a shop in New York.

However, as the date of his departure drew near, I became convinced none of these schemes was practical and there was no way to include Robert in my life. Even if he were willing, I worried that I could let slip something about my past

If I am honest with myself, I knew that I worried most that the same thing that had happened with Joseph would happen again with Robert—he would eventually abandon me, and I would never know why.

I withdrew from him. One day, I made some hasty, ill-advised remarks which I didn't really mean, but they made Robert angry enough to do the same. It was completely out of character for him. I tried to stop the rift from growing, but nothing worked. We barely saw each other during his last days in Paris. Both of us were upset and angry.

After he left, I took the ring that was the mate to his and buried it at the bottom of a drawer. I was sad and lonely and angry at him—probably to avoid being angry with myself for even contemplating some kind of future together.

Amélie and the girls came back from Normandy. I was busy and distracted enough that I could ignore for days at a time the ache in my heart. I resumed trysts with some of my regular boys. Pascal, my favourite before Robert, was delighted I was ready to take him down to the Pit again. However, as handsome and obliging as he was, Pascal could not fill the void left by Robert's departure.

Chapter 11:

Robert Returns

A few months later, almost as suddenly as he had announced his arrival the first time, Robert cabled to say that he had decided against going on to Athens. He was returning to Paris and wished to see me in six days. I was happy that Amélie and the girls were once again at Houlgate.

When he showed up at the door of the gallery, I was apprehensive. He seemed distant and distracted. On the little finger of his right hand, a band of lighter skin showed where a ring had been removed. I am sure that he noticed that my ring was gone as well. We talked about his trip. He said very little about the people he had met in Rome and how long he was planning to stay in Paris. That made me even more uncomfortable.

I had to admit he looked wonderful, though. He was tanned, had let his hair grow, and was wearing a new suit in fine wool that he must have bought in Rome. I was even pleasantly surprised by his beard. He seemed older, more confident. I had loved his boyishness. But once I got past my initial surprise, I found this new Robert even more alluring.

We had dinner in the rooms behind the gallery. Marguerite prepared a splendid repast of veal with a mustard sauce, potatoes, and haricots verts. Neither of us ate much. I'm sure we both assumed dinner would be followed by a session in the bedroom or the Pit.

After we pushed the little table back into the passage between the two apartments, I proposed shaving his body before he took his bath. In the past this always signaled a visit to the Pit. He hesitated. I thought he might refuse, something he had never done before. In the end, though, he nodded. I was relieved but more concerned than ever that something was wrong.

Once up in the tiny bathroom, it was just as thrilling as always to apply shaving soap to his naked body. I loved the feel of his skin as I rubbed the creamy foam over his chest and arms, and the way it made his cock and balls slippery. There was something particularly satisfying about the feel of the ivory-handled razor running gently across the globes of his arse. I contemplated shaving his beard but decided I was content to leave it.

Even before I had applied the lather, he displayed a full stand. While I was shaving him, there was, as before, something wonderfully boyish, submissive and yielding about him, so ready to let me take the lead.

I left Robert to wash in the tub and put on clean clothes, telling him I had several errands to run. I needed to pick up some papers in the vicinity of Saint-Eustache and decided to pick up any mail waiting for me at the *poste restante* window at the central post office which was nearby.

There was a letter from my sister Isabella who had just visited with my mother in Rome. I had not heard anything from my family in months. I tore it open and ran my eyes down the page. What I saw stopped me cold. A young gentleman from London had been asking questions about me—Jacopo that is—and about the Gottlieb murder.

Standing there in the middle of the lobby of the post office, I was in turmoil. The young man asking questions in Rome must have been Robert. What had he learned? Had he discovered I was Jacopo? Anything about Gottlieb?

I turned the matter over and over in my mind. Would he believe me if I admitted I was Jacopo but told him what I told Joseph—that Gottlieb was killed by a thief, and I only happened to see the thief leaving? Or could I perhaps admit I was there but say it was entirely an accident, a bit of play that went tragically awry? Or that Gottlieb was ill, in dire financial circumstances, and wanted to die? There was, after all, an element of truth in each of these stories.

Part of me longed finally to tell Robert the truth, but I worried that he might not believe me. And if he did believe me, knowing the kind of person he is, he might feel obligated to go to the authorities and tell them what he knew. My life and everything I had worked for was in jeopardy.

As I walked slowly home, I decided to avoid jumping to conclusions. Robert had said nothing to indicate what he had learned. I would say nothing until I knew more. If he allowed me, I would take him to the Pit, where I had some control over the situation.

I had a fleeting thought. I wondered if the Pit had always been a way to keep him and every other boy at a distance, literally at arm's length. To keep me safe. I pushed the thought out of mind.

When I arrived back at my gallery Robert had retired to the bed chamber. I went downstairs and prepared the Pit. At the last moment I thought of putting the ivory I had taken from Gottlieb's rooms on a shelf directly in front of the padded bench. If Robert had learned something about the ivory, maybe he would give me some idea what he knew.

I climbed the steps back up to the apartment with my heart pounding. I found Robert in bed face down, naked, obviously ready for me. I felt trapped in a bad dream, but I knew I needed to act. I needed to find out what he knew before I could decide my own next move.

I tied his hands behind his back and took him downstairs. It was part of our game that he would pretend to struggle. This time, I was not sure it was pretense. Once in the Pit, I strapped him to the bench and went upstairs. I took off my clothes and put on a pair of riding boots and a black robe and hood.

Chapter 12:

Back in the Pit

Paris, rue de Seine, 21 May 1879

I'm now in the Pit, standing behind Robert, watching him intensely. My stomach is churning. He knows I'm here. He sees the ivory. With mounting agitation, I realise that he is not going to say anything.

Finally, I say, "I have heard that you were asking questions in Rome. What did you learn?"

Robert cranes his neck and says, very forcefully, "I was not going to say anything yet, but since you asked. . ." Then a long pause. "I learned that you lied to me about everything. I learned you were Jacopo and that you came here to Paris immediately after the murder of Johann Gottlieb. I don't know if you killed him, but I believe you were involved."

There it was. He knows everything. Well, almost everything. Maybe not about his father and me. I never saw him so angry. He is almost shouting.

But then, more quietly: "I thought I knew you, but I'm no longer sure who you are. If you killed Gottlieb, I can see why you might never let me walk out from this room. If that is your intention, please just do whatever you intend to do now and be done with it."

I am unable to speak. My head is spinning. Earlier this evening when I considered what I would do if Robert knew about Gottlieb, I contemplated a course of action that would stop Robert from telling anyone what he had discovered in Rome. But I see now with crystal clarity that I can never hurt Robert. Despite all my anger, all my efforts during his absence to push his memory out of my mind, I have never stopped loving him.

I will let him go. I will almost certainly never see him again. What a bitter thing—to know how I really feel about Robert only at the very moment when I am likely to lose him forever.

"I am so sorry," I manage to croak. "About everything. I don't deserve this chance to tell you the truth, but will you let me?"

"I am waiting," he says in an unnervingly calm voice.

I tremble, barely able to stand. "I have lied to almost everyone for most of my life. Yes, I was Jacopo. I was a *bardassa* in Rome. I knew that I needed to escape that life, so I lied. To everyone.

"Yes, I was in the room when Gottlieb was murdered. I bear some responsibility for that. I set up a minor theft, but I did not kill him. I swear by all that is Holy, I never meant him harm.

"As a poor boy from Trastevere, I did not expect the authorities to believe me. So, I ran. I am not proud of many things, especially what I did that night. But—I know it may be difficult to believe—I want to be completely honest with you now."

Robert is still silent, so I continue.

"You might not believe a word I say. I would understand. But I'm begging you to give me another chance."

More silence. The seconds pass, and with each one, the pounding in my head and stomach increases.

Finally, he says, "What else have you lied about? If you weren't responsible for Gottlieb's death, why do you have that ivory?"

"I can explain everything if you only—"

"For God's sake, Fabrizio, whatever it is you have to say, just say it."

I pick up the ivory. "This is one of two that were in Gottlieb's apartment the night of the murder—"

"I know about the other. I saw it in the Capitoline Museum in Rome."

"In the Capitoline? How can that be? I'm sorry. Now I am confused."

"The police transferred it to the museum."

"Ah. I was not aware of that. It was the one that killed Gottlieb. Not this one. And there is one more."

"Yes, I know that as well. I saw it in my father's house. It is the same as this one except the figures are different. I suspect the young man in the medallion in London is you. But why was it made? And who is the man with you?"

"This piece or the one you saw in Rome is likely a real antique. The other is a copy made for Gottlieb. The third piece, the one you saw in London, was made at your father's request at the same time as the other copy. The medallion was designed by Jean Fortin."

"Yes I know about Fortin. You are his St. Sebastian. But who is the other man in the medallion on the ivory."

"Your father asked Fortin to have the two of us pose for it."

"The two of you?"

"Yes, your father and me."

"A portrait of you and my father? But why? Why did my father want an ivory with an image of the two of you? Unless . . . unless . . ."

"Yes, Robert. This is the part that makes me most ashamed. I didn't tell you because I was certain it would drive you away."

A very long pause.

"I think I understand now. I want to hear you say it."

"Joseph and I were lovers. He had Fortin design this image of us in a traditional pose as an older man presenting a gift to his young lover—myself, or Jacopo really. It was supposed to be a birthday present for me, but in the rush to leave Rome, both of us forgot about it."

Robert took a sharp intake breath then groaned. "Oh, my God! Oh, my God! How can this be? You knew all the time we were making love that you had performed the same acts with my father? It is monstrous. Unnatural. My uncle told me that my father was with some boy in Paris, but I never imagined it was you. I thought you were just a *bardassa* in Rome, that you provided services for money."

"I did. That is how I met your father. But that soon changed. I loved your father, although I realised it too late. I am now sure he loved me."

Robert lets out an explosive gasp. Another long pause. Finally, he says, "What about Gottlieb's death? Give me one piece of good news. Tell me that my father had nothing to do with that."

"Your father had nothing to do with it. He only knew I was involved and that the authorities would probably arrest me. He offered to bring me to Paris. I accepted."

"Of course. Of course. Now everything makes sense. But what happened? If my father loved you, why did he return to London and leave you here?"

"I have asked myself that question a thousand times. He may have found out I had lied to him. He might have grown tired of me. Or it might be that your family found out about us and put pressure on him. Maybe all those."

Robert is silent. I hear the faint drip of water from somewhere in the basement.

I think about Joseph and Robert. Joseph was such a good and honest person. Robert as well. I don't believe that I am a bad person, only one who has done some bad things for my own survival. I created a new life because I could not endure my old one. Would Joseph have understood? Is there any chance Robert will now? Or is their world just too remote from mine?

Robert eventually says, "Uncle Rupert told me the family found out my father had a boy in Paris, and they put intense pressure on him to return. They even considered bringing the boy to London, housing him discreetly somewhere. Would you have gone?"

"Yes, of course. I would have moved heaven and earth to have had that chance. But Joseph never offered."

I am weeping profusely now, full of fresh torment. Why did Joseph not take me to London? Why wasn't I the one who lived on Carlton Hill and not that silly Liam?

Did I cause the rupture? Because I was not mature enough to trust Joseph, to tell him the truth, to tell him I loved him? Why did I make the same mistake with Robert?

Was it all unnecessary? Was it only my pride and my need to maintain control that made it impossible for me to admit my love to Joseph or Robert? Was I too afraid it would give them power over me and leave me vulnerable?

My fear of Robert destroying my life seems suddenly insignificant, eclipsed by the blinding recognition of the harm I have done to him by my dishonesty. And to his father. And to myself. I put the ivory back on the shelf and fall on my knees on the floor in front of him. Tears streak my face.

"I am done. I have told you everything. I know you could destroy my life by going to my family or to the police. The world would find out who I am.

"I thought I was prepared to do something drastic to prevent you from telling anyone anything. But I cannot. I could not admit before how much I loved you. But I am telling you now, even though I suspect it is too late, and it will destroy me. I don't want to continue to make the same mistakes over and over. I do love you with all my heart."

Robert is silent. I'm still kneeling in front of him. I can feel the cold of the floor radiating into my knees.

"You are free," I say. "You can walk up those stairs and out of my life. You can go to the authorities or the newspapers or my family and tell them everything. I will not try to stop you."

Robert waits for what feels like an hour. Then he says, slowly with an icy edge that is new, "If you are not going to harm me and want me to forgive you, might I suggest a good first step would be to untie me."

"Of course. Of course. I'm so sorry." I quickly untie him. Though I am distraught, I am aware how completely in control of himself Robert appears to be. He is a different person from the man I knew.

He stands up. Then he says, "Fabrizio, you may also have noticed that I'm wearing no clothes. It is chilly down here. Take off your robe and give it to me."

No one has talked to me this way since I was a *bardassa* in Rome. I take off my robe and hand it to him. Now I'm wearing only my riding boots. I am embarrassed, an emotion I have always tried to avoid. I hide my nakedness. He puts on the robe and sits down on the bench. I kneel in front of him and try to hold his hands. He pushes me away.

"Get off the floor. You look ridiculous."

I do as I am told and stand in front of him.

I am sobbing as I say, "You probably want nothing more to do with me, but I am begging you: is there any chance you can forgive me? That we could start over and be friends at least? I dare not hope for more."

"You can stop the dramatic scenes right now, Fabrizio. I cannot answer your questions yet. I need time to think. I will tell you I believe you about your life in Rome, and I assure you I will do nothing to destroy the life you have built here."

Part of me is relieved. But ironically this assurance only makes me feel worse. I fear I will keep my life, my reputation, my gallery, my marriage, but lose Robert. My tears redouble.

Robert then says, in a nearly inaudible voice, "I will also tell you that I still love you in spite of everything."

I am overcome. I try to kiss him, but he holds me at arm's length.

"I cannot say yet whether that is enough. Enough to want to see you ever again, let alone spend any time together."

"Can you at least stay here in Paris for a while?"

"Fabrizio, even if I could forgive your lies, I am not sure I can bear to look at you without being reminded of what you and my father did in the bedroom upstairs."

There is hope! Robert says he still loves me. The words start to fly from my mouth. "You will almost certainly need to marry. Maybe you will find a woman who would understand. I think Amélie would like you, maybe even give her blessing. She may even be relieved. We once talked once about leaving Paris. Opening a shop in New York. Or London. Or I could stay here. You could return to London. We could meet regularly. Can you at least consider any of this?" I am speaking so fast I am panting. I stop to take a breath.

After my years in Rome, I vowed I would never be in the position of having to beg another man for anything. Yet here I am begging Robert. I also vowed that I would never depend on another man to make decisions that would affect my future. In everything I have done since Joseph's departure, I have always been the dominant partner, whether in business or in the bedroom. Since Joseph left, I have never let myself become emotionally dependent. If I never admitted my feelings, I could pretend to myself I didn't really care.

But I have come full circle. As I look at Robert—so young, so good, so desirable—I feel a great weight lift from my shoulders. I am now ready to throw myself at his feet and live with the consequences. For once, I'm willing to turn over control to someone else. I feel free and ready to accept whoever I will be next in my life.

"You are getting very far ahead of yourself, Fabrizio. I can't get used to the thought of you and my father together. And even if we wanted to spend time together, we both know there are almost insurmountable barriers. Family, friends, society."

"Take as much time as you need. I will wait for you no matter how long." I walk to the ledge to pick up the ivory again. "But would you not agree that it is time to dispose of this ivory? It's a painful reminder of Gottlieb and all my lies." I hold it over my head, ready to hurl it to the ground.

"Certainly not!" Robert says immediately. "It is either a genuine antique or a fine copy. Perhaps we should give it to the Capitoline Museum." To my amazement, he starts to laugh. "I would love to see the look on the face of that bloody old keeper when he is obliged to add it to the collection. But seriously, we should probably give it to a museum in Rome, or perhaps to the British Museum. It would probably embarrass people in either place, which would please me."

Robert is speaking in an entirely new way. "But what about your father's ivory? What will you do with that?"

Robert thinks for a moment. "I will not discard it. Maybe I will come to think of it as a memorial to the love we shared."

"A memorial? Does that mean you have decided? That there is no future for us?"

"I did not say that. I told you. I need time to think."

Robert turns toward the stairs. I conclude that he is about to walk out of my life forever. But as he reaches the door, he turns—as he did on that fateful third day in my gallery—and walks back to me.

"Despite our differences we share at least one very important thing. My father abandoned you. To a lesser extent, he did the same with me and the rest of my family. How old were you when you met my father?"

"Sixteen."

"I am genuinely sorry for you. My father dangled a bright future in front of you, like a toy before a puppy, then snatched it away without explanation."

"It always ends that way with men like us."

Robert shakes his head. "But must it?"

I think to myself, What about Jérôme and Hamish? I imagine there are others like them.

Robert is now walking toward me. I have no idea what he will do. I stand where I am, waiting for him to act. To my surprise, he takes my head in his hands, pulls me to him, and kisses me hard on the mouth. He squeezes tight against me. I am astonished. I'm also aware he still has on my robe, but I am still naked. Through the robe, I can feel both of us are aroused.

"Take off your boots and lie face down on the bench," he tells me. I do as I am told. He picks up one of the leather straps and starts to bind my wrist to the leg of the bench. "Maybe I can stay a while in Paris. Maybe, if there are no more secrets. Maybe, if we start again on a more equal footing. Maybe . . . "

Author's Note

Why this novel?

Partly I just wanted to tell a story. A love story, or rather two intricately related love stories. I also wanted to explore what life must have been like for men who loved men in the years before the invention of the term "homosexuality" and the trial of Oscar Wilde. Finally, I wanted to evoke the power of art and the role that it can play in communicating ideas that can't be expressed in other ways.

Readers familiar with art history may recognize that my fictional murder of Johann Gottlieb in Rome is loosely based on the death of Johann Joachim Winckelmann, widely recognized as the father of modern art history. He was murdered in Trieste by a male prostitute in 1768. I have moved this event to the mid-nineteenth century in part because I am more familiar with this era of history and in part because it was such a fascinating time. It seems at once irrevocably part of the past—before airplanes, Freud, and Einstein—and yet recognizably modern in many ways.

Perhaps because it seems at once so near and still so distant from us, this period has been oddly neglected in the histories of gay culture, falling between the better documented eighteenth century and the even more extensively studied period starting in the last decades of the nineteenth century.

For many writers the invention and popularization of the term "homosexual" in the late nineteenth century marked a milestone. They argue that it is not possible to talk about the lives of men who loved men before this event in the same way we have talked about them since. In this reading of history, there were specific sexual acts but no real gay identity or sub-culture before the invention of the term.

However, it seems to me that the invention of the term was less a cause than a symptom of more profound and gradual changes in society, changes that did not really penetrate popular culture until well into the twentieth century. It also seems to be more a reflection of the way men who loved men were viewed by society at large than the way they viewed themselves. Although gay men in the mid-nineteenth century were held to very different norms of public and private behaviour, it is difficult for me to believe that the essential internal dynamics of relationships were much different from those of our own time.

What might everyday life have been like for relatively privileged gay men immediately before "homosexuality" was a word and Wilde spoke famously and publicly in its defence? There is very little in the historical record that documents the vast majority of these men. I have tried to extrapolate from what we do know.

Some of the attitudes toward relationships among gay men can be inferred from John Addington Symonds' *A Problem in Modern Ethics*, 1891; Auguste Tardieu's *Attentats aux Moeurs*, 1857; Richard von Krafft-Ebing's *Psychopathia Sexualis*, 1886 with English translation 1893; and Arthur H. Legludic's *ArthurX: Mémoires d'un travesti, prostitué, homosexual,* written in the 1860s, published 1896.

These books allow us some glimpse into the way male homosexual culture was viewed by educated and well-off men. But they do not tell us much about the internal dynamics of relationships or sexual customs. Erotic fiction, even if not intended to represent ordinary life, supplies some insights. Two notable examples are *Teleny or the Reverse of the Medal,* anonymously published in 1893 and sometimes attributed, at least in part, to Oscar Wilde; and *My Secret Life*, by "Walter," published in instalments starting around 1888.

The academic study of gay history is relatively recent, and there is a paucity of work on the mid-nineteenth century. For my purposes the most important source was Graham Robb's *Strangers: Homosexual Love in the Nineteenth Century*, a marvellous piece of scholarship published in 2003. For Britain, there is an early work by Jeffrey Weeks, *Coming Out: Homosexual Politics in Britain from the Nineteenth Century to the Present*. More recently, Tom Crewe's *The New Life*, although a novel, was very useful in presenting ideas about homosexuality and some description of gay relationships in the late nineteenth century. For France I consulted two works by Jeffrey Merrick, one co-authored by Michael Sibalis, *Homosexuality in French History and Culture,* and the other with Bryant T. Ragan Jr., *Homosexuality in Modern France.* For Italy, although the literature is less well developed, I learned a good deal from Valeria P. Babini, Chiara Beccalossi, et al., *Italian Sexualities Uncovered, 1789-1914.*

For art and homosexuality, James W Saslow's *Pictures and Passions* was useful. The most important source for my purposes was an essay, "The Abject Gaze and the Homosexual Body, Flandrin's Figure d'Etude" by Michael Camille in Whitney Davis, *Gay and Lesbian Studies in Art History.* As some readers may have realized, the painting of St. Sebastian I describe in this novel is based on the painting by Flandrin, and my characters' reactions to it is informed by Camille's analysis of the reception of the piece.

My novel explores some relationships whose sexual expression is based on domination and submission. Since the explosion of gay literature in the late 1960s, numerous books, both fiction and non-fiction, have explored this dynamic, but most are steeped in the leather culture of the 1970s. I wanted to explore what such relationships might have looked like in the nineteenth century.

Finally, I was interested in the role art has played in creating the modern gay world. It is striking that the art of previous eras which contemporary gay men would consider overtly homoerotic was rarely discussed in those terms at the time as long as it purported to be allegorical and related to some high-minded ideal. Still, as Camille argues, it is impossible to believe that homosexual men at the time did not see and discuss this art among themselves in a way similar to the way gay men do today. It was simply not acceptable to make these thoughts public or put them in writing.

Acknowledgments

I would like to thank many friends and colleagues who were helpful to me in supplying information, reading parts of the manuscript, giving me advice and supplying blurbs for publicity. Among them are Anthony Alofsin, Susan Bielstein, Hollis Clayson, Nina Dubin, Gabrielle Esperdy, Paul Gehl, Alex Guyan, Roy Huebner, Scott Jorgenson, William Lampkin, David Masello Philip Palmer, Ellis Schmidlapp, Stephen Silha, Scott Tilden, Patrick Wirtz, Reed Woodhouse, and Mark Zubro.

I am especially grateful to David Groff who helped shape the book at an early stage, Jonathan Lippincott who provided the fine cover design, and Louis Flint Ceci who saw the potential in the manuscript, agreed to publish the book, and provided much help in putting it into its final form.

About the Author

Robert Bruegmann grew up in the Pittsburgh suburbs and received his B.A. from Principia College in 1970. He earned a Ph.D. from the University of Pennsylvania in 1976 with a dissertation on late 18th and early 19th Century European hospitals and other institutions. In 1977 he joined the faculty of the University of Illinois at Chicago, where he is currently Distinguished Professor Emeritus of Art History, Architecture, and Urban Planning. He has taught at the University of Pennsylvania, Philadelphia College of the Arts, MIT, and Columbia University. Among his numerous written or edited volumes on architectural, urban, landscape, and planning history are *Modernism at Mid-Century*; *The Architecture of the US Air Force Academy*; *The Architects and the City: The Work of Holabird and Roche of Chicago 1880-1919*; *Sprawl: A Compact History*; *The Architecture of Harry Weese*; and *Art Deco Chicago: Making America Modern*. He lives in Chicago and Palm Springs, California.